THE AWFUL TRUTH ABOUT THE NAME OF THE ROSE

by

Marco Ocram

A Tiny Fox Press Book

Cover design art by Damonza.
Library of Congress Catalog Card Number: 2019905138
ISBN: 978-1-946501-15-8

Tiny Fox Press and the book fox logo are all registered trademarks of Tiny Fox Press LLC

Tiny Fox Press LLC
North Port, FL

To my lovely wife Leona, as ever.

CHAPTER ONE

*In which Marco receives the customary first-chapter call
from Como Galahad.*

I'm afraid, Mister Ocram, you need complete rest. Your physical health is perfect—apart from your haemorrhoids—but you have mental and emotional exhaustion. Unless you take a break from your duties as a mega-selling writer, you risk a complete mental breakdown."

I nodded to show the distinguished medic her message had been understood. I wasn't surprised.

I took my legs out of the stirrups.

"Can I get dressed now?"

Since I'd published my second record-breaking book—*The Awful Truth about the Sushing Prize*—my life had gone crazy. If I wasn't being interviewed for some arts programme, I was being filmed in the White House receiving my Congressional Medal, or the president was speaking with me afterwards about how he was writing a novel and would I look at his first three chapters, or I was guest of honour at the opening night of the new film about my book, or the new play about it, or the new ballet, or at a trade conference in Beijing where a Marco Ocram mobile phone was being launched by Huawei, or...

I hadn't driven my black Range Rover with tinted windows for weeks. Worse still, I missed my Bronx mom's birthday, caught in a typhoon with Piers Morgan at a charity event in East Timor. I didn't mind missing my Bronx mom's birthday, and the typhoon wasn't so bad, but Piers Morgan was a nightmare. On top of all that, my agent Barney was on my back about my next book.

"Marky baby," he kept saying, "this is the most dangerous time for a writer, you mark my words. You wanna know what it's called? I'll tell you what it's called—it's called third book syndrome. You get the second book published, you sit down to write the third, and wham—all the creative juices stop. You dry up like a..."

I won't say what Barney said I'd dry up like—it was too rude for my mass-market sales category.

I finished dressing and put on my anorak.

"That'll be five hundred bucks," said the doctor.

I peeled off the money, then walked out to the corridor. I was looking for the word Exit among the signs for the various hospital departments—Liposuction, Facial Tucks, Breast Enlargements, Breast Reductions, Hair Transplants, Testosterone Replacement Therapy, Self-esteem Counselling—when *Que Sera Sera* sounded from my pocket. I lifted my phone to an exhausted ear.

"Publishing legend Marco Ocram speaking. How can I help you, caller?"

"Writer, it's me."

Only one person calls me Writer—Como Galahad, Chief of the Clarkesville County Police, the giant black detective who shares the unpredictable twists and turns of my plots, usually while whining about them.

"Como!"

I typed an exclamation mark to denote surprise, even though all my books start with Como calling me out the blue in the twelfth paragraph.

"How's tricks, Writer?"

"Not so good, Como. I'm on the edge of a mental breakdown and need complete rest. So if you're ringing like you usually do, to tell me about some innocuous-sounding case that ends up being one of the world's most spectacular crimes that I solve with your help, then maybe we better leave it a few weeks."

"That *you* solve? Ha!"

"I'm too tired to argue, Como. If you want to say you solve the crimes while I just get in your way, that's fine."

Which showed the psychological depths to which I had sunk.

"That's the first sensible thing you've ever written, Writer. When this book comes out I'm gonna frame that and stick it on my wall. If it ever comes out—which it won't if you keep feeling sorry for yourself with all that nervous breakdown crap. Listen. Something's come-up, and before you start bitching, it's something that's just right for a writer feeling sorry for himself, so get your sorry ass down here and I'll tell you what's what."

In a break with my well-established tradition, I didn't race down the N66 to Clarkesville in my black Range Rover with tinted windows. Instead, I pootled down the N66 to Clarkesville in my black Range Rover with tinted windows, twiddling a listless steering wheel, my legs tucked into a plaid rug. For the first time I was starting a new Ocram/Galahad book without any sense of excitement. Now I knew how my readers felt. Perhaps Barney was right— maybe I did have third book syndrome.

As I neared Clarkesville my phone beeped. It was a text from Como.

Don't meet me at PD HQ. I need 2 tell U a secret. Meet me @ Kelly's instead. B discreet. C

At Kelly's, I threaded through the boisterous revellers, wishing I could be infected with their energy, and hoping I'd spelled discreet correctly. Como was in a corner booth, his police chief hoody raised to avoid recognition. I had my anorak hood raised likewise, which was a habit of mine.

Wondering if my readers would spot the weak pun on the word habit, I squeezed into a seat next to Como's huge bulk. He surveyed the busy diner as if he suspected we were being watched. I caught his mood of caution and said nothing, waiting for him to talk. Which, it seems, was exactly what he was waiting for me to do, so we spent ten minutes without saying anything. Hardly a promising start for a mega-selling thriller. I broke the impasse.

"What gives?"

"Here."

Como passed a torn fragment of vellum under the table. I looked at it in my lap. It showed the start of a Latin text:

Lorem ipsum dolor sit amet, consectetur adipiscing elit, sed do eiusmod tempor incididunt ut labore et dolore magna aliqua. Ut enim ad minim veniam, quis nostrud exercitation ullamco laboris nisi ut aliquip ex ea commodo consequat. Duis aute irure dolor in reprehenderit in voluptate velit esse cillum dolore eu fugiat nulla pariatur. Excepteur sint occaecat cupidatat non proident, sunt in culpa qui officia deserunt mollit anim id est laborum.

I recognised the font—fourteen-point Hensteeth, as rare as a semi-colon in a Jack Reacher book.

"Where did you get it?"

"It was posted to HQ. No covering letter."

"Know what it means?"

"No. We showed it to a translator. She said it was crazy words all mixed up."

"So why did you think I'd be able to help?"

"I dunno. But when she said 'crazy words all mixed up' I thought of you."

CHAPTER TWO

In which Marco impresses the brethren with his perspicacity.

I skipped to a new chapter so I could stop looking at Como's hurtful quip.

"So why are we looking at mixed up Latin words in Kelly's Bar and Diner?"

"You tell me. You're the Writer. I don't make this shit up. All I know is that forty years ago a commune opened just outside town, near Barton Hills. It runs itself like a medevil monastery."

"Medieval, Como, medieval."

"That's what I said—medevil. They take in celebrities who wanna retreat out of the limelight—which is a joke, since they spend their whole lives wanting to get in the freakin' limelight in the first place. Anyway, three monks died up there over the last two months."

"Suspicious?"

"Not sure. Flora says it could be natural causes, or it could be a fancy new poison that looks like natural causes."

Flora was the Clarkesville County Pathologist, an icily professional scientist, or at least she was with me. Como continued his blatant exposition:

"I been hearing rumours there's something going on up there. Could be drugs, could be guns, could be anything, but I need you to investigate. If I start poking around they'll know I suspect something. But if you go they'll think you're just another crazy celebrity with more money than brains and it won't bother them. Anyway, it's just what you said you needed. Complete rest."

"But why meet here? Why couldn't we meet at Police HQ?"

Como looked straight in my eyes. "There's a mole in Police HQ. I'm going to smoke'm out, but in the meantime I'm not taking any chances, so if we need to communicate use my private number, or send a message via Barney. Here's a brochure for the commune. And guess what—it's printed on vellum."

I took the brochure, admiring its production values. The illuminations on each page were exquisite.

"One other thing," said Como, lowering his voice three semi-tones to denote extreme gravity. "Be careful."

I wondered what sort of care he had in mind. It was the kind of thing my Bronx mom used to say, albeit with a more-manly voice.

"You mean..."

"Two days ago a dead monk was found at the bottom of the cliff below the praesidium. The abbot says the monk was troubled, so suicide's the most likely verdict. But, you know..."

Yes, I knew. The *'Did he fall or was he pushed?'* conundrum was the oldest cliché in the book, or so far anyway, and I wondered how any supposedly serious writer would consider using it. I also wondered how long it would be before I got a text from a reader to say that *praesidium* was the wrong word and I should have written *aedificium*. What readers don't seem to understand is that it would take weeks to write a book if you had to keep checking everything.

"Don't worry, Como. I'll be careful. If you don't hear from me by the end of a week, look for another body below the praesidium."

We shook hands. I shuffled out from behind the table and left.

It felt like we should be starting a new chapter, but I was still only five hundred words into this one, having ended Chapter One prematurely on account of Como's hurtful quip. That just goes to show the unintended consequences of cheap jokes. I decided to write some extremely wooden dialogue to set a low bar for the rest of the book, so I called the commune on the number in the brochure. I got through to the abbot straight away, sparing my readers the tedium of a paragraph in which I get through to reception and have to ask for him.

"Is that the abbot?"

"Speaking."

"This is mega-selling writer, Marco Ocram. I was looking at your brochure and wanted to book myself in for a detox fortnight."

"That would be our pleasure, Brother Marco. However, I must let you know that we do not officially open for the season until next week. You would be most welcome at any time, but for the moment we have very few guests, and are somewhat overtaxed by the preparations for our grand opening. I am afraid you might find too little to occupy your mind were you to join us now."

I assured the abbot that having too little to occupy my mind was just what I needed.

"In that case," he said, "when would you like to check in?"

"Thirty minutes?"

I punched the address of the commune into the sat-nav, waited for her to plot the route, then guided my black Range Rover in accordance with her spoken instructions, while taking in the view through its tinted windows. Listening to the lady sat-nav reminded me that in my last book I'd got into trouble with Germaine Greer, who said my writing embodied the prejudices of a male-dominated publishing industry, with women relegated to incidental characters. Here we were, only two chapters in, and already I'd fallen into the same trap, setting my new book in a commune run as a medieval monastery, where rules of celibacy would forbid a female presence. Damn.

"Turn down the track to the abbey," said the sat-nav.

I turned obediently down the track, which wound for three miles along a snow-covered valley, the drop to its side becoming increasingly precipitous. I rounded a tight bend and there was the abbey, perched like an eagle's nest on a rocky spur of Mount Clark, surrounded by a forbidding chain-link fence which seemed almost a continuation of the cliffs themselves. The majestic preasidium grew from the highest point of the outcrop, and was roughly—no, make that exactly—square in shape, with tetragonal towers at each of its five corners, and a six-faceted heptagonal conservatory jutting from each of the towers, the battlements of which had thirteen crenellations, above which twenty one flags flew. I wondered if my readers would realise that the construction of the abbey was an architectural analogue of the Fibonacci sequence—possibly with a few other numbers thrown in to make it harder to spot—or whether I should spell it out for them.

Before I could decide, my ruminations were interrupted by the sight of a monk in the heavy woollen habit of his order, weaving up the snow-covered track as if drunk or high on some other stimulant. As he neared I lowered my tinted window. He looked at me in surprise.

"Hey, Marco."

I looked at him in even more surprise.

"Hey, Tom."

I wondered what Tom Cruise was doing under the influence of drugs at the abbey. He absent-mindedly high-fived me, then turned down a side track that led to a muck heap.

Mystified, I drove on.

As I neared the imposing gates of the abbey, a portly monk came trudging towards me, four brothers in a line behind him. I noted a large ring of keys suspended from his girdle, and imagined him to be the cellarer, a senior monk entrusted with the management of the abbey stores. I re-lowered my tinted window.

"Greetings, Brother Marco. We heard news of your arrival from the abbot."

"You are searching for an inebriated Brother Tom, I perceive."

"But how...?"

The cellarer was dumbfounded that I knew.

"You will find him by the muck heap."

"How do you know? Did you see him go there?"

This was the point at which an ordinary novelist would have said "Yes." I am no ordinary novelist, however. I decided it would be useful to remind my brethren that they were dealing with a writer of enormous intellect and observational powers.

"No, but I can assure you you will find him there," I said. The 'you you' was a reminder of the epizeuxis that characterises my best work. It rarely occurs in such an early chapter, so things were looking good.

"Thank you, Brother Marco," said the amazed and grateful cellarer. "You will find the abbot awaits you."

I drove through the gates and into the central courtyard, following the signs for guest parking. A valet monk took my keys and carried my meagre luggage to the reception hall, an imposing room with vast vaulted ceilings that continued the Fibonacci theme, with thirty four down-lighters per vault and fifty five individual LEDs in each down-lighter.

"Brother Marco, welcome."

The abbot strode to meet me, his cowl thrown back to show his fine aquiline features and silvery mane. He kissed my hand.

"Your cell is ready. Please check in. Once you are settled, I would be most grateful for an audience. Perhaps we could meet in the grand refectory after lauds."

"Indeed, Brother Abbot. I am keen to hear the ways of your community."

"So be it."

I was so excited about a joke I had lined up for my meeting with the abbot, I decided to skip the opportunity to pad-out a couple of thousand words with a detailed description of checking in and being shown around my cell by the bell-boy. Besides, I wasn't sure of all the technical terms for things like the wooden contraption you knelt-on to pray, or the monk's equivalent of a trouser-press that kept their habits fresh, or the triangular brass and ivory instruments they used to query the alignment of the planets, and the small metal things they used to bleed the radiators. So I donned my hooded robe and fast-forwarded to my meeting with the abbot.

We squeezed in behind a quiet corner table in the busy grand refectory. For a person who writes the first thing that comes into his head, I was amazed I had conceived a scene which so closely paralleled my earlier meeting with Como, even down to the hooded garments worn on both occasions. I really was wasting my talent writing this rubbish—one day I'd try something serious.

"Brother Marco, your arrival was indeed timely."

"Yes, well, when I say I'm going to be somewhere in thirty minutes, I'm there in thirty minutes. Punctuality is the whatsits of kings, don't forget."

"No, forgive me, I was not referring to the timeliness of your arrival in relation to our earlier telephone call, I meant in relation to..." the abbot looked around and dropped his voice three semi-tones, and I don't need to say what that means because I said it in the earlier scene with Como, "... a most disturbing incident."

"Indeed," I said, wishing to encourage him to speak further of the incident.

"But before I speak further of the incident," he said, entirely ignoring my encouragement, "perhaps, Brother Marco, you might explain how it was that you knew the cellarer was seeking Brother Tom, and how you knew Brother Tom was inebriated, and how you knew he would be found by the muck-heap. We are aware, of course, from your books, that you have extraordinary powers of detection, but even so, we were astonished by the perspicacity you displayed to the cellarer."

"It is easy for me to explain, Brother Abbot," I said, hoping it would be. "I knew that a person of some distinction was being sought, since the cellarer would otherwise have sent a minion rather than leading the search himself."

"Brilliant!"

"That the person sought was inebriated could be divined straightforwardly from their meandering footprints in the snow."

"Astounding!"

"That the person would be found at the muck-heap I was able to predict with confidence, since the footprints led onto the side path which ends there."

The abbot clapped his hands at my brilliance.

"And how did you know it was Brother Tom whom we sought?"

Ah, well, that was a bit trickier. I tried evasion.

"Come, Brother Abbot, you may think me guilty of the sin of boasting were I to reveal that to you."

"Yes, but far greater would be the sin of omission. You must tell me."

Lesser novelists would have been stumped at this point, but not I. I wrote the first thing that came into my head.

"The footprints were most distinctive. The snow had been fused by the warmth of the shoe far more at the toe than at the heel, suggesting lifts within the shoe that increased the height of the wearer while insulating the heel. At the same time, the briars that grow at the corner of the path had caught a lock of hair, dyed jet-black, five feet above the ground. I therefore knew that the Cellarer sought an important guest with jet-black dyed hair standing around five feet tall in shoes with lifts. To cap it all, the inebriated guest had dropped a Scientology leaflet at the bend in the path, which pointed to one famous person in particular. So you see, Brother Abbot, it was simplicity itself."

The abbot kissed the ancient Thracian cross that hung from his martyr-teeth rosary-beads, while I continued to dither about spelling abbot with a lower- or upper-case a.

"I thank the Good Lord for sending you here at such a time, Brother Marco. We have a need at present for your remarkable powers of detection."

"Indeed," I said again.

"Indeed," said the abbot. "If I might say so in complete confidence, two days ago the body of a young novice, Brother Wayne, was found at the foot of the cliff directly below the main windows of the praesidium. The young man had been deeply troubled about the meaning and purpose of life..."

I knew how he felt. I was feeling deeply troubled about the meaning and purpose of life myself, as would you if you had to write this tripe.

"... so we assumed at first that he had tragically decided to kill himself, notwithstanding the sternest admonishments of scripture about the sanctity of life. However, it subsequently occurred to me to inspect the windows above his fall, and ..."

I cut him short. "And you found them closed."

CHAPTER THREE

In which Marco tests his reader's interest with a description of the fabled door of the abbey, and invents another motive.

Brother Marco! I am astounded. How did you know?"

Because it's fiction's most predictable plot twist, I thought. What I said, however, was...

"You will come to know my ways, Brother Abbot. In the meantime, I advise you to hide nothing from me. My eyes are all seeing. Tell me what lies above in the heights of the praesidium."

"There are four upper storeys, strictly forbidden to the novitiates except with the permission of the abbot. The lowest is the studio, in which the illuminators perform their work. The next contains the personnel records of the abbey, while the third contains the library. The fourth is the ceremonium, the spacious lounge in which we hold gala dinners and other functions for our celebrity guests. Doubtless you have heard of our library, Brother Marco."

Since it was the first time the library had been mentioned, I didn't see how I could have heard of it, but I went along with the whole sorry farce anyway...

"Yes, the library of the abbey is known to all men who seek after truth, and is famed throughout Christendom for the severity of its fines. I understand that it contains rare and esoteric works."

"It does indeed, Brother Marco. And for that reason no brother is allowed unsupervised access to the library."

"None?" I asked in surprise. "You speak in riddles, Brother Abbot. Surely someone is allowed unsupervised access, otherwise how would the books be curated?"

"I am sorry, Brother Marco. I meant to say that no brother is meant to have unsupervised access apart from myself and the librarian."

His words had more than a passing resemblance to those uttered in a similar scene by the beautiful Harbour Master McBeany in my last book. They prompted a passing thought about the possibility that the librarian could be an attractive woman in a severely-cut habit, with heavily-rimmed spectacles she could whip-off now and again to flash eyes the colour of rare and exotic flours, as that might give me an opportunity to please my feminist readers.

"So, the young novice fell to his death either from the illuminators' studio or the personnel records department, or the library, or the ceremonium?" I said, overlooking the possibility that he might have dropped from the roof or from a passing aeroplane.

"It seems that way, Brother Marco, yet all were banned to him."

"A brother who would infringe the holy ordinances about the sanctity of life might not feel bound by the rules of the abbot, Brother Abbot."

"You speak truly, Brother Marco."

It struck me that including brother this and brother that in every line of dialogue was a great wheeze for padding out the word-count.

"I suggest, Brother Abbot, it would be prudent for you to show me the upper storeys of the praesidium."

"Certainly. Let us go at once."

The praesidium was built in some ways like a church, yet in others it resembled the exterior of a huge shopping mall, with its cast concrete panellations, the joints between which were sealed by the finest mastic.

I was halted by the majesty of its fabled doors. The left leaf bore the legend FIREDO, which in Latin means '*I light*'; that on the right 'ORKEEPSHUT', which in an ancient Coptic dialect means '*Who used the last of the chick peas?*'. Each leaf was cunningly wrought in treated fibreboard, machined to the most exacting of tolerances, with only minor warping evident where they met.

The leaves were mounted on the jambs by butt hinges manufactured with unsurpassed accuracy in Illinois, each secured with eight screws of zinc-plated nickel-steel, the slots of which were oriented at random to represent the random distribution of stars in the heavens.

Set into each leaf was an unilluminated window of three-eighths frosted glass through which a delicate filigree of silver wires had been inlaid, as if forming the grid of a giant religious-themed crossword. The panes themselves were retained in their recesses by glazing bars immaculately pinned to the door with forty-millimetre copper nails.

The intricate locking mechanism allowed the upper and lower bolts to be withdrawn at the press of a single bar, symbolising the role man plays in linking heaven and hell.

To either side of the doors was displayed the abbey's enormous anachronistic collection of rifles that once belonged to Chekhov. Strictly speaking, I ought now to spend three pages describing the collection in order to make the joke complete, but to save us all the bother let's just pretend I did. And if you don't understand the joke, look-up 'Chekhov's gun.' And anyway, you're not going to get the joke unless you manged to get as far as the door scene in the original Name of the Rose book, so... now that I think about it, just forget it. Forget the whole paragraph. I don't know why I bother.

I hurried through the doors before I found myself writing any more of this rubbish.

The first storey was the studio. Though the time was past lauds, the illuminators were still at their specialist work, preparing the illuminations for which the abbey was rightly famed, and which attracted huge numbers of visitors every Christmas. The illuminations were as varied as they were intricate, depicting fantastic shapes in every imaginable hue. The central theme was Father Christmas, with his helpers and his reindeer and his sleigh, all picked out in delicate lights. The ancillary themes were beyond number, including Christmas trees, fairies, snowflakes, angels, stockings, holly leaves, puddings, those funny candies shaped like a walking-stick, presents, crackers, more snowflakes, and other advent imagery of marvellous variety. There were over one million bulbs of every colour.

"Whenever a bulb fails," said the abbot, "the illuminators must replace them one at a time to find the failed one, twisting them in and out of their holders with bleeding fingers. It is demanding work, but at the same time their devotion."

"I hear reports from the abbey at Trieste," I said, "of a new technique in which the bulbs are wired not in series but in parallel, so that were one to fail the others remain lit, much as men can remain piously facing heaven even though one of their number should fall to sinful ways."

"You are indeed wise, Brother Marco."

The replacement of faulty bulbs was not the only concern of the illuminators. They laboured too on the design and construction of control boxes to flash the lights in a variety of patterns pleasing to the intellect and the soul alike.

"Tell me, Brother Abbot, is there much competition among the brethren to rise to the exalted position of illuminator?" I asked, looking for motives.

"Indeed, Brother Marco. The competition is as fierce as a nun in a nark. It is a case of dead man's sandals."

"You mean..."

"Yes. A vacancy in the illuminatorium arises only upon the death of an illuminator."

"And the young novice whose body was discovered at the foot of the cliff—did he show an interest in the illuminator's calling?"

"He did indeed, Brother Marco. He was a most assiduous student, and had studied three years as an illuminator's apprentice. He was due to have a passing-out piece displayed this very Noel."

"Hmmm," I said, undecided about whether to develop this as a core strand of the plot or as a misleading digression. "Perhaps we should view the next storey."

"By all means, Brother Marco. Please follow me."

Chapter Four

For which Marco forgot to write a summary, the idiot.

The abbot led me through passages dark and serpentine to an elevator cunningly concealed behind two sliding steel doors. We entered its box-like interior. On a panel were symbols representing the storeys of the building, below which an icon showed six monks in profile, which I understood to indicate the safe working capacity of the machine. The abbot pressed one of the numerical symbols, and we were propelled heavenward.

"If only man's rise could always be guaranteed by the push of a button," he said.

"But I see that the machine facilitates descent likewise," I replied. "What can induce virtue can also induce vice."

"You are very wise, Brother Marco."

The door of the lifting and lowering cabinet opened, and we found ourselves on the next of the four restricted storeys of the praesidium. The doors ahead of us were locked. The abbot, however, had upon his girdle an immense ring from which hung a collection of magnetic swipe cards as numerous as angels on the head of a huge pin. He selected the appropriate card and swiped our way into the personnel records department, or 'aycharium', to use the ancient tongue.

"Good heavens!" ejaculated the abbot. "There has been an intruder."

My keen detective's eye swept the scene like a powerful searchlight. The aycharium was a single enormous room containing row upon row of shelving laid out in a cruciform pattern. The shelves were filled with scrolls and parchments, sealed with ribbon and wax, many of them having rested in their positions for many years, to judge by the dust and cobwebs that shrouded them. However, certain of the documents had been strewn carelessly on the rough oak planks of the floor.

"Might it be the aycharchivist's work, Brother Abbot?"

"No, Brother Marco—he is most meticulous about his archive. He would never leave documents strewn carelessly on the rough oak planks of the floor."

"Let us examine the documents which the intruder sought, but carefully, so as not to contaminate any evidence they might bear."

The abbot and I knelt beside the parchments on the floor. I teased their curling edges apart. The abbot crossed himself as the contents were revealed.

"Why, those are the curricula vitae of Brothers George, Alfonse and Crispin—my fellow members of the Elder Council. Who would wish to view these records?"

"We shall know in good time, Your Transcendence, when my investigations are complete. Here, hold this."

I instructed the abbot to hold each of the scrolls flat while I photographed their contents with my iPad.

"Now, let us see whether the intruder has left any other signs of his purpose."

We walked warily down the main aisle to the centre of the cruciform array of shelving, where two desks lay back-to-back, each provided with a cunning set of concealed drawers which could be opened silently on runners fitted with small wheels of ivory. The drawers had been left open, as if a hasty search had been made within them, and from the richly patinated top of one of the desks began a trail of congealed blood.

"By the name of the seven holy seals!" said the abbot.

I followed the trail of blood, the abbot at my shoulder. It led to a secret door behind a mirror, down a secret flight of stairs, through the refectory, past the doors to the laudanum, across the herbarium where the monastery's famous collection of roses was developed, around the sepulchristy, past the leaflet rack at reception, into the men's toilet and out again, across the main courtyard, up another secret spiral staircase and back via yet another mirror into the aycharium, down an aisle between shelves, around a corner...

"By the eight holy lords a leaping," said the abbot. "It is the aycharchivist!"

The body of the learned aycharchivist sat on the floor, leant against the shelving. His arm lay along one of the shelves, and his cold dead finger pointed accusingly at one of the scrolls.

I stretched on a pair of rubber police gloves that I forgot to mention I kept in the pouch-like pockets of my habit, then examined the body with the all-seeing eye of the hardened crime writer. It was just as I suspected.

"Can you... have you..." stammered the abbot, carelessly omitting question marks in his confusion.

"Yes. There are many highly significant clues, indicated by the earthen deposits on the heel of the poor Brother's left sandal, a chemical stain on his right forearm, a minor burn on his knee, encrustations under his fingernails, a distinctive fraying at the hem of his robe, goat-hairs among the tassels of his waist cord, and a marked rancidity of his undergarments."

"What could it mean?"

It meant he was in the presence of a tired writer on the edge of a complete mental breakdown, of course, but I could not admit that without placing at risk the future of my book, and perhaps even the great religious order itself.

"The Lord will make his meaning clear when he is ready, Brother Abbot."

I turned my attention to the scroll to which pointed the dead digit of the aycharchivist. I broke its wax seal, unrolled the parchment, and read the following words:

Capsum ipse domatorum que nuncto passata volorem ipso sunt. Qua vontum flores namen rosica. Tabascum ipso tabasca haec paluntque nobis.

The one good thing about describing the contents of Latin scrolls is that you can write anything you like and most people won't notice that the words are randomly made-up. Even if they do, you can always say the words are a code.

The inquisitive abbot looked over my shoulder at the scroll, and crossed himself. "It looks like Latin, Brother Marco, but they are not Latin words I recognise. It is as if they have been made up by an idiot."

Which was a fair conclusion, as it happens.

"They are in some form of code, Brother Abbot, and I suspect the key to the code lies somewhere in the praesidium."

"But where shall we look for it?"

"We shall look for it where we should least expect to find it, as Satan tempts the seeker of truth to follow the obvious paths."

"And where should we least expect to find it, Brother Marco?"

"I shall tell you where we shall find it, Brother Abbot. No, wait, sorry, I shall show you where we shall find it, Brother Abbot, as to show is better than to tell."

"So the wise ones say, Brother Marco."

"We shall find it there!" I announced, flinging my hand in the direction of the staircase to the library.

"On the stairs?"

I retrieved my outflung hand and clutched it to my brow. One of these days I was going to write a book with characters who weren't complete imbeciles.

"No Brother Abbot—not on the stairs, but in the place to which the stairs lead."

"The landing at the top of the stairs?"

Rather than waste your time and mine extending this tedious gag to its awful conclusion, by having the abbot suggest the library doors, the library vestibule etc, just pretend we've been through all that and the abbot says...

"The library? But the library is a vast chamber, the dusty recesses of which are as numerous and unfrequented as those of a simpleton's mind."

I didn't argue—he should know about simpletons' minds.

"You speak truly, Brother Abbot, but the dust itself is our friend. Just as I read in the snow the story of Brother Tom's whereabouts, so I will read the dust. Come!"

I strode majestically toward the stairs to the library, leaving the abbot no choice but to follow. Hardly had I raised my sandaled foot to the first step when an unbearable shrill alarm filled the air. A deep voice sounded all around us, as if the Lord himself spake.

"This is a fire drill. Please leave the building by the nearest exit. This is.."

"A fire drill! I am sorry, Brother Marco, but we must postpone our hunt. Our health and safety policies strictly forbid anyone from remaining in the building until the drill is complete."

Phew. That was a relief. I had no idea what I was going to do in the library, so I willingly followed the abbot to the car park, where the brethren were mustering and bitching about the cold. I raised a question that was praying, sorry, preying on my addled mind.

"Tell me, Brother Abbot, does it not strike you as a coincidence that the alarm sounded at the very instant we were starting for the library?"

"What are you implying, Brother Marco?"

"I imply nothing, but it seems to me an unlikely coincidence. Might the alarm have been triggered to distract us from our search?"

The abbot stared at me as he absorbed the significance of my question. "Could such devilment be possible?"

"We will find out with swift and decisive action. Who is in charge of the fire alarms?"

"There is no single brother in charge. The responsibility is shared amongst the elders on a rota."

"Then let us consult the rota at once."

"But we cannot. The rota is in the aycharium, and we cannot re-enter it until the all clear is sounded."

I uttered a clichéd curse under my breath, and seethed with impatient rage. Someone was playing games with us. "But surely, Brother Abbot, you have the authority to override such petty rules."

"The authority is indeed vested in me, but with authority goes responsibility. My fellow brethren are impressionable. Were they to see their abbot disregarding his own rules, their faith in the hallowed traditions of our order would be undermined. I am minded of the experience of the Burgists, an order torn asunder by the great schism of 1983 which arose from a minor infringement of their sacred rules by their scapaltor, who violated the holy code with the best of intentions. His actions led to profound unease about the meaning of certain codicils to the constitution of the order."

I felt a profound unease coming on too. Why couldn't I for once, just once, write a character who did what I asked? I stared at the words on the screen, utterly fed-up. Heaven knows what the readers were feeling, but this seemed about the most annoying, unproductive and futile chapter I'd ever written. What it needed was a really good twist, so it was almost a relief when over the abbot's shoulder, I saw one of the brethren run screaming from the herbarium with blood all over his hands.

CHAPTER FIVE

In which Marco writes the premature death of a new character.

By the eight holy maids a milking!" The abbot lifted the skirts of his habit and trotted towards the distraught brother, who had fallen to his knees and was blubbing in shock.

"The herbalist, the herbalist, he is dead!"

A gasp of astonishment and fear spread among the gathered brethren, myself included. I had been planning to make the herbalist one of my key suspects, and now I'd just written that he was dead. Cursing my impulsiveness, I knelt beside the blubbing brother, hoping to ease his mind with my charismatic presence.

"Come, Brother, tell us what happened." I patted his shoulder reassuringly.

"IT IS STAN COME AMONGST US!" screamed the unhinged monk.

"Stan?" The abbot and I spoke in one voice of synchronised bewilderment. "Who is Stan?"

I realized my mistake, and retyped the line...

"IT IS SATAN COME AMONGST US!" screamed the unhinged monk.

Ignoring the reassuring pat of my hand on his shoulder, the mad monk rose and ran across the cobbles of the car park, tearing handfuls of hair from each side of his head. Reaching the perimeter fence, he hauled himself up it, tottered a moment at the top, then hurled himself into the brink. I ran to the fence, gripped its intertwining links and stared with horror down the hundreds of feet to where the crumpled body of the monk lay in its girdled habit upon the scree at the base of the cliff.

"What evil could have caused this outrage?" puffed the abbot, who was catching his breath after trotting behind me.

"I cannot yet say," I said, which was the exact literal truth, as I had only just made all this up and I had no idea where it was going. "But fear not, Brother Abbot, we will find and expunge the source. Let us inspect the herbarium."

"The herbarium? I am afraid that is not possible. No brother may enter the herbarium without the express written permission of the herbalist. It is one of the strictest codes of our order, an inviolable..."

I'd had enough. This madness had to stop. Silencing the abbot with an upraised hand, I reminded him of our predicament.

"The herbalist is dead, Brother Abbot. His written permission can no longer be sought or granted. We must rely instead on the higher permission the Lord grants to all seekers after truth. Come!"

Before the abbot could work out that what I'd said was meaningless mumbo-jumbo, I strode majestically toward the herbarium.

As I slipped across the uneven cobbles in my new sandals, I tried to refocus my mind on the gruesome task that lay ahead, namely that of inventing a few hundred words of mindless garbage about the herbarium. With all the bother about the suicidal brother, I hadn't had a chance to figure out the next plot twist, and I therefore lacked any sensible rationale for determining the key characteristics of the herbarium, such as its size, contents, appearance, age, and method of construction. Approaching its entrance at the culmination of my short walk, I had that clichéd absence of choices, viz no option, but to write the first thing that came into my head. I lost no time about it...

The famed herbarium of the abbey had been founded by Severinus the Transgressor in 1966 AD. Constructed of prefabricated softwood panels, the fifty acre greenhouse was known throughout Christendom for the astonishing variety of the scenes depicted in its five-hundred-thousand individual panes of stained glass. Year round, an endless stream of coaches delivered an endless stream of tourists which snaked endlessly between endless velvet-covered guide-ropes to marvel at the imagery.

The stained panes were the work of the celebrity guests at the abbey, who were required as part of their detox therapy to spend their mornings in silence, contemplating the wonders of the Lord while painting their individual rectangles of 4mm horticultural glass. The subjects of the paintings reflected the varied interests of their celebrity painters— award ceremonies, book launches, movie sets, lavish parties, mobbing paparazzi, villas on the Cote D'Azur, the first-class lounges of countless international airports, stretch limos, chat-shows, hotel rooms strewn with discarded needles, top-flight sporting contests of every type, rock concerts, painting studios, divorce courts, psychiatric units, election rallies, hairdressing and beauty treatments, gym work-outs, faddish diets—every conceivable topic of interest to the celebrity was depicted in the rich panoply of the herbarium's glassy roof.

The images incorporated product placements of every type, according to the contractual obligations of the painter: expensive watches and jewellery, top-end automobiles, after-shaves and eaux-de-Cologne, designer underwear, smartphones, home insurance, credit cards, open-ended unit trust investment opportunities, and countless other products and services for which the celebrities acted as mercenary pushers.

As varied as the subjects upon the panes were the crops grown under them. Cereals of every sort, berries, root vegetables, tender greens, edible cacti and other succulents, aromatic herbs, nutritious nuts, countless forms of fungi, and at least 57 varieties of baked bean. The beds of vegetables stretched into the distant recesses of the herbarium. One challenge occupied my mind—where in that giant patchwork of plants would I find the herbalist? What horror of Satan's handiwork would confront us when we found him? I sought the abbot's advice.

"Brother Abbot, can you tell me something of the layout of the herbarium?"

I waited with keen interest for his reply, a reply which might allow us to deduce the likely location of the herbalist's body within the vast greenhouse.

"Indeed, Brother Marco. The herbarium is laid out as a giant labyrinth, with paths cunningly designed to curve among the vegetable beds so that it is not possible to see more than a few paces in any direction. The paths have no names or sign-posts, and there is no pattern to the distribution of the crops within the patchwork of beds. Thus the herbarium reflects the complexity of the universe, in which man must always be uncertain of his immediate future, and must rely on faith rather than logic to guide his course."

"So the body of the unfortunate herbalist could be anywhere?"

"Indeed, Brother Marco."

"And we would have to walk every path to be sure of finding it?"

"Indeed, Brother Marco."

My eyes glazed at the tedious prospect of typing a random walk through the giant herbarium in search of the dead herbalist. Surely there was a shortcut? I waited for one to come into my head.

"There are no shortcuts," said the abbot. "We must explore every path. Come!"

Off we set. Yard after yard, chain after chain, furlong after furlong, mile after mile, league after league we paced the serpentine paths between the beds, steaming in the heat of the herbarium (the beds that is, not us). Time and again we came close to abandoning our quest, until finally we came to a widening of the way where rack after rack of seed packets were arrayed to the left of a paved area, while to the right an orderly collection of horticultural paraphernalia occupied a line of display cases: rakes, hoes, scythes, spades, forks, pruning saws, hose pipes with various attachments, brooms, cloches, plant labels, twine, insecticide, fertiliser, plant pots, gloves, kneeling pads, and a vast selection of gardening books, greeting cards, and calendars. But our eyes were not drawn to the gaudy merchandise. In the centre of the paved area, a pentangle had been hastily drawn with coloured chalk. Inside the pentangle, sprawled on the stone, lay the eviscerated body of the herbalist, its bowels spread upon the dusty floor. In horror I realised the intestines had been arranged to form a word:

CAVE

"I cannot believe it," cried the abbot. Whether he was referring to the gruesome fate of the herbalist or the whole farcical chapter I couldn't say. "What demon could have performed such an act?"

With profound reluctance, I allowed myself to type the next thing that had come into my head.

"The herbalist himself."

"The herbalist!" The abbot's disbelief was now off the scale.

"Indeed, Brother Abbot. Look!" I reached for a leather-bound, vellum-leaved note pad that lay open on the floor near the racks of seeds. "Here evidently is the herbalist's log, in which he records the daily development of his crops, cross-referencing the growth of the plants to the phases of the moon, the temperature and humidity, and so on."

"But...but..." the abbot was speechless in the face of what appeared to be a total irrelevance. I went on: "Now look at the word which has been spelled with the herbalist's entrails."

The blood drained from the abbot's face at the sound of my next words, words uttered in a voice of deadly menace...

"It is the herbalist's handwriting."

CHAPTER SIX

In which Marco remembers his mentor's advice.

The horrified abbot staggered and fell against the seed racks, a natural reaction to the harrowing corniness of the previous sentence. I knelt by his side, pulling the stopper from an ancient Thracian crystal phial that I forgot to mention I had in the pocket of my gown. I placed the small bottle to his greying lips.

"Here, Brother Abbot, this concoction will ease your distress."

He sipped it gratefully. "That is indeed a miraculous restorative. What are its principal ingredients?"

The writing on the label was too small for me to read, so I made something up. "Ginseng, extract of acacia bush, tamara root, powdered buffalo hoof, sea-horse eggs, hydrogenated cedar oil, glucose and aqua minerale. It is produced by the Sisters of Sustenance at the famous Kraft convent in Illinois."

"You are most wise, Brother Marco. But what must we do about..."

The abbot nodded toward the body of the herbalist, his words failing him. I knew how he felt. After the blatant digression about the potion bottle had bought me so little time, I now had to decide what to write. Upon my next words the course of the rest of the book might depend. What a moment of supreme literary crisis! I almost fainted under the pressure. I thought desperately. What would Como do? No, that was no help—Como would round up some obvious suspects and intimidate them physically until they cracked. I had forgotten to write-in any obvious suspects, and I was too puny to intimidate them anyway. A weak smile tugged at a corner of my mouth. I was making my old mistake—thinking. I felt in the folds of my scabrous robe for the small leathern pouch I always carry on a silk cord around my neck, the pouch that contains my most treasured possession—the gold pen given to me by my mentor, Herbert Quarry, upon which were engraved the words:

"To Marco. Never forget, always write the next thing that comes into your head."

With relieved fingers I took the precious pen from its pouch and studied the finely inscribed dedication. Herbert's theories about literature were controversial and widely derided by mainstream academics, but they had made me the publishing legend I was. Thinking is the writer's enemy, Herbert used to say. A writer should write, not think. Putting the precious pen back in its pouch, I typed the next thing that came into my head.

"Tell me, Brother Abbot, I don't suppose there are surveillance cameras, by any chance, at the entrance to the herbarium."

"There are indeed, Brother Marco; four of them, arrayed at such angles that it is impossible to enter or leave the herbarium unobserved. The cameras use the most advanced sixty-four gigabit sensors, sensitive to visible, ultra-violet and infrared wavelengths, generating images of unsurpassed vividness and detail. They were installed at the insistence of the herbalist himself only a week ago. I remember it most clearly, as the necessity for meeting the significant cost of their installation was hotly contested at the last council of the elders."

That was more like it. I felt the old magic flooding back in an inspiring mix of clichéd metaphors. The sophisticated cameras would reveal who had entered the herbarium, just as the contesting of their installation would reveal a potential suspect.

"Tell me, Brother Abbot, who was it who contested the installation of the surveillance equipment?"

"That was Brother Felonius of Syracuse. He condemned the camera as the work of Satan, a doubly evil device that encouraged voyeurism in the observer and vanity in the observed."

"Was Brother Felonius in other respects cordial and empathetic toward the late herbalist?"

"Most assuredly not. He seemed to harbour a deadly resentment of the herbalist's failure to honour him in the naming of roses."

"The naming of roses?"

"Indeed, Brother Marco. The abbey is famed in horticultural circles for the new varieties of rose it develops—cultivars and hybrids of peerless beauty, fragrance and pest resistance. The new varieties are named after individuals resident at the abbey. It is considered a great honour to be recognised by the naming of a rose, an honour within the exclusive gift of the herbalist, since it is he and he alone who decides whom to honour. It is an open secret that Brother Felonius nurses a grievance in his bosom that he, one of the most senior brethren, has been passed over again and again when new varieties have been named."

Ha! I sat back astounded. There, if any proof were still needed, was the direct evidence of the effectiveness of Herbert's advice. Just ten paragraphs ago I had been utterly at a loss about what to write next, and now, having let my auto-pilot take over, I had a suspect, a motive, a means of discovery, and—this the most amazing of all—a logic to tie it all in to the cryptic title of the book. I could have kissed the abbot. In fact, I did.

"Brother Marco! This is most unorthodox."

"Apologies, your Supreme Serenity, but your words have lifted a veil of darkness from my eyes. The way ahead is clear. Now, Your Sublimity, we must secure the crime scene."

"But should we not inform the authorities? Surely, it is a moral and legal duty to report such a crime."

I laid a reassuring hand on the abbot's bony forearm.

"Ordinarily, yes, Brother Abbot. But the Lord empowers his subjects to rise above earthly conventions when guided by pious principle. What, we must ask ourselves, would be the benefit of informing the authorities? The police, as we know from countless private-detective novels, are corrupt, bungling and ineffectual. Bringing them here would result only in the waste of the tax-payer's dollar and page after page of formulaic police procedure."

"But consider your own works, Brother Marco. Is not Clarkesville blessed with a heroic, resourceful police chief, relentless in his pursuit of miscreants? Should we not avail ourselves of Chief Galahad's investigative prowess?"

"There is truth in what you say, Your Supremity, but consider the implications," I said, wondering if that should have been Your Supremacy. "The grand opening is now just days away. Even with all of Chief Galahad's influence, he could not prevent news of a murder being published once we had activated the machinery of his office. Almost certainly, the celebrities who are booked-in for the opening week would cancel their reservations."

The frightened abbot crossed himself at the thought of the lost business. "But what should we do, Brother Marco?"

CHAPTER SEVEN

In which Marco loses his thread.

It was a good question. After my volcanic spasm of literary creativity, I felt quite spent. I decided to write some formulaic police procedure for a couple of paragraphs to allow my neurons to recharge.

"Firstly we must document the crime scene. Then we will review the recordings from the CCTV, then we will interview Brother Felonius, and then we will get back to the plot strand about a cypher that we were following up when the fire alarm when off in the praesidium."

I hunted among the horticultural products in the display cabinet and found some chalk, with which I drew an outline of the body on the floor, taking particular care around the entrails to mimic the distinctive characteristics of the letters spelling CAVE. Speaking of which reminded me I'd forgotten to develop the implications of the word as a potential plot twist. I raised it with the abbot.

"If I may beg Your Serenity's advice, what do you make of the word that the poor herbalist took such care to leave for us on the stone floor of his beloved herbarium?"

"Cave? Why, Brother Marco, you must surely know that a cave is an underground hollow, from the Latin cavus."

"Indeed, Your Supereminence, but might the letters have some other meaning? If the herbalist wanted to leave a message in such a cryptic fashion we can be sure the most literal meaning is the least likely."

The abbot looked puzzled, as if he were struggling to follow my logic, which was fair enough as I was struggling to follow it myself. "What else could he mean?"

"Cave can also mean beware, from the Latin caveo. In the Scando-Zulu tongue, as spoken in Finnish Africa, cave means cellars. In Italian it means quarries. It can mean to collapse, or succumb. It could even be the first four letters of the word evacuate, read backwards."

"Your mind is as twisted as the labyrinth of the herbarium, Brother Marco. I see now why your books have such serpentine plots. Who would have thought the herbalist's last word would pose such a riddle?"

Who indeed. I certainly didn't, but now I was stuck with it.

"Never mind, Brother Abbot, all will become clear. Let us seal the crime scene, and view the CCTV footage."

We found some rolls of waxed twine and a packet of self-adhesive plant labels, on which we wrote the words *'Crime Scene—do not cross,'* and used them to cordon the area around the herbalist's body.

"No-one must be allowed into the herbarium," I commanded. "Among the innocent, only you and I know the detail of the fate of the herbalist. We will use our knowledge to test the innocence of the other brethren. If they display any awareness of the facts surrounding the herbalist's demise we will know that they had some hand or part in it."

Immediately I wondered if what I had just typed was ridiculous. If the herbarium was a fifty acre glass-house then surely there would need to be tens of people working there to water the plants, to regulate the temperature and attend to the countless other tasks associated with cultivating produce on an enormous scale.

"It is lucky indeed," said the abbot, "that the herbarium is equipped with automatic systems for irrigation, temperature control, and other routine tasks, so that it can be left unmanned for days at a stretch."

Phew, that was a relief. We followed the trail of breadcrumbs I had laid and retraced our steps to the entrance of the herbarium, or exit, I suppose, depending on which way you looked at it. Once outside, the abbot locked the imposing doors and fastened a ribbon between their handles, sealing the bow of the ribbon with a blob of wax into which he impressed the distinctive boss of his ring.

"Where may we view the CCTV footage?" I asked the abbot.

"In the securarium. Follow me."

We took a path between the eastern wall of the praesidium and a temporary lavatory block installed to accommodate the needs of tourists. Turning a corner, we were confronted by a metal staircase that led to a lean-to building bristling with security features. The abbot swiped a card through a reader next to the door, then we stepped inside.

The securarium appeared to have been adapted from an old stable block. Its stone floor was crossed with runnels; iron rings were let into its walls where horses would have once been tethered. A hayrack, bolted above a water trough, had been adapted to house a colour monitor, on which was displayed the footage from security cameras around the entrance to the herbarium.

"The contraption is controlled from this console," said the abbot, "but its workings are unfamiliar to me."

"Who, then, is familiar with its workings?"

"Why, the herbalist. It was he who commissioned the device."

"But the herbalist is dead. Surely there must be someone else who can control the system."

"I am afraid not, Brother Marco. The system, as you call it, has been installed for just a week. The other brothers have been too busy preparing for the grand opening to pay attention to it."

"Then surely we should call-in the company who provided the system—they can explain it to us, and demonstrate how to replay its recordings."

"I fear not, Brother Marco. The system was configured by the herbalist himself, who bought its individual components second-hand from the mart of the layman known as E-bay."

I sighed a long, expressive sigh. Now I was going to have to do something I hated—writing about technology. Feel free to skip the next couple of paragraphs if the thought of them fills you with as heavy a sense of oppressive tedium as it does me.

"Never mind, Brother Abbot. You may know I have a PhD in fundamental particle physics, and am well-used to complex technological devices of every kind. I will soon discern the workings of the contraption. Let me see... Yes, the wires from the cameras enter the box here. These icons, or miniature symbols, denote the significance of the controls. This, if I am not mistaken, switches between the various cameras to determine which has its feed displayed on the monitor."

I twisted a large Bakelite knob, and the display switched from one camera to another as I did so. The pictures were indeed amazingly clear and lifelike. I had no doubt that within a few brisk sentences we would be able to identify anyone who had entered the herbarium before the herbalist's horrific death.

"Your wisdom is unsurpassed," said the abbot.

"This collection of keys can be pressed to control the replay of recordings from the cameras, which are encoded in the form of magnetic patterns on the cassette tape here." I pressed the key that opened the compartment that held the cassette tape. "By the twelve lords a leaping—the tape has gone!"

I stared in amazement at the empty tape drive, scarcely able to believe what I had just typed.

"Gone?" queried the astonished abbot. "What does that mean?"

It means I've completely screwed up my plot, I thought. What I said, however, was:

"It means that we are dealing with a fiend or fiends of exceptional cunning. They have taken the medium upon which is recorded the evidence we seek. We must track them down. Who else has a card to unlock the door of the securarium?"

"Only the elders of the abbey council."

"How many do they number?"

"Six, including myself and the herbalist."

I asked the next obvious question.

"Is Brother Felonius amongst them?"

"Indeed. He is one of the most senior monks of the abbey."

"Then let us seek him without delay."

I admit it was careless of me to have written that the tape had been removed, thus creating a dead end where there had once been a straightforward opportunity for plot development, but I was confident we would soon be back on track. We had only to confront the rascally Brother Felonious and he would crumble under the sabre-like thrusts of my interrogation. I could picture the scene: the suspected monk, shifty and evasive; myself, dominant and magnificent, unmasking lie after lie with my incisive questioning; the abbot, astounded by my performance, thrilled to hear me in action at the height of...

My creative introspections were interrupted by the cries of a breathless young monk who burst through the doorway with an expression radiating fear. "Brother Abbot, you must forgive my intrusion. There has been a terrible accident in the cannery. You must come at once."

CHAPTER EIGHT

In which Marco makes monastic mayhem.

We raced to the cannery, the abbot leading, the young monk at his shoulder, I behind them. Even my sandals slipping on the mossy cobbles of the path, causing the new leather of the straps to cut painfully into the tender skin of my ankles, was nothing compared to my mental distress. I had come to the abbey for complete rest, and here I was, spouting unresolved plot strands like a literary party popper. What I wanted was half a dozen chapters of uneventful serenity, in which I floated in the abbey's famous isolation tank, or partook of various soothing spa treatments, and instead I was back on the hamster wheel of the thriller writer, a sentence away from having to invent a whole new scenario off the top of my head. Speaking of which...

The cannery was a portal-framed shed to the west of the praesidium. Clad in corrugated steel panels, it housed the various operations through which the abbey's fabled beer was drawn from huge brewing vats and dispensed into aluminium cans twelve ounces at a time, the cans being boxed in cartons twenty four at a time, the cartons stacked on pallets forty eight at a time, and the pallets loaded onto trucks ninety six at a time. The vast sliding doors of the cannery were drawn open, as if a truck had been expected for loading. We ran through them, and even as our eyes adjusted to the harsh neon glare within, our minds struggled to accept the horrific sight they exposed.

Against the farthest wall were three giant oaken vats, each at least twenty feet tall, and each affixed with a steel-runged ladder to allow the contents of the vat to be inspected from above. About two thirds up the ladder of the left-most vat was the figure of a monk. Its head arched back, its arms flopped at either side, it was pinned in place by one of the tines of a forklift truck, pierced through its ribcage just to the left of the spine.

"By the secret sojourn of St. Stephanus," exclaimed the abbot, crossing himself. "How could such an unfortunate accident happen?"

I put my face in my hands, appalled at the prospect of the huge cliché I knew I must write.

"This was no accident," I croaked. I nodded at the young monk. "Climb up there, and see who it is."

The young man clambered onto the roof of the forklift, and managed to raise himself sufficiently far to step onto its other tine, from where he could easily peel back the cowl of the pierced figure. And no-one was less surprised than I by his next words.

"It is Brother Felonius!"

I waggled my head at the gruesome inevitability of it. Yet another perplexing dead end.

"What are we to do?" queried the baffled abbot.

"Find someone else to inspect the beer." And if my reply was tetchy and sarcastic, who could blame me, after twelve thousand words of this rubbish? "Let me guess—if I were to ask who has access to the keys of the forklift, you would say only yourself and the other members of the elder council?"

"Indeed, Brother Marco. How did you know? The forklift is a devilish contraption that frees man from many burdens and tempts him into the arms of indolence; hence its use can be entrusted only to those who are best able to resist such temptations."

"Then we shall convene an emergency meeting of the council."

"It shall be as you say, Brother Marco."

"In the meantime, I shall climb up there to inspect Brother Felonius for clues."

"Do you think it safe?"

"You are too cautious, Brother Abbot. What could go wrong? Here, lad, help me up."

I beckoned the young monk to lower his hand to help me onto the roof of the forklift. As I stepped onto the chassis the strap of my left sandal caught on the joystick that controlled the infernal machine. We skidded abruptly backwards in a tight right-hander, collapsing a huge tower of cartons that spilled a cascade of beer cans in a metallic torrent across the cannery floor. The body of Brother Felonius fell off the fork, and flopped over the abbot, who collapsed under its weight, and was now wriggling to free himself from the grisly embrace of the still-warm corpse.

"Your Eminence!"

The young monk dropped off the forklift to help the abbot to his feet, while I inspected the nasty bruise that was already showing where the knob of the joystick had pinched the skin of my foot. As if my mental anguish were not enough.

I rearranged my habit to provide some semblance of dignity, then knelt to examine the remains of Brother Felonius. The robe which enfolded his body was of the highest quality, shot with silken threads. Its pockets were of the finest doeskin, strong yet amazingly soft. And no words could describe the exquisite workmanship of the stitching of his sandals. I turned the body over. Ignoring the huge gash in its torso, I patted the pockets of the corpse in the manner of the hardened thriller writer, then revealed to the startled abbot one of the fruits of my gruesome search.

"Here, Brother Abbot, is the cassette we sought—the cassette that will either prove or disprove the guilt of Brother Felonious."

What I did not show was a second object I had found in the capacious pockets of the dead brother—a small leather notebook. I could not say why, but some instinct caused me to keep it hidden, so I secreted it in the folds of my robe.

"Let us return to the securarium, where we may inspect the contents of this cassette," I said, tapping it against my chest in the manner of a marginally repentant sinner.

Resisting the temptation to pad out an extra paragraph with a description of our return to the securarium—the echoes of our hasty footfalls, the gathering dusk, the first few tentative flakes of an approaching snowstorm, the harsh calls of the ravens, the melodious chants from the choristers practicing their carols—I decided to restart the action where I was once more looking down upon the console of the surveillance hub. I opened the tape compartment, and inserted the cassette. At last, we would see its secrets.

"At last, we will see the secrets of the tape, Brother Abbot. Please study the screen."

The screen showed the entrance to the herbarium in astonishing clarity and detail, with a set of figures overlaying the image to show the date and time at which the image was recorded.

"Those figures overlaying the image on the screen," queried the abbot, "what is their meaning?"

I tutted at his infuriating inability to keep up.

"They show the date and time at which the image was recorded."

"But that cannot be, Brother Marco. The year is shown as 1999 AD, and the time as 23.08, even though the image clearly shows the entrance to the herbarium in daylight."

"That simply shows, Brother Abbot, how symbols may mislead the uninitiated. The device has an internal clock, a clock the herbalist had not bothered to set. Now, play close attention to the image as I use my powers to reverse the flow of time." I depressed the rewind key with a thumb of majestic aplomb.

The digits on the screen counted backwards for a moment, then stopped. There followed a complex sequence of mechanical noises too unusual for me to describe, following which there appeared on the monitor in flashing red type 'Tape Sequence Error'.

"Most impressive, Brother Marco," said the clueless abbot. "What is the meaning of the cryptic message?"

As I'd only just made it up, I couldn't yet say. However, I wasn't going to allow my book to be derailed by a technical hitch. I ejected the tape and scrutinised its casing. Yes, as I suspected, there was a crack over one of the reels, and the plastic housing was slightly dented.

"The casing of the tape has been damaged, Brother Abbot, perhaps by pressure from the prong of the forklift. I must dismantle the housing and inspect the interior. Do you have a jeweller's screwdriver upon you?"

It was an odd question to pose to the head of an abbey, but I thought it worth a try. With luck, he would say he hadn't, and we would have a consultation lasting a paragraph or two, at the end of which he would conclude that we should visit the abbey watchmaker, which would give me an excuse to introduce a new character and write a two-chapter digression about the watchmaker's background, practices and workshop.

"By chance, yes, Brother Marco. The temples of my spectacles are forever working loose, so I carry a small screwdriver at all times. Here."

He proffered an ancient Thracian screwdriver, richly bejewelled, and patinated from the touch of countless hands. I snatched it with not a little resentment, and used it to unfasten the two halves of the cassette. And if I was thinking of another reason to invoke the character of the watchmaker, the abbot scotched that too...

"And please take my jeweller's eyeglass, Brother Marco, by the help of which I see the tiny screws."

I went near one of the sconces on the stone wall, where the candle it bore shed a brighter light by which I examined the interior of the cassette.

"Hmmmmmm. The cracked plastic housing has impressed a minute groove across the edge of the reeled tape."

"What does that mean?" begged the abbot.

"It means that when the groove passes the reading head of the tape machine it causes the machine to register a fault and stop."

"And what does that mean?" begged the abbot.

"It means the machine will stop after a single revolution of the reel, since the groove is a radial one affecting each loop of tape within the coil."

"And what does that mean?" begged the abbot.

"It means we can examine the contents of the tape only a few frames at a time; between each set of frames the tape will have to be withdrawn, disassembled, and advanced a fraction manually with the aid of a pencil inserted through the sprocket at the reel's centre."

"Which means," said the abbot, finally working something out for himself, "it may take several days to inspect the history contained upon the tape."

"Indeed, Brother Abbot, thus providing a cunning plot device capable of generating a continual narrative tension, which at any point might yield a revealing discovery of exceptional importance to the outcome of the book."

"Great heavens, Brother Marco, Saint Paul himself could not have written anything so marvellous. It is no wonder your books perpetually top the lists of best-sellers, much as the stars eternally bespangle the inky skies of the night."

I nodded a humble acknowledgement of his words.

"Now, Brother Abbot, we must at once set-up a roster for the continual manning of the tape machine. Your most vigilant and diligent brothers should be assigned the duty. I will instruct them upon the operation of the device, and the manual tweaking of the cassette. They must scrutinise the displayed recording and let me know at once if anything or any person appears in the image, however innocuous or immaterial it might seem—they must report the slightest intrusion to me without delay."

"It shall be as you say, Brother Marco."

"Thank you, Brother Abbot. By your leave, I must now retire to my cell for inner contemplations."

CHAPTER NINE

In which Marco calls for reinforcement.

I collected my key at reception then trod the spiral staircase to the second floor of the dormitory, where my Spartan quarters awaited. I flopped on my pallet and stared blankly at the rusting iron grille that was stopping absolutely none of the cold night air from pouring through the small window of my cell. What a day. I looked at my bespoke Rolex with the profile of my Bronx mom picked out in rubies on the dial. Too early for sleep. Remembering the notebook I'd lifted from the corpse of Brother Felonius, I withdrew it from my robe. It was an unusual format, a spiral-bound codex, roughly three inches by five, with end papers hand-marbled in gentian on an ox-bile mucilage; each of its deckle-edged folia was faintly ruled with a red margin. A fading price tag showed it had been bought in the Clarkesville branch of a major stationer. The pages were annotated in pencil in a heavy hand, the writing on one sheet leaving a discernible imprint on the sheet below it. The notes appeared to be chronological entries recording events in the abbey—a diary of sorts. I flicked through to the recent entries, the last dated only yesterday:

10th November. H apprehensive. G, C and A angry about proposal. Threats. 18th November. W dead. Whom to trust? 20th November. Saw C trailing H. Had knife. H Lost. Must look after self.

H was clearly the herbalist—but who were G,C,A and W? Where had I seen those letters? Paging back through my story, I solved the riddle. W must surely mean Brother Wayne—the young illuminator who fell, or was pushed, to his death two days ago. G,C and A were clearly Brothers George, Crispin and Alfonse, the members of the Elder Council. Which reminded me...

I brought up the photos I'd taken in the aycharium, and examined the CVs of the aforementioned elders. All had been at the abbey for many years, and, oddly, all had completed courses in a range of specialist computing topics. For some utterly inexplicable reason, I also noted that Brother Crispin was an accomplished artist and Brother George had no qualifications in either organic chemistry or olfactory neuroscience.

Fumbling in the pallet-side cabinet, I found my iPhone and turned it on. It was time to call Como. I pressed the speed-dial button for his private number, and the phone beeped—there was no signal. I went to the window and held the phone through one of the squares of the grille—still no signal. Upon a desk against the opposite wall of the cell, among the leaflets advertising various local tourist attractions, was a brown leather folder embossed with the legend *'Guest Information'*. I flicked through the alphabetically ordered contents until I arrived at the page containing a section entitled *'Telephones'*.

In keeping with our ethos, it said, *there are no telephones in the cells. Nor is there any mobile phone signal anywhere within two miles of the abbey. Guests who need to make emergency calls are asked to enquire at reception.*

Hmmpf.

I went to reception, where a young brother was kneeling at prayer behind the counter. He rose at my approach. A badge affixed to the lapel of his robe announced him to be Brother Hugo.

"Brother Marco, it is indeed a most holy honour to be graced by your presence in the abbey. Would it be presumptuous of me to ask you to bless my book with a dedication?"

With which he proffered a thick volume bound in hand-stippled porcupine hide, entitled *Veritas Terribilis de Rei Herbert Quarry, a Marco Ocram,* a Latin translation of my breakthrough mega-seller about the Herbert Quarry affair. I took a quill from the holder on the desk, dipped it in the inkpot, and scratched a felicitous inscription below the frontispiece of the book—an etched print showing Herbert Quarry dancing on a beach with Lola Kellog, while in the background wicked Chief McGee, the former head of the Clarkesville County Police, made a pact with Satan.

After blowing on the page to dry the ink, I returned the book to Brother Hugo, who gushed his thanks and asked the usual questions about the extraordinary story of the Herbert Quarry affair: Had Lola really been only fifteen? Yes. Was Herbert really my mentor? Certainly. Was it true that the published book was exactly as I first wrote it? Absolutely, it was my inviolable rule of spontaneous authorship never to change even a single word. How did I plan my plots? I didn't—I let the good Lord guide my hand. And so on.

"Yours is a unique literary gift, Brother Marco. I understand that the holy bible alone has outsold your books."

Too modest to point out that the comparison was not a fair one, the bible having been in print far longer, I tried to think of a neat segue to shift to the subject. The young monk beat me to it...

"I suppose the sales figures are in telephone numbers."

"Indeed, Brother Hugo. Speaking of which, I need to make a telephone call. Can you arrange that for me?"

"I'm afraid all requests for telephone calls must be authorized by a quorum of the elder council of the abbey."

I considered for a moment.

"Would it be extraordinary, Brother Hugo, for a phone call to be arranged by the receptionist without such authorization?"

"It would be unprecedented, Brother Marco."

"An unprecedented occurrence would be one worth noting in my next book. Would you like to appear in my next book, Brother Hugo?"

"Indeed, Brother Marco!"

"Then should you allow me to make my call, I would have to include you in my next book, as I could not resist the opportunity to document such a newsworthy event."

"Your logic is irrefutable, Brother Marco. I will connect your call at once. What number should I dial?"

I was on the point of giving Como's number, when I remembered I was at the abbey as Marco the off-duty celebrity, not Marco the crime-busting author, so I gave Barney's number instead. It would be natural for me to be calling my agent, perhaps to check the news from Stockholm, or to agree the advance for my next book.

"If you would like to step into that booth, Brother Marco, I will put the call through."

I stepped into that booth, and a within a trice Barney was on the line.

"Markie, baby, how ya doin, kid?"

"I'm good, Barney, I'm good. How's you?"

"Better now that I'm hearing from my star boy. Where are you, kiddo?"

"Clarksville, looking into something for Como."

"For Como? Jeez, Markie, has he got a case? Speak to me, speak to me, Markie. Are you boys cooking something up for good old Barney?"

"Could be, Barney. I'm fifteen thousand words in, but it's a bit early to be sure where it's all going."

Which was the understatement of the millennium.

"Fifteen thousand?" Barney whistled. "Not another of your false starts, I hope."

"Honest, Barney, I don't know. But it doesn't seem like a false start. I think I'm on to something. But I need a favour."

"A favour, for my star boy? If you're on to something, and we're not talking false starts, you can have any favour you like, Markie boy. What's it to be—drugs, sex, money?"

"Barney!"

"Calm down, kiddo. I'm only asking…"

"I need you to get a message to Como. Tell him I'll meet him at Kelly's—tomorrow, at noon. Same procedure as last time."

"Sure, kid, sure. But keep me posted. I want news, news, news."

We exchanged further pleasantries then signed off. As I left the booth, my eye caught a hooded figure dodging behind the door from reception. Had someone been listening to my call?

CHAPTER TEN

In which Marco has a brilliant idea.

I'm meant to be having a complete emotional and mental rest, and this whole thing is driving me nuts."

"Now you know how I feel, Writer—everything you write drives me nuts."

"Just be thankful you don't have to pay to read it, like everyone else does."

Como and I were in a quiet booth in Kelly's, our hoods raised to avoid recognition.

"So what's doing, Writer?"

"I don't know yet. There've been two more fatal incidents—one in the cannery and one in the herbarium."

I gave Como a potted summary of the deaths of the two brothers, hoping the word 'potted' would seem a clever choice in connection with a death in a greenhouse.

Como grunted. "Incidents, huh. Sure seem to be a lot of 'incidents' all of a sudden. You got any idea who's behind them, or what the motive is?"

"I think it might be one of the brothers on the elder council."

"Which one?"

"I don't know, yet."

"What have you got on them?"

I told Como about the entries in Brother Felonius' notebook. "I know it's not much to go on, but it's a feeling I've got—a hunch."

"A hunch, huh. You've been there two days and that's all you can give me—a hunch. Hunches don't solve cases, Writer."

"That's rich, coming from you. Christ, Como, just about every time you bang up a villain it's because of some hunch."

"Yeah, but my hunches are police hunches, not crazy made-up shit from a Writer who never knows what he's going to type next."

It was a fair point in some respects, but Como was overlooking the fact that I was having to operate entirely on my own. He worked with an entourage of detectives, beat officers, scene-of-crime specialists, and other ancillary staff, whereas I was having to investigate an abbeyful of felons single-handed, with the added burden of making it all up as I went along.

"There's too much going on for me to cope alone. I need you there as back-up."

"Don't you listen? I already told you—if I show up, they'll know we suspect something."

That was true. I looked at my pale reflection in the screen while I waited for my brain to decide what to write next. I saw my mouth widen in a delighted smile even before the brilliant new idea burst upon me.

"Como, you're talking to a genius. Why would the brothers be suspicious if you were to join me at the monastery?"

"Why d'yuh think? Because I'm the freaking police chief."

"Exactly. So to avoid such suspicions, we just need to get you a disguise."

CHAPTER ELEVEN

In which Marco has an even brillianter idea.

Don't forget—speak in a falsetto voice."

My instruction to Como was whispered at the reception desk of the monastery, while the receptionist phoned for the abbot. Como was fetchingly dressed in an XXXXXL nun's habit we had found only after scouring every fancy-dress store in Clarkesville. He'd attracted a crowd of love-hungry brethren by the time the abbot arrived.

"Brother Abbot, this is Sister Coma. It would be a boon to me were a room to be found for her in the monastery, as she attends to all my secretarial needs."

"Heavens, Brother Marco," said the abbot, staring at Sister Coma, like a child gaping at a huge sweet. "If we might speak in private a moment."

He nodded me to follow him into the back office.

"Your request is most unorthodox, Brother Marco. Ordinarily I would do all in my power to please so distinguished a guest, but I am afraid I cannot accommodate your secretary or therefore your wishes. The rules of our order strictly forbid the co-mingling of brother and sister. The Devil, Brother Marco, is quick to exploit man's weakness. Were the comely Sister Coma to be living within the abbey's precincts, the minds of the brethren might quickly be turned from piety to thoughts of lying belly to belly in unending fornication."

He took a handkerchief from the recesses of his cowl and patted his perspiring forehead.

I had another brilliant idea.

"I see your point, Brother Abbot. The Devil is quick indeed to plant the seeds of immoral thought in the fertile soil of man's mind. I have a suggestion, however, that would protect the brethren from such impious mental impregnation. Suppose Sister Coma were to hide her comeliness under a monk's cowl. Only you would know of the harmless deceit, and as abbot you would hardly be prey to the immoral thoughts that might trouble an ordinary brother."

"Quite, quite," said the flustered abbot. "Very well. I will permit the good sister to stay provided she is clothed at all times as a brother. I will ensure that a room is found for her, perhaps one close to mine, so she would remain under my protection were her identity revealed."

"You are very wise, Brother Abbot. I will speak with Sister Coma at once, and effect a suitable disguise."

We returned to reception, where Sister Coma was slapping down the importunate hands of the assembled brethren.

"I quite understand, Brother Abbot, that Sister Coma may not take-up residence here at the abbey," I announced to the disappointment of all within earshot. "I shall therefore engage the services of my other secretary, Brother Como." Wink, wink.

"Ah yes, your other secretary, Brother Como." Wink, wink. "He would be most welcome."

"Come, Sister Coma. You must return to the convent."

I led her, or, technically, him, back to the car, leaving a gaggle of leering monks at the monastery door.

Safely behind the tinted windows of my black Range Rover, Como removed his wimple in what I can only describe as a truculent manner.

"Ok, Writer. Spill the big idea. What's this 'other secretary Brother Como' business?"

"Como, you are in the presence of a genius. The old abbot said a nun on the premises would run riot with the brothers' hormones, so we've agreed you can stay if you're disguised as a monk. You'll be Brother Como from now on."

Como rolled his eyes. "Writer, I don't know how you get away with this stuff, I really don't."

Neither did I, but an inability to write anything other than unbelievable rubbish had never stopped me before, and I wasn't going to let it now. I wrote the next thing that came into my head...

We drove to the fancy-dress store where we'd bought Como's XXXXXL nun outfit, and invented a suitable story to justify exchanging it for an XXXXXL monk outfit (I'd say what the story was, if I could think of it). Como stripped in the car park, treating the shoppers of Clarkesville to several eyefuls of his Greek god physique, before donning the optional hair shirt I'd got the store manager to throw in.

"You sure I need to wear this?"

"Trust me, Como. We need it for authenticity."

"Authenticity huh. You've got a police chief disguised as a nun disguised as a monk, helping you solve a medieval murder mystery in a fake monastery outside Clarkesville, and you need authenticity."

"Yes, Como. Authenticity. If the readers have to read total nonsense, let it at least be authentic total nonsense. All great writers have signature attributes, and it just happens that one of my signature attributes is authenticity."

"So I suppose you'll be wearing one of these prickly shirts yourself—for authenticity."

"Absolutely," I said, dishonesty being another of my signature attributes.

CHAPTER TWELVE

In which Como's eyebrows perform unprecedented feats.

The abbot descended the ancient steps of the praesidium to greet us as we crossed the cobbles of the car park. Actually, I think it was more to greet Como than me.

"Brother Como, how wonderful to see you. *Again,*" the abbot added in a whisper, with a sly wink at who he assumed was comely Sister Coma under the cowl of the XXXXXXL monk's outfit. "And you too, Brother Marco." He blessed us both. "There is a small favour I would ask of you."

"Of course, Brother Abbot, of course. We would be delighted to repay the hospitality you have showered upon us. What may we do for you?"

"In preparation for the grand opening, when many of the world's foremost celebrities will be descending upon the abbey, we are increasing our security arrangements, particularly in light of the recent... ahem... incidents. You may see that we have installed an airport-style security scanner at the entrance to the praesidium. It has just been connected to its supply of electricity, so perhaps you would be kind enough to walk through the newly activated machine in order that we might test its operation."

"Certainly, Brother Abbot. Come, Brother Como."

"If you could place any metallic objects in the tray." The abbot passed me a grey plastic tray, into which I lodged my car keys, watch, iPhone, iPad, and the leathern pouch containing my special pen. "And you, please, Brother Como."

Como gave me one of his looks, then fumbled in the folds of his robe to extract a gun and a pair of handcuffs.

"Your assistant is certainly a person of admirable caution in these lawless times," said the abbot, "but the rules of our peaceful house strictly forbid the carrying of weapons, be they for offense or defence. I am sure you will not mind, therefore, if I lock Brother Como's firearm in the securarium."

"Indeed not," I said hastily before Como could say otherwise.

"Now, please step through the arch."

We stepped through, to the satisfaction of the security monk monitoring the screen of the device. The abbot, having returned my belongings, proffered the other plastic tray to Como. "My dear Sister, sorry, Brother Como, please take your...ahem...accessories." With a knowing look he encouraged Como to pick-up the handcuffs. "No doubt you use them to aid the mortification of the flesh, and to prevent the hands from straying to sin. Your piety is a lesson to us. But let me show Brother Como to the quarters I have had prepared. Come."

With his eyebrows higher than I had ever seen them, Como and I followed in the train of the abbot along the many corridors of the abbey complex. The carpeting and other trappings became more lavish as we approached the abbot's personal quarters, where the abbot eased open a thick oak door and invited us through to view the accommodation he had prepared. Como's eyebrow elevation maxed out as we stepped inside what could have been the set of a harem scene in an ultra-kitsch production of *Arabian Nights*.

"It is not too austere, I hope," said the abbot as he showed us the en-suite, where rose petals and floating candles sailed serenely on the steaming waters of an inset stone bath. "The door over there connects directly to my room, so you may consult me at any time, Brother Como, should you be troubled by impure thoughts and require instruction."

I saw Como's huge hand twitching, possibly for a gun, or a large glass of bourbon, or a chance to give the abbot a chastening smack about the ears. I decided immediate intervention was necessary.

"You are indeed very kind, Brother Abbot, but my secretary and I must begin our detailed investigation of the causes of the unfortunate incidents in the abbey, so that we may put your mind at ease by eliminating any possibility of further catastrophe. Can I ask that you provide us with some token of your authority, so that we may question whom we please and enter where we please without fear of hindrance?"

"My ring will betoken my authority. You shall have it, Brother Marco. Here."

With which, the abbot removed his ancient Thracian pinky ring and handed it to me.

I nodded my thanks.

"Come, Brother Como, let us attend to our investigations."

We bowed to the abbot and withdrew. Or, at least, I bowed to the abbot, while Como looked on with a face in which confusion and disgust vied for position. It was as we turned the corner of the corridor from the abbot's quarters that Como pressed his vocal play button and let me know the thoughts monopolising his mind.

"Writer, if that creep lays a finger on any part of me I swear to God I'll bust every bone in his body."

"Worry not, Como. He is a man of the cloth. His interest in you is purely spiritual."

"You've got some real naïve ideas, Writer. Half the cells in Clarksville County jail are full of men of the cloth, and there's nothing pure or spiritual about what they did to get there. Anyway, show me that ring."

I handed over the abbot's pinky ring, which Como examined with a deepening frown.

"I've seen one of these before, Writer."

"Come, come, Como. I suppose you'll be telling me it's a symbol of some obscure criminal gang."

"Wrong. I'm telling you it's a symbol of a famous criminal gang—and not just any old symbol: only the guys at the top wear rings like this."

I wondered for half a moment about making a joke about the Catholic Church being the famous criminal gang, but decided Barney might not be happy with it. Not that Barney's got any religious scruples, but he might think it would harm the sales figures, so instead I said:

"What gang might that be, Como? The Chinese triads? The Japanese Yakusa? The Jamaican Yardies? The French Connection? The Hungarian Goulash?"

"You can laugh all you like, wise guy, but these rings are worn by members of the Commission."

"The commission?"

"No, the Commission, with a big C." Como turned the ring between his massive fingers. "The Commission's the heads of all the American Mafia families. Your so-called abbot must be one of them."

I snatched back the ring.

"Como, this nonsense must stop, right now. I absolutely refuse to let my new book be tainted by the clichéd concepts of mediocre crime fiction. Our readers expect a much higher standard of inventiveness and originality. You'll be telling me next that a monk has been found in the conservatory, murdered by Colonel Mustard with the lead pipe."

Before Como could reply, a breathless young monk sprinted over to us, holding his robes to his haunches to prevent tripping.

"Brother Marco, you must come at once. There has been another accident."

Chapter Thirteen

In which the key to the plot is discovered.

Como, don't say it." I said, in response to another of Como's looks. We were in the conservatory, crouching by the body of an elderly monk, whose silvery tonsure was matted with recently congealed blood. A length of lead drainpipe lay on the floor nearby. "These things happen. It is just a coincidence."

"Coincidence, huh? Just like it's a coincidence that the abbot's wearing a mafia pinky ring."

"I suggest, Como, that we suspend any judgement upon the ring until we have had a chance to quiz the abbot about its provenance. In the meantime, what do you make of this 'accident'?"

"It could be an accident at that," said Como, examining the other sections of the lead drainpipe that were still affixed to the wall of the conservatory. "The stonework here's decaying, and the screws that hold the pipe into the wall are looser than the plot in your last book." He underlined his point by pulling at the pipe, another section of which came free in his hand. "If your monk here had been walking by, just as that piece of pipe dropped, it would have caught him on the side of his head."

Hmmm. I wasn't so sure. Technically, all the facts fitted with Como's idea of an accident, but an accident seemed too blatant a red herring to have at this stage in the book. I turned to the scared young monk who had called us to the scene. "Tell me, who is the unfortunate brother who has met his death here?"

"It is Brother Glaxo, the apothecary."

"The apothecary? A close colleague of the herbalist, I assume."

"Indeed, Brother Marco. He and the herbalist collaborated in the preparation of many of the tinctures, potions and infusions used by the brethren to cure or forfend maladies of every kind."

I thanked the young monk and asked him to wait outside.

"Drugs, huh?" said Como.

"Yes, Como, drugs. But not every drug is sold for twenty dollars a shot on street corners. The drugs produced by the apothecary might well have been entirely innocent concoctions allowed by the DEA. Really, you must keep your police chief cynicism in check. First, the abbot is a mafia boss; now the apothecary and the herbalist are drug barons—are you trying to suggest this monastery is a den of thieves?"

"That's exactly what I'm suggesting, and the sooner you start taking it seriously the better. Let's go visit Brother Glaxo's room."

With guidance from the young monk, we found Brother Glaxo's cell. At first sight, it seemed typical of a monk's personal retreat—old cigarette packets and betting slips littered the surfaces; empty bottles and worn horsehair socks cluttered the space under the bed. There was a dark oak bookcase against one wall, its shelves housing copies of my books and sundry self-improvement volumes of interest to an elderly celibate.

"See, Como, a simple brother's cell—so much for your paranoid criminal theories."

Como crouched at the foot of the bookcase and ran a hand over the waxed oak floorboards.

"These are scratched, and there are small pieces of grit."

"So what, Como?"

"So this." He stood and pulled the bookcase away from the wall. Behind was a hole about eighteen inches square. Como crouched again and peered into the gloomy cavity. Before I had time to decide what he might find, he reached inside and pulled out a gun.

"Still think I'm paranoid? What d'you make of this?"

I took the gun from Como's huge hand and applied my crime-writer's compendious knowledge of firearms to identify its make and model.

"If I'm not mistaken, Como, this is a nine millimetre Walther KKK, a pistol favoured by white supremacists."

Como snatched back the gun. "White supremacists, huh. If we find any white supremacists in this dump, I'll stick this up their supreme white ass. Sideways."

"Now, now, Como. We mustn't let the misguided opinions of ignorant bigots undermine our professionalism. If we find any white supremacists are involved in these heinous crimes, I want you to treat them as you would any other suspected felon."

Which, now that I thought about it, might well include a pistol up the jacksie. Como had a robustly old-fashioned approach to dealing with baddies. Not that it mattered, as he wasn't listening to me anyway. He was rummaging under the late monk's mattress.

"Here."

He showed me what he'd found—a plain plastic card with a magnetic strip, like a blank credit card.

"It looks like a blank credit card."

"Close, but you won't get any credit with that. I'd say it's a pass card, for an electronic door lock."

I remembered the huge ring of swipe cards on the abbot's belt.

"That'd make sense, Como—the abbot has a huge ring of swipe cards hanging from his belt, so there must be a lot of electronic door-locks in the abbey."

"Are you as dumb as you look?" I didn't know how to answer that without incriminating myself, so I said nothing and waited for Como to continue, which he did after a lazy blink of condescension. "The whole point about electronic locks is that the cards are programmable. You don't need a separate card for every lock—you just programme one card to access multiple locks."

That was just like Como—parading his specialist security knowledge and making me look an idiot in front of the readers. I put him back in his place.

"Which of us, Como, is writing this? For all you know, there might be special rules in a medieval monastery that forbid programming. Possibly it is viewed as the devil's work."

"Never mind all that—if you spent more time thinking and less time writing, we might start getting somewhere. Why do you think he hid the key under the bed, when no-one can tell what it's the key for anyway?"

I stared at the keyboard, stumped. Why indeed?

"I'll tell you why," said Como, thankfully sparing me the bother of working it out for myself. "Because he's not supposed to have *any* keys."

CHAPTER FOURTEEN

In which Marco writes a distracting digression upon physics.

Think about it, dumbass." Como pressed home his advantage, thereby opening the chapter with a cliché. "If he had a legit reason for having a passkey to *any* room, then he could keep this one on him, as no-one could tell what lock it fits just from looking at it."

"You are mixing metaphors, Como. I am quite happy to be lectured about the workings of modern digital locks, provided you don't tell me that swipe cards '*fit*' the locks they open. By all means use the words *activate, release, operate, engage, free, open,* and the like, but not '*fit*'."

"You can use what words you like, Writer, but that doesn't stop you being a dumbass. Anyway, let's go see which lock this fits."

"And how, Como, do you propose to do that? Are we to try every lock in the abbey? We don't even know where they all are?"

Ha. That would show him who's the dumbass. "You're an even bigger dumbass than I thought, Writer. We just need to find the system that programmes the keys. That'll tell us what this sucker's programmed to open."

"And I suppose you just happen to know where the system is, and how to gain access to it." I eyed him in a manner too nuanced to describe with fewer than seven adverbs. "Remember, Como, this is meant to be an authentic thriller—we can't just write any old rubbish off the tops of our heads."

"The system will be where it always is—in the office behind the reception desk. They'll need it there to make room keys for guests. So the plan is this—we go to reception; you keep the receptionist busy signing books; I check the system."

I nodded to acknowledge my agreement with Como's proposal—especially his use of semi-colons, which added a welcome literary touch to my dire prose.

It was as we approached reception that I spotted the flaw in Como's logic. I tugged the sleeve of his gown and twitched my head to suggest we withdraw into a side passage.

"What?" said Como, his tone suggesting that 'now, dumbass' had narrowly missed being appended to his question.

"Why do I need to distract the receptionist? We've got the abbot's ring, remember, which gives us authority to look where we like."

"Because the first time you go flashing that ring and telling someone you're investigating on the abbot's authority, everyone in the abbey will get to hear of it. We need to keep below the radar."

"Below the radar, right."

I wasn't sure what radar he meant, but I didn't want to expose my ignorance to the readers, so I went along with it and continued to reception.

The obedientiary who rose to greet me at the desk was an elderly gentleman of oriental appearance. His badge showed him to be Brother Kaku. I threw back my cowl and shook out my famous auburn afro.

"Brother Marco! What an honour."

I winked at Como to indicate that the receptionist's attention had been duly grabbed, that a suitably long digression was now to be written, and thus the search of the office could safely begin.

"If I may say so, Brother Marco, I have followed your remarkable works on the tau muon, with inexhaustible interest."

He was referring, or course, to the fundamental particle I had famously postulated before I had found my true metier as the record-breaking author of sensational crime memoirs. His words brought back nostalgic memories of those heady days at MIT, CERN, Cambridge, and Hiedelberg, where I had completed my PhD and dazzled the world of physics with my bold theories.

"It is most kind of you, Brother Kaku. Were you to have a copy of my popular science book, *The Tau Muon*, I would be delighted to inscribe a felicitous dedication within its pages."

"I have indeed, Brother Marco. Moreover, I have your true-crime stories too—as everyone has. It is hard to say which of your works is the most wondrous."

The excited monk rummaged in the folds of his habit to extract three dog-eared volumes which he laid reverentially on the faux leather top of the reception desk. I spun the first of them round to face me—it was a paperback copy of *The*

Awful Truth about The Sushing Prize, my most recent novel.

"Ah, a twenty-first edition. You came late to my work, I see."

"Your reputation for perspicacity is well-founded, Brother Marco. I had ordered an advance copy, but some computer error... you know how these things are. Such was the demand for the earlier editions that it was some weeks before I finally received my treasured version." He clapped his hands as he read the witty inscription I had scribbled. "Do you still find time to contemplate matters relating to the sub-atomic world?"

"Not as much as I would like—the occasional trouble-shooting visit to the Large Hadron Collider, calls from Higgs and others wishing to hear my views on their nascent theories, that sort of thing."

"Perhaps, then, I could seek your views on a theory of my own, relating to the established models of electrical conduction."

"It would be my pleasure, Brother Kaku."

"You will know, of course, that in all conventional teaching, the negative electrons are said to circulate in circuits, while the positive ions of the conductors remain fixed in place."

"Which schoolchild does not possess such elementary knowledge, Brother Kaku?"

"Indeed, but what if I were to tell you that I have evidence to suggest that when currents are passed through thin foils the positive ions counter rotate with respect to the electrons, albeit in smaller numbers?"

"I would be sceptical, but prepared to suspend disbelief." Which is a necessary state of mind when you write tripe like this for a living. "What is your evidence?"

"I have been performing modest experiments in my cell on the use of foil as a heating element. My idea is that rooms could be papered with aluminum foil, through which a heating current could be passed, thus allowing the walls themselves to act as radiators. In my experiments, my transformers repeatedly develop faults as a result of the build-up of large deposits of aluminium on their negative terminals. The only logical explanation is that aluminium ions are being released by the effects of the current in the foil and passing down the wires to the transformer. What do you make of that, Brother Marco?"

"It is as thought provoking as any of the mysteries of the Creator, Brother Kaku."

Brother Cuckoo, more like. Thankfully Como loomed out of the office with his thumb up, so I was able to curtail the dialogue before it became any more ludicrous.

"But you must excuse me, I am due to call CERN at any moment," I lied, "and they can be ever so stroppy when kept waiting."

"Forgive me, Brother Marco. I did not intend to keep you from your important work. If you need to call CERN, please use this phone," he said, conveniently forgetting the rule that all calls had to be approved by the elder council.

Over Brother Kaku's shoulder, Como was giving me a supremely articulate look, one conveying at least five simultaneous propositions, viz:

1) He had found the information he sought.
2) He needed to share it with me urgently.
3) What was I playing at?
4) I was a dumbass.
5) I should stop ****ing about.

That was easy for him to say, or, rather, look, but he hadn't just lied his way into an embarrassing predicament with an incidental character. Obviously I couldn't dial CERN, as I didn't know the number. I had a brilliant idea. I would dial Como's mobile number. There was no mobile signal at the abbey, so Como's phone would go to answerphone. I would invent a one sided conversation with Como's voicemail, sounding as though I was conversing with CERN in Geneva. Genius.

With a light heart, I lifted the handset to perform my innocent deception.

"This is Marco Ocram speaking. I believe you are having trouble with the Large Hadron Collider."

While I pretended to be listening to CERN's reply, Como continued his censorious look. I waved an irritated hand to shut him up.

"And you've definitely put the hadrons in the right way up?"

Como started tapping his watch. I turned away from him. If that's how he was going to behave, I would spin things out with some advanced technical mumbo jumbo, and that would teach him.

"What does the temperature gauge indicate?"

Pause.

"Try tapping it."

Pause.

"That doesn't sound good. Try flushing the injection ports with quark suppressant."

Pause.

"Yes, and double the dosage for good measure."

Pause.

"No luck? Sounds like a pulse synchronisation phase misalignment. Have you got a three eighths spanner?"

Pause.

"Try backing off the main torus lock-nut—the heat expansion sometimes makes them too tight."

Pause.

"Yes. Just a quarter turn at a time."

Longer pause.

"That's strange—it usually fixes it. Have you tried switching it off and switching it back on again?"

Pause.

"Well try now. I'll hang on the line."

For the purpose of achieving technical authenticity, I waited for the longest pause yet, ignoring the balls of rolled-up paper Como had started flicking at me.

"It's fixed it? Excellent. Glad to have been of help."

I replaced the handset and addressed Brother Kaku.

"What a bunch of dumbasses those guys at CERN are. Unbelievable, isn't it? And people wonder why we still haven't found the tau muon."

CHAPTER FIFTEEN

In which Marco procures a prop for a later joke.

S pill it."

My words were uttered in an excited whisper in a gloomy alcove off the main hall of the refectory. Como and I were alone, apart from a char-monk guiding an electric floor-polisher between the trestle tables, so my hushed tones were a device to build tension rather than a bona fide precaution.

"It's bad news, Writer. The card's programmed to open seven locks, so we're gonna have some investigating to do to find out what's what."

"Bad news!" I could have kissed him. "That's not bad news—that's brilliant news!"

Ever since I'd invented the key-card under Brother Glaxo's mattress, I'd been fretting about the risk that it would lead us to the heart of the mystery when we weren't even a third of the way through the book. But seven locks—I could write six mystifying digressions, keeping the readers in suspense about which lock was the key one, if you'll excuse the pun. Best of all, seven was loaded with mystical significance—the seven days of creation, the seven deadly sins, the seven stars, the seven streams of stoma, the lamb with seven horns and seven eyes, the seven swans a swimming, the seven samurai, the seven brides for seven brothers, the seven...

Como interrupted my septimal enumerations.

"It might be brilliant news to you, Writer, but I've got a police department to run. I ain't got time to waste on red herrings."

And there we were, back to the eternal conflict that plagued our relationship—Como wishing to wrap up a case promptly, and I needing to spin it out to seventy five thousand words to satisfy Barney.

"There shall be no red herrings in this book, Como. Crimson, perhaps, or scarlet; possibly cerise, or vermillion, or even, perhaps, given the theme of the book, rose or cardinal; but certainly nothing as unimaginative or predictable as plain red. Now, which are the locks we need to investigate?"

"Here."

Como passed me a print from the system that programmed the key cards. I scanned it with an expert eye. Among other extraneous details, it showed the card had last been programmed a little over a year ago by Brother Felonius, when it was authorised to activate locks at the following locations:

Aycharium 3
Bothy 1
Crypt 7
Herbarium 4
Herbarium 11
Infirmary 42

Vesparium 2

"Then our tasks is simplicity itself, Como. We have merely to find these locations, enter them using the card, and one is bound to contain a decisive clue."

"You know where these places are then?"

It was a good point. I knew where the aycharium and the herbarium were, but I didn't know which doors within them might correspond to the numbers on Como's printed list. As for the Bothy and the other places—I had no idea. Or, rather, I suddenly did have an idea.

"Follow me, Como."

We went back to reception, where Brother Kaku was still on duty.

"Brother Kaku, do you have such a thing as a map of the abbey complex?"

"Certainly, Brother Marco. We have one specially printed for visitors—on its reverse it advertises local hostelries and places of entertainment and commerce." He handed me the folded sheet, which I spread on the counter. "Are there certain places which you seek?"

I read out the names of the places on Como's printed list, and Brother Kaku helpfully circled them on the map with a well-chewed biro.

"Thank you for your guidance, Brother Kaku. Tell me, what is the nature and purpose of the Bothy? I see it is some distance from the abbey itself."

"You are very observant, Brother Marco. The Bothy is a little under a league distant, a small wooden hut, equipped with the barest essentials. It is a simple shelter for pilgrims caught in the savage winter storms."

"Is it much used?"

"Rarely, Brother Marco. Few celebrities now make the pilgrimage to the abbey on foot—mostly they arrive by helicopter."

Hmmmm. And I'll tell you why I typed 'Hmmmm.' The bothy was meant to be a simple wooden shelter for pilgrims to escape the storms, yet I had included it in the list of locations with advanced digital locks. Either I had made a humiliating gaffe in developing that particular plot strand, or there was something fishy going on.

"One other thing, Brother Kaku—where might we find the ornithologist?"

"Brother Audubon? At this hour he is certain to be found in the rendering plant, where he makes the fat-balls for which the abbey is famed throughout Christendom and beyond in the heathen Orient. Here." Brother Kaku helpfully put a cross on the map, yet another nuanced allusion to religion for the readers to savour.

"Come, Como. We will repair to the rendering plant."

Whether through politeness or utter confusion, Como waited until we were out of Brother Kaku's eavesdropping range before putting the obvious question.

"The ornithologist? The rendering plant? Are you out of your fucking mind?"

The true answer was quite possibly, but I couldn't go admitting insanity to one of my characters—heaven knows where we might end up.

"It is merely a practical precaution, Como. I imagine we might wish to investigate the Bothy, and if we do then binoculars might be handy. And who, Como, is likely to have binoculars? The goatherd? The brewer? The deputy assistant vellum presser? You see, Como, there is method in the madness."

The rendering plant was toward the southern edge of the abbey compound, an ancient timber building of rough-hewn, rat-gnawed planking, from which emitted reeking fumes, foul putrefactions, and pallet after pallet of bumper plastic tubs of fat-balls. The ornithologist was overseeing the production line, the complex process through which the carcasses of animals unfit for human consumption were boiled down and mixed with seeds to provide a nourishing confection for garden birds to peck. I waved to gain his attention over the unholy cacophony of the machinery. Wrenching off his ear defenders, he grasped me warmly, and somewhat greasily, by the hand.

"Brother Marco! I heard news of your arrival at the abbey. It is a miraculous visitation arranged by the Holy One. Please, if you wouldn't mind." He proffered his copies of my books. I continued the conversation as I signed them...

"I am sorry to disturb your important manufactory work, Brother Audubon, but I wondered if you might have binoculars I could borrow."

"Certainly, Brother Marco. Do you wish to observe the local avifauna? The passerine population hereabouts is sparse, but there are raptors as spectacular as they are numerous."

"Yes," I lied. "I am keen to make the ornithological most of my time at the abbey, but I have inadvertently left my own binoculars at home." I crossed my fingers that he wouldn't volunteer to take us on a bird-watching trip.

"It would be my pleasure, Brother Marco—here, I always keep them nearby." That was handy. "I have no doubt they are inferior to your own optical instruments, but they are fitted with gyroscopic stabilisers, and their lenses have been ground to perfection by Brother Zeiss of Oberkochen, so they present an image pleasing in hue, clarity, and stability."

"You are most kind, Brother Audubon. I will return them later today. Come, Brother Como."

CHAPTER SIXTEEN

In which Marco and Como discover a surprise at the Bothy.

You can't ski?"

"No, Como, I cannot ski."

"I thought you said you were a hot shot at all sports."

"I was a hot shot at all sports, Como, but no longer. My middle-ear problem, remember?"

"More like a middle-brain problem. Okay, here's what we'll do."

We were standing in the chilly locker room of the abbey, preparing for a reconnaissance trip to the Bothy. While I had been checking the spelling of reconnaissance, Como had been cadging equipment from some of the sportier brothers, and had produced two pairs of hand-planed skis in hickory.

"Put the skis on, and I'll pull you along—you can hang on to the hem of my monk outfit."

Finding a bench outside, we adjusted the bindings on our skis and affixed them to our sandals. I stood and tottered cautiously across the snow-covered cobbles. Who would believe that the hesitant figure, waving its arms like a complete beginner, was Marco Ocram, once the most revered exponent of downhill racing? A harpist plucked a rising series of arpeggios, the world dissolved into zig-zags, and the readers clapped their delighted hands as we launched one of my signature plot devices—the entirely spurious sporting flashback...

Champion skier, Marco Ocram, grips the starting poles at the lip of the infamous Diabolo *run, sliding his skis back and forth to build the momentum of his launch.*

"Tres. To. En."

Sigurd Wassmo, the veteran Norwegian starter, concludes his countdown and waves the traditional black and yellow handkerchief to signify its completion.

Now!

Marco explodes from the starting gate like a Saturn X rocket launched sideways. He eases into his famous lop-sided crouch, reaching back to tuck-in the flapping tail of his shirt to minimise drag. The flags that line the course are straining their halyards in the vicious cross-wind. The driving snow is already building up between the wales of Marco's corduroys. On the side-lines have gathered the nineteen other competitors, who as a group have declined to race in the lethal conditions. Marco alone will complete the hazardous descent—his aim to shatter his own course record.

Wham, wham, wham, wham, wham.

Like the pistons of a powerful engine, Marco's arms ram his ski-poles into the suffering piste, each thrust ratcheting up his speed. The first gate whips past. Marco leans in to the treacherous left-hander, the edges of his hand-adzed iroko skis biting into the ice. The wind and g-forces distort his face into a determined grimace measuring ten point four on the rictus scale. He leaves the ice in an impossibly long jump, cleaving the icy air like a Teflon meteor. Stewards are forcing back the crowds, twenty deep at the ropes. Three men faint in the crush. Marco tears through gate after gate, each vanishing rearwards like the chapters in a newly typed book.

But what's this?

A gasp of astonishment escapes the on-looking crowd. Spraying ice like the wake of a pirouetting speedboat, Marco performs a suicidal Christie. He skids to a stop at the side of the course, where his mentor, Herbert Quarry, has been cheering his protégé.

"Herbert, remind me—what is the figure of speech known as a psittacism?"

"It means parrot-like repetition. Now go, Marco, go!"

Wiping the snow from his spectacles, Marco thrusts himself once more into his record breaking attempt.

"Parrot-like repetition. Parrot-like repetition. Parrot-like-repetition."

Memorising Herbert's answer, Marco thunders down the mountainside like a jet fighter on full after-burn. He pierces the last gate dead centre and breasts the tape. Yes, yes, yes, ten thousand voices roar. Marco salutes the crowd as his time flashes on the display board. A new course record and personal best. Loosening his cravat, he coasts to the exit gate, where his fellow competitors raise their ski-poles in a guard of honour...

As the harp music returned, I wiped a nostalgic tear from my eye. To think I was once the toast of St Moritz, and now look at me—barely able to stand. I cursed the sloppy hygiene practices of the Bronx barber whose filthy scissors had infected my middle ear, leaving me permanently off balance. I waved unsteadily at Como, so that he came alongside and allowed me to hitch-on to his habit.

"You ok, Writer?"

"I hope so."

"Hold tight."

The three snowy miles to the Bothy took almost an hour, an hour which was tricky, tedious and tiring. Tricky, because the hem of Como's monk outfit was not quite long enough, so that the points of my skis kept interfering with the tails of his. Tedious, because I couldn't see anything much other than Como's backside. Tiring, because I had to keep my arms stretched ahead of me and my back slightly bent.

Eventually we stopped atop a ridge, beyond which a clearing sloped down to the Bothy, a crude low structure about a furlong away. Como put out a massive hand.

"Binoculars."

I pulled the strap over my cowl and handed them to him. Como scrutinised the area around the Bothy while I tried to keep upright on legs as rigid as overcooked spaghetti.

"Here." He handed back the binos. "There are footprints leading to the door, so someone's in there. I'll take a look. Stay put and keep an eye out. Don't make a sound and don't let them see you. You see any movement at all and you warn me."

"And how, Como, am I to warn you without making a sound? Thought transference? Smoke signals, perhaps?"

"Make an owl hoot."

"I can't. I'm really bad at owl hoots. I always sound like a sick parrot."

"Then a coyote howl."

"Okay."

"Just don't betray our presence."

Como took the Walther KKK from his robe, and spun the chamber, or shook the cartridge, or tapped the ammo gauge, or whatever you're meant to do to check it's got bullets. Then he undid the ski bindings from his sandals and cautiously began to drop down the hillside from tree to tree along the edge of the clearing.

To be useful, I decided to scrutinise the Bothy myself. I spun up the gyros on the binoculars—which was a bit of a bother as my fingers were frozen, so it was hard to wind the strings—and adjusted the eyepieces to accommodate my famous squint. Brother Audubon had not exaggerated—the view through the binoculars was astonishingly vivid. I could make out the individual planks in which the bothy was clad, the vegetation in its low turf roof, and the individual granules in a pyramid of grit that had been dumped by the door. What was most odd, however, was that the view seemed to be getting gradually closer, as if the binoculars were automatically zooming in on the features of interest. It was as I took the binoculars from my eyes, to see if they had some kind of zoom button, that I understood why. Freed from Como's restraining influence, my skis and I had started to glide down the slope, and were already hissing over the snow with remarkable rapidity towards the bothy. Struggling to describe my surprise and horror, I crouched in sudden fear, flinging out my arms, wing like, in an instinctive urge to help my balance, leaving the binos to dangle from my neck like an outsized pendant. My mind was crushed between the opposing forces of Como's instruction to not make a sound and an urge to scream for help. I cursed my middle ear problem, or, rather, the mindless impulse that had caused me to write that I had one. With my former skiing prowess I could have hopped down the slope backwards on one ski, but now I didn't have enough brain-body coordination for the simplest of turns. The growing rush of air tore back my cowl, unveiling my famous auburn afro, and filling the Ocram cheeks through a mouth agape with horror. The bothy was now dead ahead. On my current course, I would shortly impale my skis like crossbow bolts into the planks below the window, while no doubt the binoculars—their strap snapping under the strain—would continue their trajectory through the window to land with a thud in the lap of whomever was inside.

No matter how I turned it over in my mind, I couldn't see how the looming scenario could not be counted as a betrayal of our presence. I judged that it was time to alert Como to my predicament.

Howling like ten freaked-out coyotes, I tore down the hillside, my hair a flaming halo against the sloping backdrop of virgin snow, the very image of an avenging medieval superhero. The bothy was expanding to fill my horrified field of view. Grimacing, I closed my eyes and turned my head from the imminent impact.

Ooooooopphhhh.

For an instant I felt that an alligator had snapped at my waist while sharing a ride in a centrifuge. I opened my eyes. Missing the bothy by inches, I had stopped in a tight semi-circle, at the centre of which Como was holding the end of my girdle in one giant fist, while holding his other fist in a menacing gesture suggesting that a variety of punishments might be in order if I made another sound. I was just gesturing back to say I was in complete control, thank you very much, when my middle ear threw in the towel and I flopped into the snow. Como grabbed a fistful of habit over the middle of my back and dragged me to the side of the bothy, indicating that I should remove my skis. Having done so, we inched across the snow-covered veranda and slowly peered around the edge of the window, Como's head directly above mine.

Within the Bothy, a hooded monk was sitting on the floor in the lotus position. Whether it was some sound, some shadow or a spiritual awareness I cannot say, but the figure sensed our presence and turned its hooded face to the window. A visceral thrill ran through me as the face took shape and I began to type the idea that had just come into my head.

CHAPTER SEVENTEEN

In which Herbert Quarry acknowledges Marco's literary prowess.

Herbert!"

"Marco!"

While surprise vied with delight for control of our facial expressions, we fell upon each other for a man-hug of supreme warmth and cordiality.

"And you, Como!"

Ruining the moment somewhat, Herbert disentangled himself from my grip to shake Como's huge hand.

"Come. Sit and partake of my meal. It is simple monkish fare, but joyous to eat in such unexpected company."

Herbert proffered slices of pizza with a *Hermit's Heaven* topping of herbs and breadcrumbs, while I tried to get into the groove of writing dialogue for him. It was all about adopting a highly interrogative style with frequent use of first names, as follows...

"Tell me, Marco, what brings you and Lieutenant Galahad to such a remote bothy at the very time when I am resting within it? It is indeed an extraordinary coincidence."

I think the word he should have used was *unbelievable*, but I passed over it.

"It's Chief Galahad now, Herbert—did you not read my last book?"

"I confess not, Marco—for I have abandoned all forms of reading." He turned to Como. "Congratulations, Chief Galahad."

"I ain't so sure congratulations is the right word," said Como through a mouth full of pizza. "Being a police chief is a lot more worry than being a lieutenant and not much more pay."

"But the additional capacity for doing good must surely compensate?"

Como started choking on his pizza, so Herbert turned back to me.

"And you, Marco—are you still writing the next thing that comes into your head?"

I would have thought the answer self-evident, but I replied nonetheless.

"Absolutely, Herbert—I could never abandon the methods you instilled in me. Besides, my public demands I stay true to the artistic principle of spontaneous literary creation—that is why they buy my books. As to what brings us here, Como and I are investigating a bizarre sequence of events at the abbey."

I gave Herbert a resumé of the plot thus far.

"That does indeed sound puzzling, Marco. There seems no logic to any of it, as far as I can see."

Which made two of us.

"And you, Herbert—what brings you to the Bothy? Are you intending to join the brethren at the abbey?"

"No, Marco. I am simply a pilgrim, thankful for a night's hospitality. When we last met I had been completing a retreat at the Christian Brother's place in Pasadena. I realised that a life of denial and contemplation was ultimately more fulfilling than any of the fame and materialism I had enjoyed as a writer. Besides, I felt I had passed the baton of literary innovation to you, my protégé. I have been wandering from commune to commune in search of new insights into the meaning of life, and am on my way to the convent of Saint Raquel in Las Vegas."

"That is a holy pity indeed, Herbert. When I saw your face through the Bothy window, I had a flash of hope that you might join us at the abbey to help me make sense of my tangled plot."

"Trust me, Marco. If you follow my advice, letting the writing emerge as it will, then all will become clear."

Having finished his pizza, Como held up Brother Glaxo's key-card to remind me of the purpose of our visit.

"Herbert, since you have been here, have you noticed any digital door locks of the sort that are opened by a pass-card?"

"In this remote, crudely constructed bothy? I see, Marco, that you are writing the *very* first things that come into your head. I hadn't realised that you had developed the technique to such an unconventional extent. No wonder your books are loved by the public and reviled by the literary establishment. But to answer your question directly, no. The only door is the one through which you entered, and it has but a simple wooden latch. Unless you mean...the safe door."

"The safe door?" Como and I chorused.

"Yes, Marco. Beyond the fireplace, behind the trouser-press, there is a safe set into the wall, in which the pilgrim can safely bestow any precious items they have about them—small fragments of the true cross, perhaps, or their credit cards."

By the time Herbert had completed his announcement—a ludicrous one even by my standards—Como had crossed the room, shifted the trouser press, and knelt before the wall-safe. I gathered the skirts of my habit and went to his side.

"It's the wrong sort of lock, Writer."

Como was examining the door of the safe, which featured one of those locks that allow you to punch a combination on a keypad.

"Are you sure?" It was a stupid question, deserving the look I subsequently received. "Sorry, Como. I think I was addressing the question to myself."

Which was understandable, given what I'd just written.

But Como had already forgotten my unintended slight on his detecting prowess, and was combing through the Bothy for anything moveable that could be hiding a hatch or cupboard of some sort. He was tapping the walls, and pulling at the rough wooden planks of the floor, but found nothing.

"Let's take another look at that safe."

He knelt by the safe, this time with a candle, by the light of which he examined the interior.

"Pass me a knife, Writer."

Como took the knife and did something with it inside the safe, following which he extracted a metal panel with magnetic catches on its rear face.

"Whatcha got, Como?"

I knelt excitedly beside him and looked within the safe. At the back, where Como had removed the panel, the flickering light from the candle showed another door—a safe within a safe—and this second door had a swipe card reader!

Como fumbled Brother Glaxo's card out of a pocket in his habit and swiped it. The door of the second safe swung open.

CHAPTER EIGHTEEN

In which the clues described are indeed a puzzle.

In the safe was a white plastic carrier bag—the kind given away by small stores that can't justify the expense of printing their names on them. Como used the knife to hook the handles of the bag and lift it out, and then to open the bag so he could see inside. He turned the bag upside down, shook out the contents and spread them on the table. There were twelve small transparent plastic pouches, about three inches square. Each contained a few grams of a white crystalline substance and a strip of paper upon which a long and seemingly random sequence of numbers and letters was printed. There was also a collection of transparent plastic rectangles—each about the size of two playing cards end-to-end—held together by an elastic band twisted twice around them. I went to pick up one of the pouches, and Como rapped my knuckles with the flat of the knife.

"Ow!" I rubbed my hurt hand with my other. "What was that for?"

"It's evidence, Writer—I don't want your prints all over it."

"You might have said. Gimme that."

I snatched the knife from him and used it to pick up a pouch so I could hold it close enough to examine the string of small characters on the strip of paper inside it. There were about a hundred, printed in groups of four. About two thirds of the characters were letters between A and F—the rest were numbers. I knew exactly what that meant. Ha! Como was about to learn that while I might know nothing about the handling of evidence, I had other specialist knowledge that would shed a startling new light on the case.

"It's an encryption key."

I wondered who were the more surprised, the readers or myself, upon finding that it had been not I but Como who had spoken the words.

"Don't look at me like that," he added. "You think I'm some thick policeman? I'll tell you who's thick, Writer. You can't remember what you've written from one book to the next, can you?"

My blank look was all the answer he needed.

"Don't you remember us breaking in to the datacentre in that crazy Sushing case? You said then that I'd been head of the Cyber Crimes Unit at Clarkesville County PD, and now you think I don't know an encryption key when I see one?"

"Sorry, Como. I forgot. But, let's not forget why I forgot. Under my artistic code I must always write spontaneously. It would be a heinous violation of the code were I to be consciously remembering things. So if I had forgotten, then it was in the nature of an artistic or professional forgetfulness, whereas you seem to be trying to give the impression that it is the careless mistake of the incompetent writer. You seem to be suggesting that…"

I broke off because he was ignoring me. He was using the knife to put all the pouches and the wad of plastic rectangles back in the carrier, which he returned to the safe within the safe.

"Aren't we going to take them back to HQ for forensics?"

"I think you forgot your brains, Writer. If we take them then whoever's expecting to find them there will know we're onto them. I'll get the Bothy staked-out and we'll see who turns up. Any signal here?"

I wasn't sure whom he'd put his question to, but it was Herbert who answered as Como switched on his mobile.

"A weak one, but adequate."

It was an odd tableau. Como, a giant figure on the phone at the window, issuing instructions for the surveillance of the tracks leading to the bothy. Herbert, staring at the fire, hoping to find new insights into the meaning of life. Myself, eyes crossed with utter confusion, wondering what to write next. All three of us in monkish garb in a building that was a cross between a motel room and a primitive frontier shack. What it needed was some comforting sense of normalcy—an injection of measured, adult conversation to act as an antidote to the idiocy of the preceding pages. What it actually got was the sound of *Que Sera Sera* as my phone finally realised there was a signal.

"Publishing legend, Marco Ocram, speaking. How may I help you, caller?"

"Help me? Help me? I'll tell you how you can help me. You can help me by answering your phone. I've been worried sick. My poor fingers are red raw with dialling. And I've got all this food. You might have told me you weren't coming home. I had Mrs Goldman's daughter here yesterday for nearly an hour. I'd baked all day. Come and meet my boy Markie, I told her. And where were you? Such a sweet, lovely girl. She would have been just right for you, Markie. Just right. She's got two sisters too."

"Sorry, Mom, but I had to go on an urgent mission."

Como and Herbert exchanged looks at the mention of my Bronx mom. Como tapped his watch, and made various other gestures to suggest I should kill the call, or at least try to keep it below the one or two hours it usually takes to complete any conversation with my Bronx mom.

"A mission! He has to go on an urgent mission, he says. What's so urgent that you can't take two minutes to tell your mom you're going away?"

"Sorry, Mom, but it's an urgent police mission for Como."

Como fanned his hands in a gesture signifying that I should keep his name out of it. Too late now, of course.

"For Como! Are you crazy going off down there? You should have told him to come here. I could have fixed him with Mrs Goldman's daughter's friend. She'd be just right for Como. Just right. Is he there now? Tell him about Mrs Goldman's daughter's friend. Tell him, Markie."

"Just a minute, Mom." I put my hand over the microphone, and made an apologetic face to Como. "I've told him, Mom. He says he's really sorry he's not there to meet Mrs Goldman's daughter's friend, but he'll come up as soon as this case has finished."

Como's hand-fanning escalated to the point at which I thought he might be generating enough down-draught to take off.

"He's such a nice boy to your mommy, Markie. Why can't you be a nice boy like Como? But I've got all this food he could have eaten. Is he getting enough to eat?"

I looked at Como's huge bulk.

"I think he's getting enough to eat. Mom, I've got to go now. I'm making a plan with Como and Herbert."

"Herbert?" My mom screeched the name so loudly that Herbert heard it. He looked up at me. I turned down the volume, fearing what might be coming. "Don't tell me you're with that Herbert Quarry, Markie. What are you doing with that sick paedo scumbag?"

Thinking it might be undiplomatic to try to persuade my mom that Herbert Quarry wasn't a sick paedo scumbag while Herbert Quarry was listening to me saying he wasn't a sick paedo scumbag, I resorted to a simple subterfuge.

"No, it's another Herbert, Mom."

"Is he a nice boy?"

"Yes, he's a really nice boy, Mom."

Herbert pointed to his chest, the look on his face querying whether he was the nice boy in question.

"Put him on the line. Let me have a word with him."

"Mom, I can't. We need to get back to the abbey. I need to see the abbot."

"The abbey!!!??? The abbot!!!???"

I shouldn't have mentioned the abbey and the abbot.

"The abbey!!!??? You mean with Catholics?"

"Not really, Mom."

"Not really? Not really? Are you telling me he's a Jewish abbot? Have you got plenty of clean underwear?"

I think my second mistake in the call—assuming you ignore the mistake of answering it in the first place—was telling my Bronx mom that monks didn't wear boxer shorts. She found it hard to come to terms with the horsehair shirts, and struggled to imagine how you could pack fourteen of them in a bag for a fortnight's stay. Thankfully a higher power intervened, and my phone lost the connection. I put it on mute, and dropped it back in my pouch.

I was starting to tell Como about Mrs. Goldman's daughter's friend, when a car horn sounded.

Chapter Nineteen

In which prayers lead to violence.

When the door to the bothy was nudged open, Como, Herbert and I were kneeling in a circle—technically it might have been a triangle—our cowls raised, our rosary beads dangling, seemingly deep in prayer. I peeped and saw the bottom half of two figures in the doorway—both male, to judge by their stance and footwear, although that could have been blinkered gender stereotyping on my part.

Our visitors were evidently unsure what to make of the scene before them—which was fair enough—as they were silent and motionless for about two minutes, which seems a lifetime when you're kneeling on a hard floor worrying about what to write next. When I say motionless I was not entirely truthful, because one of the two figures seemed twitchy and impatient. I judged it was he who spoke first.

"Say something, Donny."

It was an edgy, whispered instruction, suggesting that the speaker habitually looked to Donny to take the lead in difficult circumstances.

MARCO OCRAM

"Excuse me, Fathers," said a deeper, slower voice. "Only we didn't count on anyone being here."

I decided Herbert should answer, as of the three of us he was the only one with the right kind of voice and bearing to pass-off the role of a venerable man of God—Como would have been too terse and aggressive, while I would have seemed too jokey and nervous.

"That's quite alright, my son. Please, join us in prayer."

Join us in prayer! Where had that come from? Genius! I knew I'd been right to give Herbert the lead.

They shambled uncertainly to join our circle, Donny on Como's left, the other on his right.

"Lord, welcome these weary travellers. Make them feel your peace." said Herbert. "Let us join hands in prayer."

He grabbed Donny's right hand and my left. It was insane, but under Herbert's mesmeric influence a circle of hands formed. My eye hopped around it. Herbert's hands, calm, warm, shapely, and full of humanity. Donny's, large, hard, and heavy. Como's much bigger still, the size of boxing gloves. Those of the twitching man, small, dirty, heavily tattooed.

Tension shrouded us like a volatile gas. I wanted to shriek with laughter or fear. In an instant it happened. In an instant, they knew and we knew that this was no holy prayer circle. The hand in my right hand snatched away, like a striking cobra on rewind. I saw a knife in it. Donny's right hand pulled free from Herbert. Whether he would have used the holstered gun under his jacket I can't say, as his hand never reached it. Faster than I could type, Como yanked the twitching man forwards, butting him square in the face, then used the limp body's weight as anchorage to pull Donny forward off his knees to meet Como's huge bunched fist. Two baddies down in less than two seconds.

Lacking anything more useful to do, I made the sign of the cross.

"You okay?"

It was to me that Como put the question. For all his carping, my safety was always his overriding concern. I nodded to show that I was okay, apart from having come close to pooping myself. Como hunted through the pockets of the two unconscious men.

"I know these guys. Small time crooks. Donny hires himself out to anyone who needs muscle. Jeb here's a crackhead—he's in the pen more time than he's out."

While he was talking, Como was looking at the incriminating personal effects he was finding on the men—sachets of powder, a ball of resin, implausibly large amounts of cash, and various accessories useful for street-fighting. He also pulled out two smartphones.

"We'll keep these. Might have interesting contact numbers."

"Good thinking, Como," I said, anxious to encourage him to retain the initiative so I didn't have to take it myself. "What next?"

"You tell me—you're the writer, Writer."

So much for my encouragement.

"Do you think these men dangerous?" It was Herbert's question.

"Now, or when they wake up?"

I thought Como's sarcasm was a little uncalled-for, but Herbert seemed to take no offense.

"I'd been planning to stay here another night. The sense of isolation is an exquisite aid to contemplation."

"I don't think there'll be much contemplating when these guys come round. Here's what we'll do."

Taking back the initiative, thankfully, Como announced his plan. We'd take the money, drugs, and phones, so the baddies would think we were just three monks on the make. We'd leave the guys to wake and do whatever they were going to do with the contents of the safe. When we got a chance, we'd come back to check. In the meantime, Como would get someone to analyse recent calls on the phones.

"Okay?"

"Okay," said Herbert and I.

Como checked that the two unconscious thugs were still breathing, then we went outside.

"No way," I said, when Como indicated I should re-fasten the skis to my person. "I'm not getting on those death traps again. Besides, Herbert hasn't got skis."

"No," said Herbert. That settles that, I thought, until he continued, "But there are two pairs in the loft here."

In the end, I agreed to ski, on condition that instead of holding Como's habit's hem I would be supported by Herbert and Como either side of me, so at least I wouldn't be bent double and I could enjoy the view.

So much for theory. In practice there were far too many obstacles for us to spend much time three abreast, and I lost count of the number of times I fell over. It was with a huge sense of relief, therefore, that I found myself coasting the last few feet across the car park to hug the wing mirror of my black Range Rover, noting that the reflection in its tinted window showed a Writer on the edge of exhaustion and mental collapse. Herbert, too, noticed my state.

"Here, Chief Galahad, give me a hand."

They helped me to a bench, where Herbert knelt to unfasten my skis.

"Are you sure, Herbert, that you would not rather stay at the abbey for a few days?" I said, looking down at his back.

"No, Marco, I must continue my quest. There is one favour, however..."

"Anything, Herbert. Ask away."

"My sandals have been chafing somewhat, so I thought I might complete the remaining leg of my pilgrimage to St Raquel's by aeroplane, rather than walking so..."

"...you'd like a lift to the airport." I said. "It would be my pleasure."

"Ah...yes, well, you're very kind, my friend, and a lift would be most welcome, but I was thinking actually of money for the fare. I have renounced all but spiritual wealth, you see."

"Ah, yes, of course, Herbert, of course. Would five hundred cover it?"

"I was thinking, Marco, of a first class fare, actually."

While Como made a face over Herbert's shoulder, I peeled five thou' from a wad in my pouch. It was a small return, given that Herbert's advice had made me the world's fastest earning author, so I gave the money with a willing heart.

"Now, Herbert, let me drive you to the airport."

I stood unsteadily to walk to my black Range Rover with tinted windows.

"Are you sure you're up to it, Marco?" asked Herbert, scanning my face anxiously.

Protesting that I was fine, I collapsed into Como's arms.

CHAPTER TWENTY

In which Marco learns the history of the abbey, and finds an unexpected clue.

When I awoke from my swoon I was in my cell, my bespoke Rolex telling me I had been out for a little over three hours. Propped on my pallet-side cabinet was a note in Como's distinctive scrawl.

Gone to take H to airport in your car. Meet in refectory for supper. C.

He and Herbert must have carried me in. As a precaution I checked my pouch—the rest of my wad was still there, so perhaps it was just Como who carried me in. I'm not saying that Herbert's untrustworthy, just that he has unconventional ideas about morality.

I had a few hours to kill before Como's suggested rendezvous, so I fired up my iPad and started to look at some ghost-writing Barney had asked me to do for JKR. I don't know if you've ever tried ghost-writing for another big author. The trick is to get their voice into your head, after which you can just let it flow. The problem is if you get them mixed up, and you end up writing an idiotic wizard story for someone like Ruth Rendell. It drives Barney nuts when I do that.

There was a tentative knock on the door. I lay down my venerable iPad, crossed myself, and said "Enter."

The brother who answered my invitation was clad in the distinctive habit of the Post-Modernist order, with a purple corduroy cowl and suede sandals. He had thick spectacles, a heavy black beard, a copy of the Times Literary Supplement poking from the pocket of his gown, and a black plastic suitcase on wheels with an extending handle.

"Brother Marco, I trust I am not disturbing your meditations. I am Brother Umbert of Eco. I heard that the monastery had been graced with your presence. Taking it as a sign that a beneficent Lord had answered my prayers, I hurried at once to seek your advice."

"Upon what topic, Brother Umbert?"

"You will not be surprised if I say writing, Brother Marco, as your name is revered among those of the brethren who wish to be authors."

"Ah, if only writing were sufficient to make one an author. Please be seated."

"Indeed, Brother Marco. I have written so many words, millions of words, words as numerous as the grains of sand in distant Nevada, but my prodigious toil in the scriptorium has led only to these."

With those words Brother Umbert passed me a package of letters neatly tied with a bow of twisted horsehair.

I undid the bow and extracted the first of the letters from its envelope. *Dear Author*, it began, *thank you for your submission. Unfortunately your work isn't right for our agency. We get so many books sent to us that we can't comment on them individually, but we hope you have better luck elsewhere.*

"What am I to make of their devilish words?"

Brother Umbert's face creased with perplexity.

Not having an answer to hand, I parried his question with one of my own.

"What have you made of their words, Brother Umbert?"

"I cannot be sure, for they do not make sense to me. They imply that my work lacks some combination of qualities, but how am I to know which, if my submissions are rejected without explanation? It is as if the Lord were to condemn us as sinners without defining sin; how then could we repent?"

"Perhaps if you could show me a sample of your work, I might shed some glimmer upon your predicament."

"Nothing would give me greater pleasure, Brother Marco. I took the liberty of bringing my manuscripts, in the hope you might review them. Here."

He opened his black plastic suitcase to extract heavy bundle after heavy bundle of yellowing paper, which he landed with a depressing thump on my oaken desk. I smiled to indicate my appreciation, and took at random one of the bundles.

"You have an interesting choice of font, Brother Umbert."

"You are too kind, Brother Marco. It is called *Comic Sans*. I do feel it matches the mood of my work, and I imagine it pleaseth the literary agents for whose attention my work is intended."

As I scanned the first few paragraphs of Brother Umbert's prose, the play of expression on my delicate features told its own story.

"You find something wrong with my work, Brother Marco?"

"Not wrong, exactly, for there are no rights and wrongs in literature, Brother Umbert, merely prevailing preference and prejudice. However, among the prevailing preferences of the literary agents is the belief that it is better to show than to tell, while your work telleth greatly."

"I have heard of the great show-or-tell debate, Brother Marco, but I confess that I cannot make sense of it."

I wasn't sure I could either, but I had a go.

"Let me illustrate with an example. Your opening sentence in this manuscript of *Mission Five to Mars* is *'Umbert was a top astronaut at NASA'*."

"Indeed, Brother Marco. I wished to hook the reader's attention without preamble."

"Hooking is good, Brother Umbert, but the true hooker attracts through showing rather than telling. Perhaps instead of telling us that Umbert was a top NASA astronaut, you might have described Umbert's face distorted by immense g-forces as the mighty Saturn VII rocket accelerated to reach escape velocity on NASA's historic first launch of its Mars Explorer programme; that way the reader can work out for herself that Umbert is a top NASA astronaut."

"But the launch does not come until Chapter Eleven, Brother Marco. At the opening of the book, Umbert has not flown a mission for many months, and he is unsure whether he will fly again."

With my customary benevolence to all lesser authors, I managed to suppress a tut of irritation at Brother Umbert's thick-headed inability to get the point.

"Then you must adapt the principle to the circumstances. How about starting like this:

"Umbert gripped the lance of his top-of-the-range Karcher K1708 pressure washer and directed its powerful

jet at the folds and creases of his spacesuit. As he cleared the mossy deposits from the chromed letters of the NASA logo on the breastplate, he wondered if he would ever don the suit again.

"In such an opening, the reader is shown many things about Umbert. That he has a spacesuit shows he is an astronaut. That the spacesuit has a NASA logo shows Umbert to be employed by NASA. That the spacesuit is much begrimed shows it has not been worn for many months. That he has a top-of-the-range pressure washer shows that Umbert is no ordinary astronaut. And the mention of the Karcher brand could lead to a lucrative product placement deal, offering discounts on a wide range of pressure cleaning accessories."

"Your wisdom is as all encompassing as the heavens, Brother Marco. Could you, perhaps, give an example from your own work of showing rather than telling?" "Come, come, Brother Umbert—surely you cannot be that unobservant." A blank look was Brother Umbert's response to my rebuke. "When you entered my cell did I tell the readers you were a failed novelist?"

"Certainly not, Brother Marco."

"No, I showed them, by having you produce rejection letters from literary agents. Did I tell them you had a resentful, obsessive personality?"

"Certainly not, Brother Marco."

"No, I showed them, by having you retain your rejection letters in a bundle tied with horsehair. Did I tell them you were slow-witted?"

"Certainly not, Brother Marco."

"No, I showed them, by having you fail to grasp the significance of my initial suggestion about the launch of the

Saturn IX rocket." It might have been a Saturn VI rocket, but I was too bored to check.

"Your lessons are very clear, Brother Marco; but tell me this—in showing have you not substituted one form of telling for another? Is not all showing telling in the end? There is no logic to the debate."

"You must not fetter the dove of fiction with the iron shackles of logic, Brother Umbert."

I don't know about you, but I was beginning to wish I'd never brought Brother Umbert into it. I decided to change the subject, before he had a chance to figure out that most of what I'd said was complete nonsense.

"Perhaps, Brother Umbert, you could repay my lessons by teaching me about the abbey and its ways, and particularly about the abbot and the council of elders."

"I would be delighted, Brother Marco. The abbot, as you know, has been at the abbey only a few months, his predecessor having died in strange circumstances."

That was the first I'd heard of it. I highlighted it on my iPad to remind me to link it to a plot twist later in the book.

"The abbey itself is on the site of what had been intended to be a sports complex, built by a visionary, local billionaire who wished to bring the winter Olympics to Clarkesville. Alas, her vision was never fulfilled. She hosted a visit by the International Olympic Committee, showering them, in the fashion of such transactions, with bribe after bribe, but a rival venue leaked a confidential report from the CCGSMB..."

"The CCGSMB?"

"Sorry, the Clarkesville County Geological Survey and Meteorological Bureau. The report revealed that the topology and climate of the Clarkesville mountains brought the risk of catastrophic earth tremors and avalanches. You may readily imagine the consternation this spread amongst the Committee. Even the most minor tremor could result in appeal after appeal in the curling arena, while the death of all of the world's winter sports athletes in a devastating quake would jeopardise future games and their associated sponsorship deals. Notwithstanding lavish bungs, the Committee reluctantly decided to hold the games elsewhere. The complex fell into disuse, until it was bought cheaply by the monks of The Order in the nineteen sixties. Which brings me via my rambling route to the council of elders, since one among them—Brother George—was the original paymaster of the abbey. He had a business which provided security to those wandering bands of minstrels known as rock groups, a business which had various lucrative side-lines. He is still reckoned to be the most influential of the brethren, even if he lacks the ceremonial authority of the office of the abbot."

That was another important plot hook I didn't want to forget, so I stalled Brother Umbert with a gesture until I had time to highlight it, then begged that he continue, hoping he might introduce the other members of the council.

"The other members of the council [gives wink to readers] are all brothers of the highest piety, the deepest devotion, the broadest knowledge of scripture, and yet..." Brother Umbert looked around cautiously "...one hears the most startling things said."

"What sort of things?"

"I would feel guilty of propagating profane gossip were I to tell you, Brother Marco. In any case, doubtless some of the talk is prompted by the forthcoming elections to fill the empty seats on the council—all of the brethren have candidates they favour or despise, and they are apt to speak of them accordingly."

"Come, Come, Brother Umbert. I am but a simple chronicler, a student of man's affairs; I have no interest in friary gossip in itself, but only as a guide to the workings of the evil one. When one understands his ways one is better able to avoid them. I consider it your duty to share the gossip with me, however juicy, sordid, sinful, and salacious, and however painful it might be for you to recount."

"Very well, Brother Marco, although you will scarce believe your ears at what I have to say." He leant closer. "What I have heard is ... cmmf... excuse me... ghmmf... I am sorry... chmmm... gchmmp... " Brother Umbert doubled over as he made a series of unhealthy coughing sounds too complicated for me to spell.

Dropping my iPad, I rose to comfort him.

"Are you alright, Brother Umbert?"

"Yes, yes, I am quite... crmmmf... hrrgclrchh... grclcthrmc... rcthrmmgrthpj..."

In spite of his doubly affirmative reply, Brother Umbert's paroxysm of coughs and gasps morphed into more violent retching, now with spots of crimson bespattering his manuscripts as his tortured lungs expelled his very life blood.

"Brother Umbert, here, quickly, take this."

I uncorked my ancient Thracian tincture phial, but alas too late. Brother Umbert had collapsed over my desk. I watched as the blood oozing from his gaping mouth slowly obliterated the copyright notice at the foot of the first page of *Mission Five to Mars*. I didn't need to tell the readers he was dead; he had shown it for me. At last Brother Umbert had learned his lesson.

I fell back on my pallet, horrified. On the brink of startling revelations about the elder council, Brother Umbert's mysterious death was such a corny plot twist that even I was struggling to accept it. God knows how the readers felt. But courage, Marco, I thought—if anyone knows how to deal with clichéd plot twists it is you. Or should that be me, or I? Anyway, let's not get bogged down in pedantic trivia. I felt inside my robes for the leather pouch, comforting myself with the solid feel of the special pen it contained. Remembering Herbert's inscription, I wrote the very next thing that came into my head.

I eased poor Umbert's body off my desk and onto the worn oak planking. It was now my sacred duty to perform the ceremonial rites of the post-modernist order.

I folded the dead monk's arms across his chest, arranging the fingers of each hand into a V sign to the literary establishment. A few deft folds and creases transformed his copy of the *Times Literary Supplement* into a passable echo of the death mask of Flann O'Brien, which I laid reverently over Brother Umbert's face. The piles of yellowed manuscript I divided in two: one half to serve as a cushion for Brother Umbert's head, the other to support his sandaled feet. Now for the rejection letters—in the hallowed tradition, they would be shredded and sprinkled over the body. Where had he put them? I felt in the capacious pockets of his robe. Something quite unexpected met my touch. I closed my fingers around it, and brought it out.

CHAPTER TWENTY-ONE

In which Marco writes a digression involving his old foes.

So how come he has recent calls on his iPhone?"

Como's question was what we authors call a stumper. I couldn't make any sense of it. Twelve thousand four hundred and seventy six words ago I had written that there was no mobile phone signal within three miles of the abbey—or was it two?—and now I'd just found that Brother Umbert had a mobile phone with recent calls on its log. How was I going to explain that?

"That, Como, is the essence of a good thriller—a mystery. Let us consider the possible answers to the riddle. Perhaps Brother Umbert had left the abbey compound to make his calls."

Como knelt to examine Brother Umbert's sandals.

"Not in these shoes, Writer—they've not seen the outdoors for days. You're gonna have to try harder."

"Must you be so negative, Como? Might he not have outdoor shoes for the purpose of his telephone expeditions? Overshoes, perhaps? Use your imagination."

"Imagination's your department, Writer. Mine's facts."
Como rummaged through the other oddments in Brother
Umbert's case, thankfully producing no more clues to add to
the stack I was already struggling to resolve into a coherent
plot. "Let's go look at his room."

Brother Umbert's room proved to be the twin of Brother
Glaxo's, but, to Como's disappointment and my relief,
lacking any secret compartment behind its bookcase.

"Any idea where he hides those overshoes?"

Given that the room contained only a bed, a stool, a
desk and a bookcase, I concluded that Como's question was
intended to be a rhetorical stab at my incompetence in the
plotting department, rather than one I was expected to
answer.

"If I remember correctly, Como, a chapter or so ago we
had a locker-room in the book. I would expect a police chief
in ruthless pursuit of facts to be heading there to examine
Brother Umbert's locker, not mocking his Writer with
sarcastic questions. In the locker room, I am sure, we will
find what we seek."

In the locker room, what we actually found was that
Brother Umbert had no locker.

"I ain't saying nothing, Writer."

Como waited for me to acknowledge the facts.

"Very well, Como, I admit it looks likely that Brother
Umbert has no outdoor shoes, and that he cannot have
travelled from the abbey compound in search of a mobile
phone signal. But aside from satisfying your police chief
obsession with facts, and making me look foolish to the
readers, where, pray, has that got us?"

"Where it's got us is that you need stop writing crap and
we do this my way."

Half an hour later, having decided to do things Como's way, we were in Como's police chief Range Rover where he'd left it in the car park outside Kelly's. Como had called HQ—that's Police HQ, not Herbert Quarry—to get a trace put on Brother Umbert's recent calls. While we waited for the results of the trace, Como was on the phone catching up with some of his less interesting cases. I overheard his half of a dialogue about some evidence incriminating the owners of a lumber yard out at Barton Hills. It was nothing to do with the incidents at the abbey, but I decided to let Como run us out there for a nosey around, as I was sick to death of writing about monks.

"What's the deal, Como?"

We were on the N66, still about four miles from the Barton Hills interchange. Como was driving in what seemed to be an unusually erratic manner, possibly because he was continually scratching the irritated patches of skin where his horsehair shirt had been rubbing.

"The lumber yard's owned by Stella McGee. She's been..."

"Stella McGee?"

"That's what I said, Writer. She's been..."

"Stella McGee? Spelt em cee gee eee eee?"

"Uh huh."

"Christ, Como, she's not another of *the* McGees?

"A McGee's a McGee, Writer. What other sort are you thinking?"

I clutched my non-typing hand to an anguished brow. The McGees of Clarkesville were the world's biggest collection of crooks, leaving aside politicians that is. Certain late members of the clan had been exposed as baddies in my previous books, and their surviving relatives bore an enormous collective chip on their shoulders—a chip with my name on it. And now we were driving to a lumber yard owned by McGees, a location so densely packed with dangerous machinery that there would be no shortage of opportunities for a tragic 'accident' of one sort or another. I could imagine the headlines: *Ocram Buried in Six by Two Lengths*. And that, I concluded, was what happens when you let Como influence the plot.

"Christ, Como. Why does it always have to be McGees? Couldn't you pick someone else to be the baddie for a change? Fu Manchu, perhaps. Dr No. The Joker."

"I only know one joker round here, Writer, and he's sitting next to me. You can make up any old crap you like, but I've got to stick to facts."

"What I do is not making up any old crap, Como—it is known, technically, as fabulation."

"You can call it what you like, but I know crap when I hear it. Anyway, you'll be okay while you're with me. None of the McGees is crazy enough to bump you off with me around. Except maybe Orville McGee."

"Orville McGee?"

"Yeah," Como checked the mirror before making the turn to Barton Hills, "a real nasty piece, even by McGee standards. He swore he'd kill you, after Chief and Scoobie McGee died in your first book. So you can guess how he was when Steve McGee died in your second."

"That wasn't my fault—I can't help it if his relatives get topped."

Which wasn't exactly true, but Como wasn't to know.

"Stop worrying. Orville McGee hasn't been seen for months. Seems he got religious, or something, so maybe he'll turn the other cheek. Anyway, at least when we see the McGees there'll be none of that 'Oh please sign my book, Mister Ocram' hocus pocus."

That was true. The only thing a McGee would want me to sign would be my own death warrant.

"This is it." Como turned at a sign that announced *Clarkesville Timber Processing*.

I wrote that the lumber yard was an old, untidy, weed-infested site down a curving track alongside a shallow river that ran over a pebbly bed between low banks shaded by trees. There were five rickety timber buildings, like bigger versions of the bothy, in the nearest of which freshly cut lumber was stacked to dry, while further into the site was the shack that housed the milling equipment—a wicked circular saw about four feet across, driven by a sagging belt from a stationary diesel engine that belched unhealthy fumes. The site was littered with rusting equipment—some of it sunken into the rutted ground—and abandoned cars beyond economic repair. A handful of dungareed hillbilly types were moving the timber around, guiding logs along a series of rollers that fed them into the path of the saw.

So, having written all that, it came as a huge surprise to find that Como had actually driven us into an enormous modern compound about the size of a major airport, into which a stream of giant trucks brought what seemed to be an endless supply of tree trunks, and out of which another stream of giant trucks was taking lumber, plywood, fencing posts, chipped bark, and various other freshly created wood products. There seemed to be about a hundred forklifts and cranes unloading and loading the trucks. None of the milling machinery was visible, all being housed in smart, metal-clad buildings into which the tree trunks vanished on conveyors through curtains of thick plastic. There was not a dungaree in sight. All of the employees sported stylish overalls and hi-viz tabards.

Como pulled into a carpark in which his Range Rover seemed the least prestigious vehicle—quite shabby, in fact, alongside the Porches, Maseratis, Aston Martins, and other flashy autos of the lumber yard staff.

We got out of the car, Como donning his police chief hat.

"Over here."

Como indicated that I should follow him to what seemed to be a bonsai sky-scraper, about six storeys, clad in bronzed mirror glass which reflected our silhouettes as we approached—mine unimpressively thin, Como's towering and beefy.

"Let me do all the talking," said Como. "You keep an eye on Stella—see how she reacts to what I say."

We entered a plush reception, and took chrome and leather seats after signing in. Como was busy checking messages on his phone, so I flicked through some of the dog-eared trade magazines left to entertain the waiting visitor—*Forestry Today*, *Timber Processing Monthly*, *The Oregon Weekly Logger*, *The Sawmilling Gazette*, *Country Logging*. I was reading about new trends in heat recovery from sawdust piles, when a young woman in a smart business suit asked us to follow her.

We were zapped through a security style and taken to the elevators. Our hostess made small talk to put us at ease en route to Stella McGee's office. *How had our trip been? Did we find the site easily? Wasn't it good that average prices for marine grade ply were at an all-time high? Wasn't the weather cold?* Finally we were shown into a large office that seemed to take up most of the top storey of the building.

Stella McGee closed a folder on her desk and rose to greet us. I wasn't sure how to describe her. If I made her a stereotypical, glamorous, able-bodied, heterosexual businesswoman of average age I'd be slammed for my lack of diversity; if I didn't, I'd be slammed for including a token minority. I decided to leave it to the reader's conscience.

"Chief Galahad and Doctor Ocram." She shook our hands. "It isn't often we get such distinguished visitors. Please take a seat." She gestured at a long, highly-polished conference table that ran along one side of her office. "Are you here for business or pleasure, Doctor Ocram?"

Como and I exchanged looks. We both knew that people who call me Doctor Ocram usually turn out to be the bad guys, or gals in this case. It was with redoubled caution, therefore, that I gave my suavely evasive reply. "Err, pleasure, hopefully. I'm booked into the abbey. You know, for a chill-out fortnight. Complete relaxation. Doctor's orders and all that. Mustn't do anything stressful like investigating crimes or anything—just take it completely easy."

"Really?"

"Absolutely."

"So why are you here with Chief Galahad?"

Clearly this was a master criminal with a rapier-like intellect. I parried her thrust.

"He was just giving me a lift, and we were going passed, sorry, past, and he said would I mind if he popped into the lumber yard to check something, and I said no, not at all—haven't got anything I need to get back to abbey for or anything. Besides, I've always been interested in timber processing, and I've always wanted a chance to look round a lumber yard. So we popped in."

"I see. And you, Galahad. How's the Mayor? Are you still going round to hers every Saturday for those long, intense debriefing sessions? I always wondered how you got to be Chief."

"Cut the crap, Stell—you know there's nothing between me and the Mayor."

What!?!

In spite of Como's instruction to keep my eyes on Stella McGee, they swivelled to his face in response to Stella's startling insinuation. He definitely had what we cliché lovers like to call a shifty look. Under brows that were now a good inch higher, my eyes re-swivelled to Stella McGee.

"Is this an official visit, or an unofficial one?" she asked Como.

"Unofficial—for now."

"So how can I help?"

"Two days ago a car was found on fire near the Hacienda Apartments."

"That's hardly news."

She was right. The Hacienda Apartments are the run-down dump I always use as the backdrop for any scene that involves the underclass scum of Clarkesville. They probably burned cars there every five minutes.

"No, but this car had a body in it."

I wasn't sure even that counted as news, such were the levels of criminality in and around the aforementioned apartments.

"So?"

"The body was Tan Falconi, known drug dealer."

"So a known drug dealer gets torched at the Hacienda—big deal."

"We traced Tan Falconi's calls. Seventeen times in the last two weeks he's called your switchboard, Stell. Why would he do that?"

"You tell me. Why would he do that?"

"Come on, Stell. I'm not saying it's anything to do with you or the business."

"What are you saying, then?"

"It's an unusual pattern of behaviour. We need to follow it up."

"Right. Have you followed up all his calls yet, or just the ones to my switchboard?"

"We've gotta start somewhere, Stell."

"Well I can't help you. We get hundreds of calls a day. How am I meant to know who they're from or what they're about?"

"I'm not expecting you to know," said Como, "but you could help us find out."

"How's that meant to work?"

"Show us the switchboard logs. Let us speak to the switchboard operator."

"And if I do that, and if you find nothing, then this little game stops?"

"Sure, Stell. What other reason would I have for poking my nose around?"

I was deeply uneasy at the direction the dialogue was taking—twenty three paragraphs without a single joke. If I didn't introduce an absurd note soon, I'd be in danger of sounding like a real author.

"Okay." Stella McGee made a decision. "You can talk with the switchboard operator now."

"What about the logs?"

"I'll have to get someone to look into that."

That was fair enough. I wasn't even sure a switchboard had logs, so it seemed reasonable to give Stella a chance to investigate. It would also give me a chance to think whether I could make a joke about telephone logs in a timber yard.

Five minutes later, in a small meeting room near reception, Stella McGee introduced us to the switchboard operator.

"Gentlemen, this is Thaddaeus McGee. I'll leave you to it."

Thaddeus McGee was gaunt, unshaven, white haired, and about a hundred. He had a huge hearing-aid clamped behind his right ear—an unpromising handicap for a switchboard operator. Como opened the discussion diplomatically.

"Thank you for your time, Mister McGee. I'm Chief Galahad, and this is a colleague of mine." Como clearly thought it inappropriate to mention the name Ocram in the presence of an elderly McGee.

"I know very well who you are, Como Galahad—I knew your grandma. Fine woman. Shame about that disgrace of a bum she married, begging your pardon. Your friend here looks just like that Ocram character that caused all the trouble. Sorry, Mister," he addressed me, "I don't suppose you can help what you look like, but it's a mighty shame to look like the double of Marco Ocram when you're in McGee territory, I don't mind telling you."

I smiled to show that I didn't mind either.

"I'm wondering if you can help me with an enquiry," said Como.

"No McGee would have truck with that pesky Ocram. Hang 'im on a nail faster than you'd shoot a skunk. It's every McGee's dream to finish-off that piece of shit."

"I'm sure," said Como, virtually inciting the man. "I appreciate how you must feel."

"And as for those so called books of his. Muckraking libellous trash, all of them. Dang knows why everyone buys 'em. They should be burned—along with him too."

I kicked Como in the shin to move things along a bit.

"But to return to the point..."

"What point was that, young man? Say, aren't you Como Galahad? I knew your grandma."

"Mister McGee, you took a number of calls over the last couple of weeks from a particular number."

"Did I?"

"Yes, from Tan Falconi's number. Do you know Tan?"

"You mean Ronnie Falconi?"

"No, Ronnie was Tan's uncle—he died about a month ago. You were at his funeral—remember?"

"Was I? Every day's like every other day. Hard to remember what I did five minutes ago now. Hey aren't you Como Galahad?"

Como nodded, with about a million times more patience than I would have shown in his shoes. "Those calls, Mister McGee, those calls from Tan Falconi."

"What about them?"

"Do you remember who you put them through to?"

"Who says I did?"

"So was he calling to speak to you?"

"Who was? Say, aren't you Benedicta Galahad's grandson?"

"Mister McGee, you've been very helpful. Thank you for your time." Como stood up.

"Glad to be of help. She was a good woman, your grandma." He turned to me. "Nice to meet you, young fella. Take my advice, if you meet any more McGees tell'em right off you ain't that Marco Ocram asshole, cause you sure look like him. Same stupid expression, begging your pardon."

I took his proffered hand, smiled, then nudged Como to get us out of the room before I had to write any more of this outright nonsense.

Stella McGee had been awaiting our exit, a sheaf of papers under one arm. "I hope my great uncle gave you every possible cooperation."

"He's been very helpful. I appreciate you arranging it." Como's reply was miraculously free of irony.

"I've spoken with my IT people about those logs."

I remembered to make a joke. "They must be used to dealing with logs...*in a lumber yard.* Ha ha ha ha ha."

Neither Como nor Stella echoed my grin, which I thought showed some degree of ingratitude—I had invented them, after all.

"You're welcome to take these," said Stella, handing the papers to Como, "but I'm afraid they will be of limited help. The logs record calls to and from the office; they don't record internal transfers."

Hmmm... I wasn't convinced. That sounded far too convenient.

"Surely," I said, "A modern digital switchboard is capable of tracking internal transfers."

"That's exactly what I said to my IT people, Doctor Ocram, and they tell me the statement is correct. However, our switch has never been configured to log them. Why would it be? We're a lumberyard. Why would anyone want to trace internal call transfers in a lumberyard?"

Because they are trying to figure out exactly what combination of serious felonies allows the lumberyard to make so much money that its forklift operators can afford to drive Ferraris, is what I thought; but what I said was "Quite. Not that it's my business, since I'm in Clarkesville to have a complete rest and not be involved in crime fighting in any capacity."

"I'll take them anyway," said Como, "since you've gone to all the trouble of having them printed."

Como's radio beeped the kind of beep which meant he had to excuse himself to talk to someone at HQ, leaving me alone with Stella McGee.

"Since you have such an intense interest in timber processing, Doctor Ocram, why don't you let me show you around?"

My mind froze in a spasm of indecision. I wasn't sure Como would be happy with me sticking my nose into one of his cases, and I wasn't sure that walking around a sawmill staffed by resentful McGees would be entirely good for my health. On the other hand it might spawn opportunities for fantastic new plot twists.

"That would be nice," I found myself saying. "A walk around would do me good."

"I wasn't proposing to walk, Doctor Ocram."

CHAPTER TWENTY-TWO

*In which Marco sees the sights of Clarkesville from an
unexpected angle.*

Are you sure it's not too much trouble?" I coughed to
dislodge the nervous catch in my throat. "I'd be quite happy
to walk."

"She's my new toy, Doctor Ocram. I hate to miss any
chance to take her up."

Stella McGee continued her pre-flight checks, while I
tried to remember how we'd ended up in a helicopter. And
not just any helicopter—Stella's new toy was an electric blue
Bell Predator Turbo, the GT model with the low-profile
rotors, extra dials, and chromed exhaust nozzles.

"All set?" She adjusted the choke and eased off the
handbrake. "Chocks away."

We kangarooed forward in three jerking hops.

"Ooops, not enough revs. One of these days I'll get the
hang of it. Hold on to your hat."

Stella floored the throttle, and we roared upwards. I
clutched my seatbelt with both hands, like Tarzan grasping
a vine, and wished I could avoid staring out of the

windows—an insufficient word for the giant hemispheres of glass which the designers of the Predator Turbo had substituted for any actual bodywork. No matter which way I looked, I could see I was high in the air in a contraption as substantial as an anorexic dragon-fly.

Stella frowned at the dashboard. "Hand me those other glasses in the glove compartment, would you—I can't read a thing with these."

The glove compartment bore only a half-full gin bottle, or, now I think about it, a half-empty one.

"Never mind," Stella poked the bridge of her inappropriate spectacles to sit higher upon her nose. "We'll just have to wing it."

My feet pressed with alarm against imaginary brake pedals as we shot forward over the expansive lumberyard, an area the size of one point three million Olympic ping-pong tables.

"Over there," said Stella, nodding to the north of the compound, "is where we keep our lumber reserve. Ordinarily the raw material's coming in as fast as we can deal with it, but we need some stocks in case of transportation problems in our supply chain."

I began to feel a little more comfortable as I realised that what lay ahead were a few explanatory paragraphs about the workings of the timber processing plant— paragraphs I could knock-out straightforwardly after reading the trade magazines in reception.

"Those tanks at the back are where we keep the chemicals for the treated timber. Lots of arsenic in the mix, which is why there are bunds around the tanks—we couldn't afford the fines if there was a spillage.

"The big silver building is the main mill—the logs are taken in on conveyor, stripped of their bark by tungsten scarifiers, scanned in three dee, and computers work out the best way to cut each one for maximum yield.

"See the heat haze over those chimneys? That's the kiln for drying the wood. You wouldn't want to be stuck in there when it's fired-up, or you'd come out like a piece of biltong.

"Just below us is the sheet production plant, where we make ply, particle-board and other sheet products. Mainly it's about applying massive pressure to squeeze the materials flat."

It seemed to me that Stella's lumberyard was a smorgasbord of deadly hazards, in contrast with which, being in a spiralling helicopter piloted by a half-blind beginner was starting to feel the safer option.

"Let's open this baby up."

I changed my mind about the safer option as Stella signalled *full speed above* to the engine room, and we shot up like an express elevator on steroids. I had earlier agreed with Stella and Como that she would drop me back at the abbey—it seemed that we were to take the scenic route.

"Great view, huh?"

In fairness, the view was, technically, great. As we approached what seemed to me to be the fringes of outer space, spread below were the countless unforgettable scenes from my record-breaking books. I saw the small cove where Herbert Quarry once had a house on the beach overlooking the ocean—the scene of the brutal murder of Lola Kellogg by Chief and Scoobie McGee. I saw the stretch of coastline along which I had sailboarded to Clarkesville after my black Range Rover with tinted windows had been torched by vigilantes. I saw the quiet curving road by the cliffs, where Como and I had narrowly escaped death in two separate books; the port complex where we had found a body squashed between shipping containers; the still blackened sites of the burned out warehouses where millions of copies of a book had been stored—a book at the centre of a conspiracy to break my record as the world's fastest selling author. Finally, my nostalgic eye settled upon the Clarkesville County International Airport, the vast transportation hub from which Como and I had departed in the private jet of the mad Professor Sushing, a man so resentful of my success that he was prepared to crash his $2 billion airplane just to see me dead.

At the recollection of the Professor's evil plot, a fresh fear gripped me—what if Stella McGee's bungled attempts at piloting her 'toy' were feigned incompetence? What if it was the build up to an 'accident' in which she long-sightedly pressed the wrong button on the dashboard, causing my side of the helicopter to swerve into something large and solid just as we were landing, crushing me to a clichéd pulp? Or perhaps she'd crash it on its side by the tanks of preserving fluid, slicing open one of the tanks with the rotor, and squashing me under the wreckage so I drown in the escaping torrent of arsenic. Or maybe we crash onto the conveyors into the main mill, my side of the helicopter inching slowly towards the merciless tungsten scarifiers as a puzzled computer tries to figure out the best way to get maximum yield from the oddly shaped electric-blue log. Or maybe she'd wedge my side of the helicopter into the kiln, 'accidentally' jamming the temperature control on maximum, so that I...

Stella broke in on my panicky speculations. "Perhaps you're wondering why a McGee is showing you around Clarkesville in a helicopter?"

I made a vague noise that Stella interpreted as a polite laugh at the humorous irony of her question. If only she knew.

"While it's true most McGees fantasise about your demise, Doctor Ocram, some of us benefit from your continued success."

I fractionally loosened my grip on my seat-belt. "You surprise me, Ms McGee." Which was the literal truth.

"It's Stella, please. The lumber yard isn't my only business—just a side-line, in fact. Tourism makes the money, or at least it has since you took an interest in sleepy little Clarkesville."

I dithered about whether to say '*You surprise me, Ms McGee*' all over again, or to write a long expositional paragraph explaining how the Clarkesville tourist industry had exploded with the phenomenal success of my books; how coachloads of visitors of every nationality thronged the hotspots along '*The Ocram Trail*', and followed the sensational footsteps of my adventures with Como; how Disney had opened '*The Awful Truth*' theme park; how Marco and Como lookalikes conducted perpetual turf wars for the right to charge tourists ten bucks for selfies; how countless other tacky exploitations of my work had erupted like a rash over Clarkesville County. Before I could decide, however, Stella continued...

"I make more money from Lola Kellog dolls than I do from selling timber. Want an idea for your next book?"

"I never say never." My attempt at a James Bond voice was tainted by nervous strains of Kermit the Frog.

"At the back of the lumberyard there's the original site of the old McGee sawmill. My great-great-great grandma bought it from some deadbeat who was losing money. Those were the days when the timber grew thick on the hills. Old Nanny McGee had the idea of straightening one of the streams for a flume to bring the logs down the mountainside. She cut her transportation costs and put all her competition out of business. Good old Nanny McGee. Without her there'd be no McGee clan in Clarkesville."

Good old Nanny McGee indeed. I must remember to strew poison ivy on her grave.

"I was thinking," Stella continued, "how brilliant it would be to open the old mill as a tourist site. Imagine if we could turn the old log flume into a ride."

Stella went on to elaborate her big idea—that in my next book I should stage some sensational scene at the old sawmill, so she could open an attraction there to sucker the tourists into yet another of her speculative schemes. I asked what would be in it for me.

"Can't you guess? You do that for me, and I use my influence to call off the McGee vendetta. You won't have to keep looking behind you for the rest of your life. What do you say, Doctor Ocram?"

It was a hugely appealing proposition, but there was one obvious flaw in her thinking. I explained to Stella that, much as I appreciated the spirit of her suggestion, it was against my artistic principles to make conscious decisions about the contents of my novels—that I was committed to Herbert Quarry's principle of literary spontaneity, and always wrote the next thing that came into my head.

"It's the only pure way of writing. You have to let the story come out of your sub-conscious in its natural form."

I continued in that vein for several sentences, stressing to Stella the purity of my artistic pursuit of freeform literary expression. I could tell from the way she started snatching at the gear stick that she wasn't happy.

"I thought all that stuff about writing the first thing that came into your head was just marketing crap to explain why you wrote awful books. Well, I'm sorry you can't accept my proposal."

But not as sorry as you'll be, said the look on her face, as she took the Predator Turbo GT into a vicious dive toward the abbey.

CHAPTER TWENTY-THREE

In which one ring prompts the appearance of another.

The abbot came to meet me as I walked from the helipad.

"Brother Marco, I observed your descent from the heavens. A most suitable metaphor. But is your... erm... assistant not with you?"

"Sister Coma? She is following me overland, and is due to meet me in the car park in half of the hour's time."

The abbot's face brightened. "I would like to be present to greet her, lest she forget the way to her chambers."

"You are most considerate, Brother Abbot. I am sure my assistant will wish to repay your kindness in any way she can." Notwithstanding Como's concerns, I thought it best to encourage the abbot's interest, in case we needed to find an excuse to enter his rooms on an undercover mission. "In the meantime, I am most interested to learn the ways of the infirmary, which is famed throughout Christendom for the variety of its treatments. Might I intrude upon Your Supremacy to show me around?"

"Indeed Brother Marco. Come."

The abbot picked up the hem of his brushed velvet gown, and we traipsed through the snow to the doors of the infirmary—large sheets of plate glass that opened miraculously at our approach. While the abbot signed us in, I kicked the snow off my sandals and looked around reception. There was the usual rack of leaflets offering medical insurance plans, a hatch through which biological samples could be dropped, and a number of brethren reading old magazines.

"Please, Brother Marco..."

Having completed the formalities of registration, the abbot indicated that I should precede him through a security style which he had opened with one of his key-cards.

"Are you alright, Brother Marco?"

The abbot's question was probably prompted by my pre-occupied look, as I tried to remember the significance of the word key-card. That was it! I'd written that we'd found a key-card hidden under Brother Glaxo's mattress...and...and...it was starting to come back to me...yes, and we were going to explore all the locks it was programmed to open, one of which was in the infirmary. So *that's* why we were here. It was all starting to make sense, surprisingly. I hurried through the style, noting the number 2 stencilled next to the slot through which the abbot had swiped his key-card.

"Tell me, Your Predominance, what is the significance of this numeral?"

"It is the serial number of the lock, Brother Marco. Security within an institution as complex as an abbey is most important. We have many ranks among the brethren, and many rules which determine which places may be visited by monks of which rank. It is a holy conundrum indeed to keep track of who is allowed to go where, so a system to identify the locks is indispensable."

Ha! I'd cracked it. I couldn't wait to tell Como. I pretended to the abbot that I had a stone in my sandal, to give me a moment to page back on my iPad to the list Como had printed from the digital lock system. The fifth location on the list was *Infirmary 42*. All I needed to do was to get the abbot to take me through every part of the infirmary, and keep an eye out for a lock with *42* stencilled against it. Eat your heart out, Hercule Poirot.

With suitable words of encouragement from me, the abbot led us through department after department. We passed audiology, gynocology, ER, medical imaging, nephrology, hepatology, leeching, exorcism, trepanning, blood letting, phrenology, billing, and many other departments too difficult for me to spell, but at none did I see the number *42* stencilled beside a lock. Finally, we returned to reception.

"I trust you have found your tour informative, Brother Marco. I would have lingered longer in each of the departments had I not been anxious to greet your assistant upon her return."

"Indeed, Your Paramountcy, but did we visit all the departments?"

"Certainly, Brother Marco—the tour was comprehensive. Do you have reason to believe otherwise?"

I laughed a disarming laugh. "I confess you might find what I have to say odd, Your Prepotency, but through my years as an investigator, I have developed an unnatural cast of mind that causes me to be an obsessive observer of numerals. I saw all of the holy numbers between one and seventy nine stencilled against the locks of the infirmary, except for one." I studied the abbot's face with a steely intensity as I confronted him with my knowledge of his deceit. "The lock bearing the number 42 was not among those we passed."

"Goodness, Brother Marco, your powers of observation are miraculous indeed. I cannot imagine how we might have overlooked a department, though possibly in my anxiety to provide succour to your assistant I might have been distracted from my purpose. Shall we return to the car park, as the appointed hour of her arrival cometh?"

With undignified haste, the abbot puffed his way to the car park. I followed, cursing Como for derailing another of my finely reasoned schemes. As we arrived, my black Range Rover with tinted windows was crunching over the snow-covered cobbles, a noticeable list to port showing that Como's huge bulk was indeed in the driving seat. I waved to attract his attention, and he drew up beside us and eased himself out of the car, tossing the keys to me in the customary fashion.

"Sister Coma," said the abbot, with a leery wink, "I am pleased you have returned to us without mishap. The path to the abbey is treacherous in this snowy weather. Have you dined this evening?"

"Thank you, your abbotness—I grabbed a burger at Kelly's." Como leant his head down to hiss in my ear "Ask him," at the same time tapping his right pinkie with his left forefinger. It took me a moment to twig what he meant.

"Tell me, Your Supremacy," I said, "this ring which you gave to me as a token of your authority, can you tell me something of its provenance? It has a most unusual appearance."

I held the ring before me to distract the abbot's attention from Sister Coma's statuesque figure.

"Indeed, Brother Marco. It was given to me upon his death by my superior when I was the deputy abbot at a monastery near Chicago. He begged I should wear it in his memory after succeeding him in the office of abbot."

I gave Como a look which conveyed the message that, as I had expected, there had been a perfectly simple explanation for the abbot's possession of a mafia pinkie ring; that I hoped he would learn his lesson, and that he should not be so melodramatic and paranoid in future.

In return Como gave me a look conveying the message that if I believed a word of the abbot's story I was an even bigger dumbass than he thought, and that was saying something.

I gave Como a second look that said if anyone was a dumbass it was...

"Oops!"

I interrupted my look by accidentally dropping the abbot's stupid ring, which disappeared into about a foot of snow atop a low wall next to the path upon which we stood.

The abbot made his views clear. "My ring! Tell me it is not lost! This is the Devil's work. It must be found!"

Not waiting to see what sort of look the abbot might now be giving me, I uttered a sycophantic apology and assured him that my assistant would find the ring in a trice.

"Who, me?" said Como, pointing at his chest.

"If you would do me that kindness it will absolve you from your penance for your earlier sins," I said.

With a look too rude to include here, Como bent over to begin patting the soft snow for the feel of the ring.

I swear it was an accident, but somehow I pressed a button on the remote control for my black Range Rover with tinted windows, causing the tailgate to slowly swing heavenward. As it did, its nearer corner caught a fold of

Como's cloak, lifting the entire lower portion of Como's habit, and unveiling for a spectacular instant the rounded black mysteries of Como's nether portions. To my eyes the sight had a certain gruesome novelty to it. To the abbot's it must have been a temptation of apocalyptic proportions— Sister Coma's immense globular buttocks, bent over and framed in a miniskirt of horsehair.

"Found it."

Como stood, unaware of his momentary exposure, to find the abbot trembling with a feverish appearance.

"I must... I must repair to my chambers to give thanks to the Lord for revealing the ring. Excuse me, please."

"Seems a lot of fuss over a cheap ring," said Como, as we watched the abbot trotting to the praesidium. "I'm telling you, Writer, there's more to this than meets the eye."

Chapter Twenty-Four

In which the boys discover the laboratory.

Back in the discomfort of my cell, I flopped on my pallet and tried to marshal what passed in my head for thoughts, while Como surveyed the compound through the grille of my unglazed window. The counter at the bottom of my iPad said we were 28,735 words into the book—barely a third of the way through, and already I had as many loose ends floating around as a colony of polyps on a coral reef. Dan Brown once told me that he keeps track of his plot lines by writing significant topics on post-it notes and sticking them on the wall. There were two problems with that approach: one, I didn't have any post-its, and two, I'd need a cell with bigger walls. There must have been a hundred things I needed to follow up, but which ones? The death of the herbalist in the chalked pentangle? The significance of the word CAVE he had written with his own intestines? The frame-by-frame review of the footage from the security cameras? Brother Glaxo's gun? Brother Felonius' notebook?

"Which building is that?"

I joined Como at the window and followed the line of his pointing finger. "No idea. Why?"

"Look for yourself, smarty pants. The clue's staring you in the face."

I looked. The building was a simple single storey affair, with dressed stone quoins, rubble walls, asbestos roof sheets and a twin-wall chimney pipe with a matte black cowl. Aside from my elegant play on the use of the word cowl in a monastic setting, I could see nothing remarkable about it.

"Nope. Nothing's clicking, Como. Just looks like any old building to me."

"Not the building itself—look at its context."

I looked. All I saw was a shabby collection of diverse buildings given some semblance of coherence by a uniform coating of snow.

"Okay, Como—you win. Dazzle me with your detecting prowess. What should I have spotted—the ash from a rare Cuban cigar on a window ledge, perhaps? A Cuban cigar sold only in the twenty-four-seven store by the Hacienda Apartments, where Tan Falconi's associates bought their nicotine fixes?"

"Much simpler, Writer. You see the smoke from the chimney?"

"Yes."

"You see the lights on inside?"

"Yes."

"You see the snow's melting on part of the roof?"

This was getting tedious. "So there's someone inside. So what?"

"How did they get there?"

"Through the door, presumably."

"Take another look, Writer. There's deep snow in front of the door—nobody's been through that door for days."

"Wow! That's genius, Como. Just a sec." I went back to my pallet and felt between its slats where I had dropped my map of the abbey complex. I smoothed the folds of the leaflet against the wall by window, and matched the images on the map to the collection of buildings on view outside. "That's... it's not on the map!"

"Let me see." Doubting my map reading prowess, Como pinched the leaflet so he could see for himself. "Something crooked's going on here, mark my words. C'mon. Let's take a look."

A paragraph later we were peering round the corner of the praesidium toward the mystery building. Its windows were shuttered, but there seemed to be gaps between the shutters sufficiently large to allow a look inside. I nudged Como's arm. "What about the snow. If we go over for a look through the cracks in the shutters we'll leave footprints. It'll tip them off."

"Good thinking, Writer. You follow me. Step in my footprints. We'll walk back backwards, so there'll only be one set of footprints leading to the window. If they notice, it'll confuse the hell out of them."

"Okay."

We set off across the virgin snow towards the side of the building. Como's legs must be about a foot longer than mine, so I was having to leap from one of his massive footprints to the next, but luckily his feet are twice the size of mine, so the footprints were hard to miss. Since Como was the first to arrive at the window, he had the first peek through the shutters.

"What can you see?" I said.

"Looks like some kind of lab."

"A dog?"

"No, a science lab. There's all sorts of weird looking kit."

I tugged at his habit until he turned to look at me.

"Which of us, Como, is the world-renowned scientist, familiar with laboratory equipment of every type?"

"You, according to you. But how do I know that ain't more of your fabulating bullshit?"

"If you're not prepared to take your Writer's word for it, my extensive listing on Wikipedia would be a good start. Now, let me have a look through that crack."

I put the stronger Ocram eye to the gap between the shutters, and allowed it to rove over the inside of the strange building—an Aladdin's cave of specialist scientific instrumentation. There were crucibles of perfect sphericity. Pestles and mortars of exquisite quality, capable of grinding dusts to subatomic fineness. There were programmable Bunsen burners, with touch-sensitive controls. Callipers and weighing scales of unsurpassed precision. Mile after mile of fine glass tubing. A neutrino tunnelling microscope, with deluxe velvet eye-cups. And all was illuminated by flicker-free neon lights of exceptional radiance and hue.

"That is no ordinary laboratory," I announced over my shoulder. "It has leading-edge instruments of the utmost degree of specialisation. If I am not mistaken, it has a bank of eight piezo-electric manipulators—devices capable of adjusting the positions of individual atoms in complex molecules."

"Right. So not the normal monk stuff?"

"No, Como, not the normal monk stuff." I had an idea. I felt in my habit and produced the key-card we had found under Brother Glaxo's mattress. "Let's see if this will let us in."

We manoeuvred to the door, Como first and I literally in his footsteps.

"I don't think that's gonna help, Writer."

"Nonsense, Como—don't be so defeatist. Let me try."

Como stepped aside to let me try.

"Oh, right."

There was no card-activated digital lock. The door was made of heavy oak planks bound with thick iron straps, and studded with pointed nail-heads. Above the knob was an escutcheon for a massive key.

"That door hasn't been opened in years, Writer. We need to find the other way in."

I put my good eye to the massive key-hole.

"There's an open trap door at the far end of the building. I can make out steps leading down to a dimly-lit tunnel."

"Which way's it headed?"

I sighted along the wall of the building to gauge the alignment. There could be no doubt about it—the tunnel was headed directly to the centre of the herbarium. I informed Como.

"There can be no doubt about it, Como—the tunnel is headed directly to the centre of the herbarium."

"Okay, let's get back to the cell and make a plan."

This was the point at which I regretted typing that nonsensical suggestion of Como's about walking from the building backwards in order to leave confusing footprints. The challenge of jumping from one of Como's footprints to the next was bad enough when walking forwards. Doing it in reverse was almost impossible. I had an increasingly ratty argument with Como about the stupidity of it all, until he made a practical suggestion, for once, and offered to carry me. It was therefore in the manner of a reversing Christ and St Christopher that we arrived at the steps of the praesidium, to find ourselves greeted by a bug-eyed abbot.

Chapter Twenty-Five

In which observers become auditors to exploit a loophole.

Brother Marco, I observe that you are helping your assistant mortify her flesh. If you tire of that duty and would like me to take its burden upon myself please let me know." The abbot perspired heavily at the thought of riding around on Sister Coma. "In the meantime, I was searching for you to let you know that an emergency meeting of the council of elders is to start at any moment. I am most anxious that you should be present to apply your investigative powers to the proceedings. Perhaps you could bring your assistant with you to act as your secretary."

We agreed to the abbot's suggestion and followed him through the labyrinthine passages of the praesidium to the governance chamber, an elaborately decorated room of lavish proportions, cunningly shaped like a large rectangle. Along its richly patinated panelled walls were photographs of the abbot's predecessors, a venerable procession of saintly celibates stretching back to the formation of the abbey in the remoteness of the 1960s. At the exact centre of the room was a semicircular conference table with a gleaming Formica surface, into which were set the symbols of the seven savants in the most intricate marquetry. Around the curved edge of the table were nine executive chairs, each adjustable for height, squab angle, and back-rest angle. The central chair was more luxurious than the rest, with adjustable arm-rests and castors of superlative smoothness.

In the far corner of the room was a top-of-the-range espresso machine, around which three monks were exchanging whispered thoughts. They turned at the sound of our entrance. I had never seen three faces so varied in countenance. One was almost entirely round, with wide-set, bulging, toad-like eyes under orange brows, above which a completely bald pate receded to meet a curtain of straight orange hair which covered only the rearmost segment of the head. The second was gaunt and dark, with deep-set black eyes, below which the nose alone was visible within the wiry tangle of a beard. The third was olive skinned and effeminate, with a small upturned nose and delicately arched eyebrows, like a cross between Michael Jackson and Greta Garbo. The abbot introduced them as Brothers Alfonse, George, and Crispin, before directing Como and me to take the outermost of the nine chairs.

"Brethren, the Council is quorate," said the abbot. "Please be seated. *Pax in nobis jam profundis.*"

"*Pax in nobis jam profundis,*" echoed the three elders.

"I have called this extraordinary meeting of council to invoke the succession planning protocol following the tragic deaths of the herbalist, brother Glaxo and Brother Felonius. I will issue a *decree obversi*, following which... Yes, Brother George?"

Brother George, having raised his hand to speak, now spoke. "By whose authority are these observers present?" meaning me and Como, I assumed.

"By my authority," said the abbot.

"You do not have the right. The rules of the Order are clear—only the elder council may invite observers to its meetings. It is explicitly stated in the fourth codicil of Rufus. The abbot may not decide matters without a vote."

The abbot blanched with fury at this challenge to his authority. "Your knowledge of the arcana of our order is greater than mine, Brother George, so I will not question your statement. We will put the matter to a vote. Will those in favour of the continued presence of the observers please raise their right hand."

Brother George's hand remained resolutely clenched on the Formica top of the conference table. Brothers Alfonse and Crispin looked uncertainly between the abbot and his challenger, then lowered their eyes, their hands clasped as if in prayer.

"Very well. If the will of Council demands it, I will ask our guests to leave."

I couldn't believe what I'd typed. How could I have allowed my plans to be thwarted by three incidental characters we had only just met? I had an idea. I raised my hand, much as Brother George had done a few paragraphs ago.

"Yes, Brother Marco?" The abbot invited me to speak.

"Your Sublimity, my knowledge of the regulations of the Order are somewhat rusty, but I recall that the fourth codicil of Rufus specifically refers to *observers*. Is that correct?"

"I have already said so," butted in Brother George.

"Then I suggest, Brother Abbot, that rather than leaving the chamber, my assistant and I will close our eyes, thus ceasing to be observers. I recollect that the fifth codicil of Rufus empowers the abbot to appoint auditors, with no requirement for a vote."

An enraged flash of his black eyes confirmed that my sly suggestion had not met with Brother George's approval. The abbot, however, was all for it.

"Your offer is accepted, Brother Marco. Do, please, remain seated, with your eyes firmly closed."

I lowered my eyelids, sneakily leaving them open a fraction to see Brother George smite the table with the side of his fist.

"This buffoonery makes a mockery of the Council. I will not participate in the corruption of its hallowed procedures."

Brothers Alfonso and Crispin watched uneasily as Brother George stormed out, forgetting his espresso in his wrath.

"Brother George has exercised his democratic right," continued the abbot. "Those of us who remain must continue the business of the meeting."

"But..."

"You have an objection, Brother Crispin?"

"We are no longer quorate, Your Excellency. We would be acting *ultra vires* were we to conduct the formal business of the Council whilst so few in number."

This was getting ridiculous. Yet another good plot strand thwarted by monkish nonsense. I raised another hand.

"Yes, Brother Marco."

"Your Honour, sorry, Your Holiness, I believe you will find it a well-established tenet of monastic law that any council, congress, diet, assembly, conclave, synod, or any other formal regulatory gathering, however so constituted, remains quorate if, having started quorate, its numbers are reduced by the departure of one or more members with the deliberate intention of frustrating the business of the council, congress, diet, assembly, conclave, synod, or gathering. The precedent was ratified with unquestionable authority at the international conclave of abbots in Sienna in 1308."

"Your holiness, I object," said Brother Crispin.

"Objection overruled." The abbot banged the gavel that I forgot to mention was on the table in front of his seat. "I propose to issue a decree obversi, giving the brethren of the abbey until noon tomorrow to submit their nomination for the vacancies on the Council. Those in favour raise their right hand."

The abbot stared with such ferocity at the two remaining members of council that their right hands raised almost against their will.

"Thank you, gentlemen. The court is adjourned," was what I typed before I realised I had once again slipped into Scott Grisham legal potboiler mode. I honestly don't know why, but it always seems to happen around the 33,000 word mark. Anyway, please ignore the abbot's last statement, which will be expunged from the official records of the abbey, and pretend instead that he said:

"Bless you, brethren. Let us pray for the restoration of harmony within our number."

Following the example of the abbot, Brothers Alfonse and Crispin bowed their heads in prayer. I used it as a chance to nod at Como that we should withdraw and leave them to it, as I had a new problem to deal with. Then I remembered that we were both supposed to have our eyes closed, so I supplemented the nod with a cough and a nudge.

"What?" said Como, after I'd closed the door of the governance chamber behind us.

"I need to think—give me a second."

I paced a few small circles—well, probably ellipses really—on the echoing stone flags of the ancient corridor. Have you noticed that there's been no real idea of the passage of time since I first arrived at the abbey? It might have been this morning or some days ago. *The Penguin Dictionary of Literary Terms and Literary Theory* has an entry entitled 'Temporal Indeterminacy', which goes into some detail about that aspect of my books, claiming it to be a post-modernist challenge to the primacy of time in the ordering of narrative coherence. That's all a load of rubbish—the truth is that I'm just crap at keeping track of time when I write, which is why one of my golden rules is never to set fixed dates or times in my plots, as they tie you in knots as an author. Yet only a few paragraphs ago I had stupidly set a deadline of noon tomorrow for the nominations, which meant that everything I wrote about from now until then would have to fit a sensible schedule. I looked at Como. How was I going to explain that suddenly our behaviour was going to have to change, and instead of performing a spontaneous stream of unconstrained detecting work, we'd have to stop for meals, sleep, showers, and all the other boring repetitive activities that make realistic fiction so tedious to read? I needed time to figure it out.

"Como, I'm beat. I've been flat out since I checked in, and I'm meant to be here for a break. You said it would be a complete rest, remember?"

"Okay, Writer—you look beat too. Let's check out of this crazy house and get back to the real world to clear our heads."

Somehow I didn't think that mooching around Clarkesville with Como would rank among the world's top head clearing experiences, but anything was better than the abbey. Or so I thought.

CHAPTER TWENTY-SIX

In which Marco returns to the rough side of town.

We repaired to the burger bar where Como and I always go when we need a chance to gather our thoughts and make a token gesture to realism by eating.

"What I don't get," said Como, "is why the herbalist spelled a word with his guts, like you said he did. Why didn't he write it with the chalk he used to draw the pentangle, or just in his freakin' notebook?"

I swallowed enough of the burger in my mouth to make room for speech, albeit slightly distorted speech diverted through one cheek.

"What do I always say, Como? That's the difference between true crime and the made-up crap everyone else writes. In true crime things happen that you can't explain. In the real world people do crazy things."

"That's true enough. A police chief hangin' around with a crap Writer, for example."

"Exactly, Como."

"So what else have we got?"

"Christ, Como, I don't know where to start. I never got a chance to investigate any of the deaths that happened before I arrived, but I've already got enough leads for an army of dogs."

"Ok, take me through them in order—the order you wrote them in."

I tried to remember back to the start of the book, all those chapters ago, helping myself to a handful of Como's fries as an aid to concentration.

"The first thing was the young monk found dead from a fall at the foot of the praesidium. He'd been tipped for one of the illuminator jobs, so someone else going for the same job might have killed him to cut the competition."

"Unlikely, Writer. How many murders happen in the US every year? Thousands. And when did you last see news about someone topping someone else to stop'em getting a menial job they were after? Never."

I was too tired to argue. "The next was the dead aycharchivist. He had a scroll." I munched some more of Como's fries. "I think there was a coded message on it, but I never got to find out because the fire alarm went off."

"Okay. Might be worth following up. What else?"

"The herbalist installed security cameras only a week ago, so he must have known something was up."

"What d'they show?"

"Nothing, yet." I explained to Como the freak combination of circumstances that had caused the video tape to be nicked by a tine of the forklift, rendering it playable only a few frames at a time.

"Jeez. How long's it gonna take for them to check the whole tape."

"Hard to say, but could be ages yet."

"Ok, what other crazy fucked up clues have you found?" Como put so much spin on the word clues that I nearly put it in italics.

"There's the notebook I told you about—the one I found on Brother Felonius."

"You got it on you?"

I patted my pockets.

"No."

"Let me guess—either you've got it locked in the car in a tamper-proof evidence bag ready to be checked-in at HQ, or you've left it in your cell, along with your brains, where anyone can take a look at it."

"Good guesses, Como." Or one of them was.

"And is that the end of it? Everything else happened after you called me in?"

"I think so." In truth I was too tired to remember.

"So we've got that lot to chase up, plus the key-card, the Walther, the phone screen covers from the bothy, Brother Umbert's phone, and the lab in the mystery building."

"For now, yes."

"For now? You ain't telling me, I hope, that you're gonna be finding any more so-called clues we haven't got time to follow up."

Como's phone buzzed. He eased it out of a pocket and took the call.

"What?" I said, when he'd finished.

"They traced the calls on Brother Umbert's phone. Seems they all went to mobile numbers for SIMS bought in a batch two months ago."

Wow. I hadn't expected that.

"Who bought them?"

"Let's go find out."

After arguing over the bill, we took my black Range Rover with tinted windows, Como suggesting that an unmarked car would be less likely to announce our arrival than his police chief Range Rover would be.

"Announce our arrival? Where are we going?"

"You'll see."

Como gave me a series of instructions which I followed to drive us through the centre of town and over the railway tracks. As the incidence of burned out cars and boarded up shop fronts increased, I figured we were headed into the rough part of town. It was with a gruesome sense of inevitability, therefore, that I took the next left turn, and there down the shallow hill were the Hacienda Apartments, the epicentre of the Clarkesville blue-collar crime epidemic.

"Pull up on the right," said Como.

"Are you kidding?" I now realised that Como might have had another reason for taking my car and not his, namely a preference for retaining his alloy wheels.

"What?"

"They'll trash the car."

"This might be a rough part of town, Writer, but they still respect the cloth. They won't touch the car. Now come on."

CHAPTER TWENTY-SEVEN

In which more of the history of the abbey is revealed,
following a confrontation with young hoodlums.

I followed Como through the warren of underground passageways that connected the various parts of the rundown housing project, the slap of our sandaled footsteps echoing through the harsh urban townscape. Notwithstanding our monkish garb, the prostitutes and drug pushers proffered their services as we passed—but we were too busy to stop. We turned up a ramp, at the top of which four young hoodlums were harassing an elderly lady, circling her in a menacing way on garishly decorated bicycles. I thought of my Bronx mom in the place of the old lady, and a wave of compassion rocked me—those poor thugs.

I drew Como's attention to the old lady's predicament.

"We can't just ignore it."

"I'll tell you what, Writer—you sort it. Meet me at the twenty-four-seven store in ten minutes."

"Me?"

"Who else is gonna meet me in the store?"

"No, I mean me sort the predicament of the old lady?"

"They're only kids, Writer. Even you should be able to handle them. Man up a bit."

With which he strode off, leaving me to join the old lady in the predicament department. I scratched the receding Ocram chin as an aid to thought. It was easy for Como to dismiss the thugs as kids, but to someone a good foot shorter than he, and two hundred pounds lighter, they seemed a tougher proposition. I decided poise and a commanding mien might compensate for what I lacked in brute physical presence, so I approached the hoodlums with a firm besandled step.

"On your way, holy man."

The head hoodlum swung his thumb towards another of the exit ramps, indicating a direction in which I might be on my way. Impelled by a pleading look from the old lady, I stood my ground.

The leader stepped forward, a knife held low.

"You just made a big mistake, buddy."

Hyena-like, the bullies advanced as a pack, each bearing the unmistakable signs of a debauched amoral lifestyle—carelessly pressed denims, scuffed shoes, and tee-shirts emblazoned with not a single reference to literature.

The menacing muggers were now within slashing distance—I'd run out of time to think. Typing the first thing that came into my head, I threw back my cowl, shook out my famous auburn afro, and grinned the self-effacing grin loved throughout the book-reading world.

"Marco Ocram!"

Five exclamations burst as one from five astonished mouths, as hoodlum and victim alike rejoiced at the unmasking of the world's foremost celebrity author. I nodded in humble acknowledgement, high-fived the thugs, hugged the old lady, then posed for photos while my fans took turns at being cameraman. With the old lady comforting one of the thugs, who had stupidly left his at home, the others proffered their battered copies of *The Awful Truth about the Herbert Quarry Affair*. They chattered excitedly as I signed witty dedications in their treasured paperbacks.

"Gee Mister Ocram, this is such a thrill."

"Your book is like the best EVER!"

"Is Tom Cruise really gonna be you in the movie?"

"The tsunami at the end blew me away, dude."

"What's your next book about, Mister Ocram?"

It was a good question; but before I could explain that I didn't know, the old woman laid an enquiring hand upon my forearm.

"Mister Ocram, can what we learn from the media be true? Do you really make up your books as you go along, never going back to edit a single word? Surely that cannot be true of books so perfect, so moving, so authentic, so thrilling, so..."

"Absolutely. It's Herbert Quarry's golden rule of authorship. Never think ahead, and never go back to change anything. Just write the next thing that comes into your head."

"So could we be in your next book?" It was the turn of the thugs to adopt a pleading look.

"You already are."

My words prompted another round of high-fiving, hugs and excited chatter.

"No freaking way dude!" said someone—possibly not the old lady.

"Wow, my mom will go like crazy."

"Hey—who'll play us when they make a movie of it?"

I was about to write the next thing that came into my head, when Doris Day sang *Que Sera Sera* in the pocket of my anorak. Answering the call, I held up a hand to shush the jubilance of my incidental characters.

"Writer, it's me. I've picked up a lead on the Tan Falconi murder. Give me thirty minutes and I'll see you at the store."

On the good-idea scale of nought to ten, I rated Como's suggestion around the minus three mark. I responded accordingly.

"You've only left me five minutes and I've already nearly been stabbed. How am I meant to cope on my own for half an hour at the Hacienda Apartments?"

But Como would have none of my impassioned expostulations. Assuring me that I would be 'alright', he killed the call.

On an impulse, I offered to walk the old lady home. It was the 'maybe she can protect me' impulse, rather than anything nobler. At her apartment, she invited me in to repay my kindness with a cup of tea, an offer I gladly accepted to get myself off the crime-ridden street.

"It's so nice to have some intelligent company for a change," said the old lady. I knew how she felt. "Tell me, Mister Ocram, have you found religion?"

"Oh, this?" I lifted the skirts of my habit a fraction. "No, it's... it's a sort of disguise. I'm working undercover at the abbey, doing research for my new book."

The old lady clapped her hands. "Oh how exciting! It's so long since I was last up there."

"At the abbey? I didn't think they allowed women to visit?"

"No, no, it was before it became the abbey. My late husband, Bertrand, was an architect. He was employed by

Christina Bow to design the facilities there. He was so proud of his commission. He said it was his greatest work."

"Christina Bow?"

"Yes—she was the billionairess who funded the development of the site. I'm surprised you don't know her, Mister Ocram."

"Really? Should I have known her?"

"Why yes—she was the mother of Elijah Bow."

"Elijah Bow!!!"

Three exclamation marks might seem a tad excessive, but Elijah Bow was the cross-dressing industrialist at the corrupt centre of the conspiracy to frame Herbert Quarry in my first mega-selling book.

"Here. I have a photograph of the opening of the sports complex. About half the town was invited." She handed me an eight by twelve photo showing a woman I took to be Christina Bow cutting a ribbon across the door of what had since become the praesidium. I had a thought.

"Did Bertram, by any chance, keep any blueprints or plans for the site?"

"He certainly did, Mister Ocram. I couldn't get him to throw any of them away. And since he died I've kept them— it would seem like an act of betrayal to dispose of documents he guarded so carefully."

"Might I see some of them?"

"Of course. I have kept his study exactly as it was when he was alive. I would be delighted to show it to so distinguished a visitor. Bertram would have been thrilled to know that you took an interest in his work."

Phew, that was handy.

"Here."

She opened the door to a time-capsule of a room, which abounded in memorabilia of the 1960s, including magazines showing pictures of the Kennedys, of the Beatles, Sputnik, Vietnam, and old NASA rockets. An architect's drawing board was positioned at the far end where it would receive light from a north-facing window. Beside it, a number of cardboard tubes were stood on end, leaning against a grey filing cabinet.

"I'm sure the plans for the complex are in those cardboard tubes," said my kindly hostess.

I picked up one of the tubes. In purple ink in the tidy hand of the professional draftsman were the words 'The Bow Complex—layout plans.'

I eased out its rubber stopper, then angled the tube to shake out its contents. There were perhaps twenty sheets of tracing paper. I took them to the drawing board and unrolled them, slipping their edges under spring-loaded clips that held them in place. I saw at once that the top sheet was the master plan for the site—a much larger version of the map on the leaflet. Each of the buildings on the plan was labelled with a number, and it didn't take my huge brain more than five minutes to realise that the numbers corresponded to those upon other sheets showing the individual buildings at a larger scale. Wasting hardly any time eating cake and showing Mrs Goodman photos on my iPad of my Bronx mom and all her friends, I went straight to the drawing of the mysterious building Como and I had inspected in the snow. It was, indeed, described as The Laboratory—presumably a drug testing facility for the winter Olympics that never happened there. Hmmm...

I had one of those rare moments of authorial doubt— did they do drug testing at the Olympics back in the 1960s, or had I just made a huge technical gaffe, one that might undermine my hard-won reputation for authenticity? A quick check on Wikipedia confirmed that all was well—1968 was the first year when drug testing was mandatory at a Winter Olympics. Phew. Where was I? Oh, yes...

Did the plan show the trap-door I had seen towards the back of the building? You bet—along with a dotted outline showing the start of an underground passageway, an arrow from the end of which was labelled 'to the caves'.

The caves? I looked back at the master plan—there was no mention of caves on it. I consulted Mrs Goodman.

"Mrs Goodman. Do you remember your husband saying anything about caves in connection with the development of the complex?"

"Excuse me." Mrs Goodman covered her mouth with her hand to stifle a giggle. "You must think me awfully rude. I was just thinking how funny it was that you're the second person in a monk's habit to have asked me that exact same question in as many months."

I was astounded. I admit the chapter might be laughably implausible, but the least she could do was keep a straight face.

"Ha ha, yes, that is a bit spooky. Who was the other person?"

"I can't quite remember the name. It was Brother something." That was a big help. "I was at home one afternoon when this monk called and asked if it was possible to see Bertram's plans."

"Mrs Goodman, this is really, really important. Can you remember which plans the monk looked at?"

"I definitely can, because the whole episode was so remarkably like your visit this evening, Mister Ocram, starting with a look at the site plan and then the plan for the laboratory."

Unbelievable. I could barely summon the will-power to type.

171

"And what did you say when the monk asked you about caves?"

"I said Bertram had mentioned that there was an extensive cave system in the area, and that it had been mapped in the 1950s by students from the speleology department of the Clarkesville County University. Bertram had ideas about using the cave system to link the buildings, so that it would be possible to move safely between them even if there was very heavy snow, but the cost was too expensive, and Mrs Bow cut the budget once she knew the Olympic committee had picked Grenoble instead of Clarkesville."

I wasn't sure American counties had universities, but I was too astonished by Mrs Goodman's revelations to check.

"And what did the monk do next?"

"She thanked me for my time and left."

CHAPTER TWENTY-EIGHT

In which Marco develops a fotofit picture.

She? You could have knocked me down with a feather—a hummingbird's armpit feather.

"Pardon me, Mrs Goodman, but I understood your visitor was a monk."

"No, Mister Ocram—I said a person in the habit of a monk."

I looked back thirteen paragraphs—she was right. My mind raced. I had an idea.

"Are you sure it was a she?" I remembered the monk on the council of elders with the effeminate face—Brother Tarquin, no, Crispin. "Did the facial appearance of the person suggest to your mind an enchanting fusion of Michael Jackson and Greta Garbo?"

"She was definitely a she, Mister Ocram, and didn't look anything like Michael Jackson or Greta Garbo."

I was utterly stumped. In all my writing career I had never typed anything quite like it. However, I wasn't about to bore the readers with pointless speculations—I had plenty of other things to be boring them with. Speaking of which...

Having thanked Mrs Goodman for her help, eaten the rest of her cake, and heard about her last three visits to the hairdressers, I raced to the twenty-four-seven store, eager to share the news with Como.

He looked pointedly at his watch as I approached.

"Half an hour, we said."

"Sorry, Como. I got distracted. But it was worth the wait. Guess what?"

"What?"

I summarised the startling facts I had learned at Mrs Goodman's.

"Nice work, Writer. Just as I thought this was the most screwed up case that even you could imagine, you go and screw it up even more."

"Como! Don't be so negative. Can't you see the bright side? This gives us more hot leads to chase up."

"Writer, you and I have different views of what makes a side bright. I got a PD to run, and a seventy-two-inch TV I've hardly switched on since I bought it. A bright side to me is wrapping up a case in a neat and tidy bow five minutes after opening it, then getting home early to watch the big game. A bright side to you is making up endless crap."

"Hardly endless, Como. Have not our previous cases all been wound up eventually? I say nothing of their spectacular denouements or the prestige they have conferred upon you. Don't forget, you would still be a lowly detective were it not for our cases, Como."

"True. I'll tell you what, Writer—I'll help you work on the leads we got, but on one condition."

"Which is?"

"When we solve this crazy case you get me a new job. I sure as hell can't cope with this one much longer—it's driving me nuts."

"I make no promises, Como, but I will see what I can do. Now, with all this self-indulgent career planning aren't we forgetting something?" Como's blank look suggested that at least one of us was forgetting something. "Aren't we meant to be chasing up one of our other smoking hot leads about the purchase of SIM cards?"

Como acknowledged that we were, and led the way into the twenty-four-seven store—the furtive entrance of two hooded monks seeming not to phase its occupants in the slightest. We went to the counter, behind which a swarthy disreputable individual whom I took to be the storekeeper was ostentatiously oiling a shotgun.

"How can I help you?" she said.

"You get many dealers in here?" said Como, presumably meaning dealers of the illegal stimulant variety.

"What's it to you, brother—you wanna buy, or take their confessions?"

Como pulled a tablet out of his robe and showed a picture of Tan Falconi.

"Seen this guy?"

Before I had a chance to say to the store keeper *whatever you say, don't say maybe*, she said:

"Maybe."

If there's one thing that triggers Como's mean streak it's criminal underclass scum with firearms responding evasively to his direct questions. Faster than I could type, Como flashed out an arm and snatched the shotgun by its barrel. Before the storekeeper's startled eyes, he wedged the end of the barrel behind something solid and heaved upon the stock. Then he laid the shotgun back on the counter, now with a noticeable bend in it. I wouldn't have believed it possible if I hadn't written it myself.

"So have you seen him, or haven't you?"

"It's Tan Falconi. Everyone knows Tan Falconi. So what?"

"You keep good records of what you sell in the store?"

"What is this—an IRS bust?"

"No, but it might be if I don't get cooperation."

"Cooperation? I don't have to cooperate with freakin monks. I'm sick to death of you guys."

I saw that look in Como's eye that usually presages the exercise of his muscles in pursuit of rough and ready justice, so I stepped between him and the counter.

"Excuse the hastiness of my colleague, madam. Am I to understand that we are not the first holy brethren to bestow our trade upon your delightful emporium?"

"Are you kidding me?"

"Not in the least, madam. We are simple friars, new to the area, and anxious to assimilate the habits of the local brethren."

"Two months ago someone bought a batch of twenty SIM cards in this store," interrupted Como.

I wish he wouldn't keep doing that. It's really tricky to write dialogue when there're more than two people chipping in. Perhaps for the remainder of this scene I should identify the speaker explicitly at the start of each line of dialogue, to make it easier ~~for me to write~~ for you to follow...

Criminal underclass scum storekeeper. "Two months is a long time. You expect me to remember?"

Como. "I expect you to maintain adequate records to prevent felonies, in accordance with the provisions of the XXXX act."

I didn't have time to look-up the name of the XXXX act, so you'll have to imagine it for now.

Criminal underclass scum storekeeper. "Are you guys cops, or is this some kind of joke?"

Anxious to avoid the blowing of our carefully established cover, I wrote the next thing that came into my head.

Publishing legend and top physicist Marco Ocram. "Okay, we'll level with you. But this *must* remain absolutely secret. Agreed?"

Criminal underclass scum storekeeper. "Sure."

Publishing legend and top physicist Marco Ocram. "We're from the EACB, investigating possible improper activities at the abbey."

Criminal underclass scum storekeeper. "EACB?"

Publishing legend and top physicist Marco Ocram. "Yes." I lowered my voice the customary three semitones. "The Ecclesiastical Anti-Corruption Bureau. With orders from the very top." I added a wink, lest there be any doubt about the meaning of *'the very top'* in such a context. "My colleague and I believe that a batch of SIM cards purchased at this store might have been acquired for the purpose of facilitating activities not enshrined in scripture. The most holy blessings will be lavished upon your loved ones should you cooperate with our enquiries."

Como. Says nothing, but rolls eyes.

Criminal underclass scum storekeeper. "How do I know you're on the level—you got any ID?"

Publishing legend and top physicist Marco Ocram. "Ring this number."

I gave her a mobile number that had been given to me at around this point in my last book, when I had shared a flight to Panama with a certain pontiff whose identity I am currently prevented by gagging clauses from disclosing, although I have every reason to expect they will be quashed once my legal arguments are heard in a sufficiently senior court. She dialled the number. I watched her eyes grow wider as she heard the well-loved voice answer her call.

Criminal underclass scum storekeeper. "I'm sorry, Your Holiness. I didn't mean to interrupt your massage. Please forgive me." Kills call with astonished finger.

Publishing legend and top physicist Marco Ocram. "Please, Madam, let there be no more procrastinations. Tell us what you know."

Criminal underclass scum storekeeper. Crumbling. "It was about two months ago, just as you said. It was a Saturday, about six thirty. I remember two monks came in. I thought they'd just be looking at the top shelf magazines or buying hooch like the monks usually do, but these guys were kind of shifty."

Publishing legend and top physicist Marco Ocram. "Guys? You're absolutely sure they were guys?"

Criminal underclass scum storekeeper. "Well they're not likely to be gals. What idiot would think that?"

Publishing legend and top physicist Marco Ocram. "Quite. Please continue."

Criminal underclass scum storekeeper. "I remembered because they wanted twenty SIMs and there weren't twenty on the rack, so I had to go to the safe to get the rest."

Como. "How did they pay?"

Criminal underclass scum storekeeper. "Cash. Brand new notes. I remember checking them in case they were counterfeit."

Como. "You remember what they looked like?"

Criminal underclass scum storekeeper. "Sort of."

Como. To me. "You still got that photophit app on your iPad?"

Publishing legend and top physicist Marco Ocram. "I think so. Let me see." Spends five minutes searching through icons on iPad.

Criminal underclass scum storekeeper. "Bros, I ain't got all night, Pope or no Pope."

Publishing legend and top physicist Marco Ocram. "Here it is. Here it is." Clicks icon. "Ooops, no, that's not it."

After a few false starts I fired up the photophit app, and patiently took the storekeeper through the innumerable steps through which a rough outline of a person is gradually refined into a lifelike image.

"What've we got?" said Como, after the storekeeper had pronounced herself satisfied with her work.

I spun the iPad around to show him. On it was a lifelike image of two monks, their faces entirely shrouded by their cowls.

Como said something unbecoming a monk.

CHAPTER TWENTY-NINE

In which Marco sings a spontaneous tribute to the late Professor Stephen Hawking, RIP.

We were back at Como's place, where he had kindly offered to put me up for the night to save me the bother of writing a scene about checking into a motel. In order to protect what was left of our collective sanity, we had agreed to ban any talk about the case. After downing a delicious steak, we were in the kitchen, an apron-clad Como washing the dishes, I drying them.

"So tell me, Como. Were I to consider writing a new job for you in a future book, what job would you have in mind?"

"We already talked about that in the last book, but clearly you don't remember."

"Not true, Como. I do remember. We talked about you being the police procedure advisor to Steven Spielberg when it comes time to film *The Awful Truth about the Herbert Quarry Affair*. The difficulty there, Como, is that the movie business is old fashioned and slow. They don't know the meaning of deadline. It could be months before production starts. There is no end to the preliminary procrastinations. Would you not prefer, in the meantime, to continue your sky-rocketing progression through the ranks of the police profession?"

"I ain't so keen on that, Writer, to tell you the Lord's honest truth." Como's rubber-gloved hand passed me the last of the dripping plates. "The higher you get the less real policing you do. More and more of the work is politics, and you have to be a lot more slippery than I am to do that political shit."

That was true. Como might have many shortcomings, but no-one could accuse him of slipperiness.

"Could you, perhaps, move into another branch of law enforcement—the CIA, maybe, or the FBI? Interpol, perhaps?"

"You've been watching too many movies, Writer—they wouldn't take someone like me."

"Nonsense, Como. You have resourcefulness, courage."

"Yeah, but I also have a huge handicap, don't forget."

"What's that?"

"You. If I was the director of the CIA, the last thing I'd want is you writing stories that fuck everything up. C'mon."

We retired to Como's Victorian lounge, where he knocked a blaze from the coals in the grate while I stepped to the windows to close the curtains against the bone-chilling cold of the night outside. Now the time for action had passed, and our adrenalin levels were subsiding—each of us was in a sombre mood. I studied the evening papers as he tapped out a wistful cover of Schubert's serenade in G minor on his vibraphone. It was unusual for Como to play classical pieces. He preferred razz—the experimental fusion of rap and jazz to which I had introduced him in our first book—and would often exhort me to improvise topical lyrics to accompany his beats.

"Hey, Writer—you heard that Stephen Hawking's gone to the big lab in the sky?"

"Yes, Como. A sad time."

"You knew him?"

"I did indeed, Como. He would often consult me about some of the more difficult sums with which he had to grapple in order to reveal the origins of the universe."

"You fancy doin' him some real razz honour, you bein' a fellow physicist?"

"Why not, Como—that's an excellent suggestion. Hit me with a beat."

Como let his vibraphone sing, and I clapped my hands for a few beats to get the rhythm before letting the rap flow...

He let his voice box do the talking
And we all knew him as Stephen Hawking
He was rightly famous across the nation
For discov'ring Hawking radiation
He became more famous by and by
For analysing Swartzchild radii
And for showing the likes of you and me
How to calculate black hole entropy
And one thing we like that's really ace
Are the worm holes he found deep in space
No wonder his eyes were tired and bleary
From nights spent tackling quantum theory
When you saw his conclusions on a graph
They made the Higgs Boson look really naff
I think he's so very wise
He should have won a Nobel Prize
Some say he was a bit of a miser
For having such a cheap old synthesiser
That gave him that distinctive voice

But we know really it's a fashion choice
So hats off to clever clogs Stephen Hawking
Whose days and nights of blackboard chalking
Have helped us understand our place
In the continuum we call space-
Time.

"Yo, give me five, Como."

As I clapped an exhilarated hand against Como's massive palm, the sound of a vehicle utterly unlike a hansom cab, drawing up on the street, announced that we had an unexpected visitor.

"A thousand apologies, Como, for disturbing your evening of domestic peace. It seems as if someone has discovered I am staying with you, and is anxious to consult me upon some matter of extreme urgency. I shall see who it is."

I arrived at Como's front door just as its bell was rung. Opening it, I found myself wondering who would be more astonished, the reader or I, as the figure behind the door revealed itself to be a young monk in the last extremity of exhaustion.

"I need to speak with Chief Galahad. Immediately." She said, and collapsed into my arms.

CHAPTER THIRTY

In which Marco forgets he is not Sir Arthur Conan Doyle.

Como, Como, quick!"

I was in the hall, painfully pinned against Como's walking-stick holder by the weight of the collapsed monk. Abandoning his vibraphone, Como rushed to my aid, easing the insensible postulant over his shoulder and carrying her into the lounge. He laid her gently on the settee, a pillow cushioning her weary head. I patted her hand to encourage her to wake from her swoon, while Como patted her clothes for ID.

"Here."

He showed me an official identity card that announced our visitor to be Special Agent Leona Dyson, FBI.

Get it? Dyson—Hoover—FBI. Yes, the old magic was still there.

My eyes went from the face on the card to the real face on the settee. It was a face of courage and purity, with a high noble brow, a wide determined mouth, and a resolute jaw. Her eyes, as she awoke, were dazzling opal, with intriguing amber hints. She raised a queenly hand to take the brandy flask Como had placed to her lips, upturning it to down its contents in a single glug.

"Thank you."

Wiping a smear of brandy from her chin, she waved the flask at me in a manner suggesting that a top-up would be appreciated.

Como tightened the tasselled cord of his dressing gown, sat back in his armchair, half closed his eyes, steepled his fingers in a clichéd aid to thought, and said:

"You have come from the lumber yard via the burger bar, I see."

"That is astonishing. How did you know?"

"There is a crust of sawdust on the welt of your sandal, overlaid by a crushed segment of gherkin in chilli mayonnaise—the combination is distinctly suggestive."

In my imagination I clapped to acknowledge the acuity of Como's observations. Well done, *mon brave*. I handed Leona the brandy bottle, checked that she was seated comfortably, then flexed my fingers in preparation for typing a long passage of expositional dialogue.

"Please, Agent Dyson, tell me your story from the beginning," said Como, now speaking in full Sherlock Holmes mode. "Omit no detail, however trivial it may seem."

Agent Dyson winked at Como and nodded her head towards me.

"You need not worry about Doctor Ocram—the faithful chronicler of my detecting prowess. You may speak as freely in his presence as in mine."

"Is he security cleared?"

"No, but he is so imbecilic he will hardly understand a word you say."

On I typed, with aloof indifference to Como's cruel taunts...

"My name is Leona Jasmine Dyson of 1504 Picasso Boulevard, Connecticut," she said, taking the trivia point a little too far, I thought. "I was orphaned as a baby and raised on a farm full of silent lambs by a maiden aunt who valued truth above all else. Although poor, my aunt saved every cent to send me to police college, where I excelled in my studies and won a scholarship for a training course with the Federal Bureau of Investigation, or FBI as it may more conveniently be typed by authors in a hurry. I graduated top of my year, and was the youngest ever to join the fast-track promotion scheme, through which I took on many cases of immense geo-political significance.

"Some months ago the Bureau noticed a disturbing increase in certain types of criminal activity. At first it seemed to be a series of unrelated cases, but through my pioneering application of big data techniques, a pattern was established. We identified that the head of the most powerful mafia family had moved from Chicago, claiming to have renounced his criminal ways, and taken up the position of abbot at the commune here in Clarkesville."

Como held a hand in the air. "Would you mind repeating that last sentence, please."

"Certainly."

Como stared at me while Agent Dyson repeated her last sentence about the abbot being the head of a Mafia family.

"Please continue your singular narrative." said Como.

"The Bureau needed a volunteer to go undercover to the abbey. I was a natural choice, owing to my proven prowess as an agent and my in-depth knowledge of monastic life."

"Your in-depth knowledge of monastic life?" Como raised an eyebrow in my direction.

"Sorry," I admitted, "I'd meant to say something earlier about Agent Dyson having completed a module in medieval monastic studies at police college."

"Pray continue, Miss Dyson."

"I infiltrated the abbey as an itinerant pilgrim, and befriended a number of the brethren, among them Brother Wayne, the young monk found dead at the foot of the praesidium some days ago. A monastery is a hothouse of gossip, and there is a commonly accepted belief that a small faction within the abbey is conducting experiments which may lead to business opportunities of inestimable value to criminal organisations worldwide."

"What sort of experiments?"

"I have no direct evidence, but I believe them to be drug related."

"Kindly focus upon relating facts—leave the development of absurd and fanciful theories to Doctor Ocram."

"As you say, Chief Galahad. The experiments involve monks as subjects. Brother Wayne admitted to me that he had been enrolled in some form of clinical trial. He had been asked to consume a drug of some sort and to log his experience of its effects. Alas, he was not to live long enough to make any record. The drugs appear to be developed in the laboratory. I have not been able to observe which monks are engaged in the work, as they enter and leave the laboratory along a secret passage through a trap-door inside the building."

"Come, come," I interjected, unable to contain my impatience at Agent Dyson's incredible narrative. "Surely a top agent would have the gumption to look through the cracks between the shutters of the laboratory windows?"

"That is true, Doctor Ocram. I did indeed look—only an idiot would have failed to. However, some of the brothers are members of an order which requires the cowl to be raised at all times, so it is difficult to identify individual monks. I have discovered that the secret passageway leads to a system of caves. Through watching the movements of the brothers, I have identified entrances to the caves in a number of buildings in the complex."

"Are they the Aycharium, the Bothy, the Crypt, the Herbarium, the Infirmary and the Vesparium?" Como repeated from memory the locations associated with the key-card we had found under the mattress of Brother Felonius.

Agent Dyson looked at Como with astonishment upon her queenly features. "How did you know?"

"I have my methods. Have you managed to enter the caves?"

"No, the entrances are all protected by digital locks, and I have been unable to find a swipe card that will open them."

Well, we'd soon fix that.

"Why did you come to see me?" asked Como.

"If I may say so, the name of Como Galahad is revered among the crime fighting fraternity. Your incisive exposures of the awful truth about the Herbert Quarry affair, and the awful truth about the Sushing Prize, are legendary. Your articles in *The Journal of Crime Fighting and Detection* are mandatory reading for all Bureau staff."

"Ahem." I coughed to remind Agent Dyson that Como wasn't the only person in the room who had played a pivotal role in exposing the awful truth about the sensational cases she had mentioned.

"Being in Clarkesville, it was natural that I should seek your help," said Agent Dyson, completely ignoring my cough.

"I quite understand," said Como. "It was a sensible decision in every respect."

"Ahem," I coughed again. "Agent Dyson, would you excuse Chief Galahad and me for a moment?"

I yanked the cord of Como's dressing-gown to get him to follow me into the kitchen.

"What?"

"Can we trust her? If she was a real FBI person, why's she down here talking to us? She'd have all kinds of FBI back-up. And as for all that nonsense about you being a legend—how do we know she's not just trying to hoodwink you?"

"Writer, I've seen more fake IDs in my time than you've written crap words, which is saying something. Her ID is legit, and if I thought it wasn't I could get it checked in five minutes. You're just jealous because for once someone's owning up to the awful truth about which of us actually does the crime fighting and which of us just goes round making up shit."

We went back to Como's Victorian lounge.

"Agent Dyson," said Como. "I suggest you return to the abbey at once and continue your observations. Doctor Ocram and I will join you there in the morning. Be in the canteen at ten thirty."

I showed out our visitor, and returned to the lounge, where Como was filling a pipe from a Turkish slipper full of shag. I flopped on the settee and drained what little had been left in the brandy bottle by Agent Dyson. I don't know about you, but this Sherlock Holmes pastiche was one of the most sickening things I'd ever had to type, involving, as it did, an unnatural and wholly unconvincing reversal of roles, with Como as the crime-fighting savant and I the unimaginative foil.

"You want another night-cap?"

"No thanks, Como. I'm beat. I think I'll turn in."

Turning in turned out not to be the most restful of experiences. Having offered to put me up, Como revealed he had no spare bed, so I would have to share his. Top to tail, I spent the night shrouded in the miasma emanating from Como's huge feet—feet which moved restlessly beside my pillow with all the grace of two elephant seals fighting on a beach. I'd have slept better on my pallet.

CHAPTER THIRTY-ONE

In which Marco decides to crack the case quickly.

That was delicious, Como. The cornflakes and raw squid were an unusual touch."

We had just finished breakfast, a novel re-imagining of pancakes with maple syrup which Como had rustled up from a sparsely stocked refrigerator. "Shall we make our way to the abbey?"

"You can make your way to the abbey if you like," Como was tying his Clarkesville County Police Chief tie, "but I've important things to do."

"But you said we'd meet Agent Dyson in the refectory."

"That was down to you, Writer. You should have checked my schedule before you started writing commitments like that. I've got an 8am with the Mayor to go through budgets for next year, a weekly meeting with my direct reports at 8.53, a review of ammunition stocks at 9.20, an update to the health and safety policy to finish by ten, a..."

I let him drone on. I was beginning to wish I'd never promoted him to police chief. He'd changed so much since those carefree days as a detective—days when he and I virtually lived in his police car, free to focus on the fighting of crime.

"Very well, Como. If I must shoulder the entire burden of fighting major organised crime without your help, so be it. But don't blame me if I uncover startling developments of a sensational nature involving sinister power brokers, international intrigue, and nefarious activities libellously attributed to living figures."

"The way I see it, Writer, is that you're gonna be up to that kind of mischief whether I'm there or not. At least if I'm not there I can pretend it ain't happening. That's about the only thing keeping me sane right now. I'm off. Lock the door when you go, and leave the key under the mat."

Making a final adjustment to his hat, he grabbed his gun and left me to wonder what to write next. To buy time, I rummaged through his cupboards to find his shoe-cleaning kit and set about polishing my sandals. As I worked the wax into the seams, I reflected on the satisfying trend of the last few chapters, chapters which had seen a considerable clarification of the plot, culminating, if that's the right word, in the appearance of Special Agent Dyson. I contrasted her youthful idealism with Como's jaded view of the world, or at least of the bits of the world that involved me. Would Agent Dyson be another incidental character, coming and going in the space of a few chapters, or might she evolve to be a lasting member of the team? Was the Ocram/Galahad duo about to become a trio? Admittedly she had, to date, shown a marked tendency to big-up Como while ignoring the importance of my role in the proceedings, but that was understandable. Como, after all, was a member of her fraternity, someone on her level, someone to whom she could instantly relate. I, on the other hand, must appear a remote and lofty figure—how could she hope to bond with a publishing legend in an entirely different intellectual league?

I put a final pass of the brush across my sandals, and buckled them tight. Perhaps today I would spend time with Agent Dyson, helping her to understand that I had an approachable side. Having packed my satchel, I locked the house and blipped my way into my black Range Rover, noting that its tinted windows were heavily smeared and in need of a wash. As I drifted with the lazy current of the Clarkesville traffic my phone beeped. It was Barney.

"Heeeyyy, Markie baby. How's the boy?"

"I'm good thanks, Barney. How's you?"

"I don't know yet—that's why I'm calling. How's the book going?"

"Great, Barney, just great. All that third book syndrome has gone. We just made a big breakthrough with the case."

"A big breakthrough? Whoa there, Marco."

"Whoa there?" That was the first time I had ever known Barney be concerned about me writing too quickly. Usually he was on my back to be more productive. "What's with the 'whoa there'?"

"Are you still at that abbey place?"

"Yeah. I'm headed there now."

"Great! It was on the news this morning. There's a big campaign brewing about the celebrity opening."

"What sort of campaign?"

"One that sells lots of new dresses. They're saying monasteries are sexist. They're picking on the abbey 'cause it's high profile. There's gonna be a big gate-crash by women on the opening night. Oprah told me she's leading it. Meryl's gonna be there, and Hilary, and J-Lo, and Madonna, and Beyonce, and..."

Barney rattled off a dozen or more names, most of them clients.

"Well it's about time, Barney. Gender-segregated communities are indefensible ethically. I've always argued that there should..."

"Never mind all that ethics crap. What counts is the coverage. Don't you see? This thing is gonna be huge, and there's my star boy, Markie, right at the heart of the action with a new book. If you can spin the story out to cover the opening night, every website in the world's gonna be streaming it live. You can spin it out, can't you?"

I imagined Barney's features rearranged in a hugely concerned look.

"I wouldn't worry about that, Barney. The case is so complicated, I can't see it being wrapped up any sooner."

"That's my boy. How's the big guy?"

"Como's grand, thanks. He's stuck in meetings this morning, but I hope he'll be back in action this afternoon."

"Hope? Hope? There's no hope about it, Markie. We can't have a Galahad adventure without Galahad."

"A Galahad adventure?"

"Anyway, gotta go. Keep writing."

A Galahad adventure? Since when have my books been Galahad adventures? If it wasn't galling enough to have Agent Dyson treating Como like the star of the show, now my own agent was up to the same trick.

The steering wheel of my black Range Rover with tinted windows had a hard time for a block or two as I squeezed it with a grip of intense resentment. Here was I, the person upon whom the existence, success and financial security of my characters depended, supposedly at the abbey for a complete rest, actually at the abbey in the mode of overworked author on the point of a nervous breakdown, and was I getting any sympathy? Was I getting any recognition? Was I getting any thanks? Well I'd show them. Stuff Barney and his coverage. I was already the world's biggest author. I didn't need another mega-seller. I'd crack this case *before* the celebrity opening, with or without the help of Como Galahad, and woe betide anyone who got in my way.

A siren sounded behind me.

CHAPTER THIRTY-TWO

In which Marco is held up.

Please step out of the car, Sir."

I had pulled to the side of the road in response to the lights and sirens of a Clarkesville County Police prowler. The officer who had been driving the car—a round-figured Latina past middle-years, whose badge announced her to be Carmina Dyaz—was standing the regulation distance from the door of my black Range Rover, one tinted window of which I had lowered to hear what she had to say. I stepped out, lowering, as I did so, the cowl of my habit.

"Gee, Mister Ocram, I didn't know it was you."

"That's quite alright, officer. Why should you have? What seems to be the problem?"

"You went through a couple of red lights back there, as if you had something other than driving on your mind."

I was impressed by her faultless diagnosis. Como could learn a lesson or two from this woman.

"I'm so sorry, officer." I'm in a hurry to solve a major criminal conspiracy, is what I wanted to add, but with Como's mole still to be smoked out, secrecy sealed my lips.

"I was returning to the abbey to continue my treatment—my doctor says I need complete rest. And no stress," I added, hoping she would take the hint.

"You've put me in a holy pickle now, Mister Ocram. You know I'd like to just let you go, but I radio'd the number of your car there through to HQ, and they'll have traced it to you by now, and...well, you know what Chief Galahad always says—we have to be as tough with our friends as we do with our enemies, otherwise standards start to slip. I'm gonna have to ask you to come along with me to give a statement. Hopefully that will be the end of it and I can let you go. By the way..." she looked round to check we weren't being watched "...could you just sign these?"

Having signed her copies of my books, I sat in the rear of her prowler and answered her questions about tau muons as we drove to a police station. I had no idea whether it was standard police procedure to take statements from drivers who jumped red lights, but I thought the sooner I wrote it the sooner I'd be back at the abbey.

"This way, Mister Ocram."

I followed Officer Dyaz through the dingy police station to a corridor off which were a number of small interview rooms. My own interview consisted of formalities too boring to be recorded word-for-word in a fast-paced thriller. Officer Dyaz asked for my name, date of birth, occupation, address, driver's licence number, insurance details, and current medications, inserting between each of her requests a rambling narrative that featured her husband, her mother, her hairdresser, a visit to the Grand Canyon, her nephew Marlon, the disgracefully high cost of pet insurance, a medical condition I would prefer not to relate, a lost mobile phone, the Clarkesville County Police Department gospel choir, two of the Three Tenors, Cheryl Crow, the pilot light on her gas boiler (Officer Dyaz' gas boiler, not Cheryl Crow's), and no apparent point or purpose. It was more than an hour before my sparse details were captured on her pad of forms.

"I thinks that's everything, Mister Ocram. It all looks fine. We can take you back to your car now. Just keep an eye out for those red lights next time."

I assured Officer Dyaz that I was anxious not to repeat the experience, and we got in her car.

"Santa Maria, I forgot to take your prints. I'm sorry, Mister Ocram, but we have to take your prints."

We got out of her car. I followed her through the now familiar dingy police station to another corridor, depressingly like the first, off which were cubicles for completing various police procedures, one being the taking of prints. With a loquacious commentary, Officer Dyaz stretched on latex gloves, opened a thin flat plastic box containing an inked pad, pulled a blank print-sheet from a stack in a tray, and rolled each of my finger-tips in turn on the pad and then on the print-sheet. I was offered wipes soaked in solvent to remove the ink from my fingers, then asked to sign the form.

"You just sit here, Mister Ocram, while I get these logged."

Forty one minutes passed, during which I could hear Officer Dyaz down the corridor repeating to some other victim most of the narrative she had kindly shared with me during my interview. She returned.

"That's it, Mister Ocram. All done. So many forms to fill."

We got in her car, and this time made it as far as reversing out of the parking slot.

"Santa Maria, I forgot to take your photograph. I'm sorry, Mister Ocram—you being such a celebrity and everything, I'm getting all mixed up."

This time Officer Dyaz followed me into the police station, as I knew where I was going.

"We'll have to wait, Mister Ocram. They're photographing someone else just now, and she's in a wheelchair, so they can't use the fixed stand. When you can't use the fixed stand it takes just ages."

By the time a photograph of the wheel-chaired law-breaker had been successfully captured without the aid of the fixed stand, my bespoke Rolex with the picture of my Bronx mom on the dial said it was thirteen minutes before the time at which I was due to meet Agent Dyson in the refectory.

It was forty seven minutes past the time at which I was due to meet Agent Dyson, when I next entered Carmina's patrol car, the intervening hour having been spent waiting for Oma—*he knows everything about cameras, Mister Ocram*—to find and study the manual in order to figure out how to insert and format a new SD-card in the camera, the remaining capacity of the old card having been squandered on unsatisfactory images taken without the aid of the fixed stand.

"Traffic's heavy, Mister Ocram," said Carmina, after we had made less than a mile from the police station in a little over twenty minutes. "Let's hope Gertie doesn't blow."

"Who's Gertie?"

"This baby." Officer Dyaz patted the rim of her steering wheel. "Don't like heavy traffic, do ya Gertie?"

I decided to put Carmina's loose lippedness to a productive use. "What do you know about Tan Falconi's death?"

"Tan Falconi? Sorry, Mister Ocram—Chief Galahad has said we mustn't tell you anything about official police business."

"Are you sure he said that? It's hard to believe... ha ha... that Chief Galahad would mean to exclude me from the opportunity to help the Clarkesville County Police fight crime. The idea's laughable. Surely you've mis-understood."

"I don't think so, Mister Ocram. He was very clear about it. He had everyone gather in the Clarkesville County Police gym, and he laid it on the line. He said you were coming for a rest at the abbey, and that if any of us came in contact with you we weren't to say anything about official police business, and if he caught any of us saying anything to you about official police business it would mean an automatic disciplinary."

"Ha ha... oh that's so like Como to be concerned about me. I told him I needed a complete rest, so he was probably just trying to make sure that I wasn't inadvertently burdened with worries about your workload. But it's quite alright, Officer Dyaz, I am almost fully recovered after my rest at the abbey, so there is no-longer any reason to for Chief Galahad's kindly precautions about my health."

"No, it definitely wasn't anything to do with your health, Mister Ocram. Chief Galahad said that if we told you anything you'd only start interfering and who knows where we'd end up once that asshole Ocram gets involved, begging your pardon. Oh no, Gertie's blowed!" Thankfully, Carmina's humiliating revelations were interrupted by a jet of steam from some forward part of the prowler. "I knew she'd start blowing, with traffic being so heavy. Don't like heavy traffic, do ya Gertie?"

Officer Dyaz nudged Gertie onto the sidewalk.

"Shall we try to fix it?"

"No way, Mister Ocram. When Gertie blows she blows good'n'proper. She'll need the tow-truck. But don't you worry—shouldn't be more than an hour."

Two hours later...

"Santa Maria, where's that tow truck?" Carmina radioed the Clarkesville County Police Transportation Department for an update while I banged my head against the un-tinted window of the prowler. I would rather drag myself to the abbey by my eyelids than suffer any more of this tedious digression.

"Carmina, can I get a taxi?"

"A taxi? In this part of town? I doubt you'd get a taxi in under an hour, Mister Ocram. I tell you what, though, my nephew Marlon lives nearby. I'll get him to pick you up and take you back to your car."

Carmina made the arrangements, and in less than two hours Marlon had arrived, produced his books for me to sign, taken a grinning selfie with me in front of his Aunty Carmina's immobile prowler, and helped me into his Toyota. He had barely started his engine and moved off when we stopped again.

"Here we are, Mister Ocram?"

"Where?"

"Your car."

We'd pulled up alongside my black Range Rover with tinted windows, about a hundred yards down the street from where Officer Dyaz was having a long cozy chat with Gertie. Resisting the temptation to bang my head repeatedly against the passenger side of Marlon's windshield, I asked him why he thought his aunty had put him to all this trouble just to save me a minute's walk.

"This is a rough area, Mister Ocram. Carmina wouldn't forgive herself if you got hurt."

I think he meant to say 'hurt physically,' since Aunty Carmina had seemed quite comfortable subjecting me to mental torture for the last four hours. However, I took him at his word, and followed up with a query, hoping he might be less tight-lipped about police matters than his relative had been.

"Is there much crime hereabouts?"

"Sure is, Mister Ocram."

"Have you heard of the Falconis?"

"Sure have, Mister Ocram. They're a big crime family in Clarkesville—almost as bent as the McGees. Half the local prison's full of Falconis."

"Do the Falconis and the McGees fight?"

"Not any more, Mister Ocram. They used to, until Stella McGee went into partnership with Al Falconi. Now they're thick as thieves."

"Al Falconi?" I paged back to the start of the scene with Stella McGee, wondering whether I'd made another continuity error. "Don't you mean Tan Falconi?"

"No, Mister Ocram. Tan's just a bum. Al's his uncle, a real smart guy. I think he works up at the abbey."

Chapter Thirty-Three

In which Marco meets Brother Leon.

After my nightmare at the hands, and voice, of Officer Dyaz, it was almost a relief to be back in the lunacy of the abbey. A breathless abbot appeared as I was getting my key from reception.

"Thank Heaven you have returned, Brother Marco. There has been apocalyptic news of an outrage to be visited upon our grand celebrity opening."

"I have heard of it already, Your Fabulosity."

"What are we to do? Consider the impiety of it—harpies from Hollywood and elsewhere, violating the sanctity of the abbey."

"I cannot counsel you on such lofty matters, Your Superlative. My expertise lies strictly within the earthly plane."

"But there is already so much evil at work within our community. I fear the arrival of women will create no end of havoc with the hormones of the brethren."

Which was rich coming from him, the randy old goat. Speaking of women at the abbey reminded me of my missed appointment with Special Agent Leona Dyson. I must make contact with her. I looked around to make sure we were not to be overheard, then spoke to the abbot in hushed tones designed to convey the message that what I was about to say was a matter of utmost secrecy concerning my investigations...

"Your Sublimity, I am looking for a young monk."

The abbot patted me on the forearm, and replied conspiratorially.

"I quite understand. Happily you are in the right place for that." He looked around too, repeating my precaution. "Perhaps you and your young monk might care to join me and Sister Coma in special devotions." Wink wink.

I was really, really, really beginning to wish I had written an altogether more pious character for the abbot. All of this unseemly allusion to physical frolics with Sister Coma was starting to threaten my sanity. God knows how the readers were coping with it.

"No, no, Your Exaltedness. The particular monk I seek is one gifted in the practicalities of detection. I believe his name may be Brother Leon."

"Young Brother Leon? I was not aware he had any detecting prowess, although he does exhibit the three most important qualities of a novice monk."

"You mean..." I hesitated, dreading the corniness of the imminent joke.

"Yes—vocation, vocation, vocation. I will consult the work rota to determine Brother Leon's likely location. One moment." The abbot bid me follow him into the office behind the reception, where he tapped one-fingeredly on a keyboard to consult the programme that managed the allocation of work among the staff of the abbey.

"Brother Leon is working in the laundry this afternoon—you will find him there until tea time."

I thanked His Pre-eminence, and hastened to the laundry, a crude lean-to on the western face of the praesidium, its open sides offering no protection against the snow-laden winds that whipped through the complex. Within the laundry were a series of steaming vats, heated by fires, in which the bed-sheets and undergarments of the brothers were boiled with salt, camphor, juniper leaves, and fabric conditioner. A hooded monk upon a step-ladder was stirring one of the vats with a cedar paddle. I attracted his attention with a suitably corny comment.

"If only the souls of men could be cleaned so readily."

"Indeed Brother... Doctor Ocram!" Agent Dyson dropped her paddle and clambered down the ladder. "Excuse my astonishment. I did not know what to imagine when you and Chief Galahad failed to keep our rendezvous at 10.30."

"I am sorry for that, Agent Dyson—Chief Galahad and I have been detained on matters of the most supreme importance. However, having traced you here through the application of my unique detecting skills, I am anxious to continue our investigations without a moment's further delay."

"But..."

"But what, Agent Dyson?"

"If I leave the laundry now, with the work incomplete, I will arouse suspicion."

"Come, then. Let me help. The work will be done in half the time with the two of us. How do these contraptions work?"

Agent Dyson explained the workings of the various knobs and dials which controlled the laundering process, and showed me which of the feed-drawers took the detergent and which the conditioner. Together we moved the items of soiled cloth which had been dumped in trolleys at the entrance bay, through the varied steps through which they were cleaned, rinsed, dried, pressed, and folded, ready to be returned to housekeeping. Our labours complete, we knelt in prayer for the benefit of any passing observer, then we went to the dry-cleaning racks, where we pretended to be sorting through the habits looking for items past their due collection dates.

"I am anxious to enter the cave system," I whispered. "I believe a key-card in my possession is programmed to provide access, but I need you to direct me to one of the entrances, preferably one where we are least likely to be challenged."

"The best way is via the morgue. Hardly anyone goes there."

"Lead me to it."

Our cowls raised, we walked through the snowy precincts of the abbey to the infirmary. I flashed the abbot's pinkie ring to quell any nonsense from the security monk at reception, then followed Agent Dyson to the morgue, which thankfully was just like all the other morgues you've seen on TV, so I don't have to bore myself to death typing a description of it.

"It's that door at the back there," said Agent Dyson, "between the vending machine and the rack with the undertaker's leaflets."

We walked to the specified door, and no-one was less surprised than I to see the number *42* stencilled against its digital lock. With excited fingers I swiped the key-card. A red light on the lock changed to green, and a click announced that its mechanism had been activated. Cautiously, we pulled open the door.

CHAPTER THIRTY-FOUR

In which an ancient painting is found to be not entirely so.

My emotions upon opening the door were best described as mixed. The blend consisted of perhaps twenty percent relief at having finally progressed the central plot after so many stupid digressions, ten percent excitement about the scope for writing a stellar plot twist, and seventy percent fear—I hate being in dark enclosed spaces.

The door revealed a downward passage hewn out of the cliché-lover's living rock. At intervals along the wall were bulkhead lamps of barely adequate wattage, the curving line of which showed the passage to be bending to the left. I pulled out my leaflet map—that would mean we were headed for the herbarium. Excellent. This was going to be a piece of cake.

We followed the passage for perhaps a hundred yards until we encountered a large natural chamber, roughly shaped like seven octagons fused to a central heptagon. From each of the forty nine outer faces of the seven octagons, other passageways led away through arched openings. Not so excellent.

Agent Dyson asked the obvious question.

"Which way?"

I was about to ask Agent Dyson how did she expect me to know, when I remembered that I was meant to be impressing her with my intellectual prowess.

"We must seek signs to guide us from this muddling nexus. Let us have more light."

We adjusted the wicks on the oil lights I forgot to mention we were carrying, and raised the lamps to illuminate the upper parts of the chamber. Agent Dyson let out a gasp at the details thus revealed. Carved into the rock above the forty nine external archways were the Latinised names of the forty eight contiguous US states plus Washington DC. Above the seven archways linking the individual octagons to the central heptagon were written the following strange devices:

SVPERARE MONSTRVM
CENTVNCVLVS AD OPVLENCIAM
REGENERATIONE
INVESTIGATIO
COMOEDIA
TRAGOEDIA
NAVIGATIO E REGRESSVS.

"What can they mean?" asked a bewildered Agent Dyson.

I was feeling pretty bewildered myself, but I made a brave face of things. "The Latin inscriptions within the central heptagon are obviously the seven basic plots."

There was nothing obvious about it, but I threw in the word to convey an impression of omniscience.

"The seven basic plots?" said Agent Dyson, conveniently giving me an excuse to explain them to the readers.

"It has long been held by philosophers that all works of fiction are variations on a small number of fundamental themes. The theory is misguided, of course, but has maintained some currency among those whose powers of memory exceed their powers of independent thought."

"And what might be their significance in this context?"

It was a good question. I had no idea. I wrote the next thing that came into my head.

"That is for us to discover. What do you notice about the arches of the central heptagon, Agent Dyson?"

"I... I can't see anything special about them."

"You see but you do not observe, Agent Dyson. The signs to which I allude are as visible to you as they are to me—you must analyse what you see. Upon the floor, for example, what can you see?"

"The floor is worn with the passage of many feet."

"Excellent. But how does the degree of wear vary?"

"The degree of wear is greater through some arches than through others."

"Excellent. And is the nature of the wear the same in each case?"

Agent Dyson lowered her lamp to examine the ancient linoleum.

"The wear through certain arches is indicative of the passage of stiletto heels. There are also signs of wheeled abrasion."

"Excellent. And what do you see upon the ceilings?"

"I see soot, from the passage of many oil lamps."

"Excellent. And is the soot of a uniform sootiness?"

"No, the soot is darker above certain arches than others."

"Excellent. What conclusions may we draw from our observations?"

"That some passages are busier than others, that some are frequented by people wearing stilettoes, and that some are traversed by wheeled devices."

"Exactly! Now, let us consider those wheeled devices. Lend me your tape measure."

With Agent Dyson's FBI-issue tape, I took various measurements of wheel scuffs on the lino.

"Just as I thought—two feet seven and three eighths inches. That, Agent Dyson, is the ANSII imperial gauge of a hospital gurney. You will note that most of the wheel scuffs are through the arches that connect SVPERARE MONSTRVM and REGENERATIONE."

"And the stiletto wear seems to correlate with the wheel scuffing."

"Well done, Agent Dyson. The conclusion being...?"

"That the hospital trolleys are being pushed by nurses in stilettoes?"

"That is certainly a plausible hypothesis, given the circumstances." The circumstances being that a certain writer's imagination was running off the rails after being cooped up with monks. "However, speculation is the mother-in-law of procrastination. We must not speculate, we must act."

"But which octagon should we explore first?"

"COMOEDIA, or comedy, is the octagon through which we entered the nexus. I have a deep reason to believe that any of the arches we take from that octagon will simply return us to the abbey compound. I have a hunch that we should investigate INVESTIGATIO. Come."

I trod boldly through the aforementioned archway, leaving Agent Dyson no choice but to follow. Now we were confronted by seven other archways, each bearing the name of a US state.

"Which arch should we take?"

I wasn't sure if it was me or Agent Dyson who was meant to have said that. I don't suppose it matters, so feel free to take your pick.

"My instinct is to take the arch inscribed MISSOVRI." I said. "You will see it has the lightest soot staining and yet the most heavily abraded linoleum, suggesting that it is the most brightly lit. And where there is most light the Lord reveals the greatest truths."

It was complete nonsense, of course, but Agent Dyson seemed happy to go along with it, so we headed down the passageway. At first it led gently downward, but after a turn to the left it switched sharply upwards before opening into an immense grotto of unimaginable grandeur and beauty. We stopped and stared, stunned by the spectacle before us. Colossal stalactites and stalagmites, larger than any seen on National Geographic, peopled the cavern like the majestic columns of a huge cathedral. Rich veins of all the precious and semi-precious metals threaded through the rock like a giant glittering Jackson Pollock. Everywhere were the purest and largest crystals of every conceivable mineral— adamite, bassanite, coesite, dolomite, ekanite, fingertite, locktite, marmite, striplite, watertite, and countless others.

Stunning as these natural wonders were, it was a man-made spectacle at the far end of the cavern which had attracted the most attention over the years, judging by the wear on the lino before it. On a smooth pale stretch of wall an artist among our remotest ancestors had painted a scene so vivid and lifelike, it might almost have been real.

"I believe this is the real treasure of the grotto," I said, as I videoed the amazing mural with my iPad.

"That? It's just a painting."

"Not just a painting. A painting of immense symbolic significance." I spotted another opportunity to impress Agent Dyson with my intellectual prowess. "You will know I am famed for the authenticity of my novels. Such accuracy does not arise by chance—I complete meticulous research upon every topic. It happens that one of my forthcoming novels—*The Awful Truth about Little Bighorn*—touches upon the cultures of the indigenous American, and in preparation for writing it I have completed research of unparalleled scope and depth into the cave art of the native Americans. To me, this series of images reads as clearly as a book."

"What does it say?" asked Agent Dyson, conveniently giving me an excuse for another long paragraph of expositional dialogue.

"Consider firstly the manner of dress among the subjects depicted. The group to the left are low-ranking people in the most-simple ceremonial garb. The figures here are great chieftains. However, the most significant is this figure—the one with the hide of a jackal on one shoulder, and a miniature bushel of corn on the other—she is a shaman, or shochnassai in the Chinook tongue. She has evidently administered a powerful hallucinogenic to the cross-eyed floating chief here, whose resulting visions are shown upon the clouds over the mountains. The drug she has administered is one she has created by her own hand— you can see a crude pestle and mortar in the entrance to her tepee, and small plastic pouches in which the doses of the drug are packaged. The decorated brown-grey rectangles on the bookshelf inside the tepee are writing tablets made from birch bark. The symbols upon the tablets are glyphs of some ancient tongue of Mesoamerican origin, a language that spread northwards with the retreating glaciers in the cobolazoic period. I cannot decipher them with certainty, but I believe the glyphs show the recipes for various types of drugs. What is most striking is the profusion of pink flowers in this bed—they are clearly being cultivated for the purpose of supplying the shaman's ingredients, as denoted by the trail of petals leading from the cultivated strip to the shaman's herb cupboard. May I borrow your glass?"

Agent Dyson handed me her FBI-issue magnifying glass.

"They are roses. There can be no doubt about it—the spacing between the sepals and the pedicel is an unmistakeable signature of the family Rosea. I should say they are a primitive version of Rosa Woodii, a variety native to North America and capable of flourishing in mountain climes."

"What can it all mean?"

I don't know about you, but I was getting a bit fed-up with Agent Dyson's endless questions. I'd just exhausted myself inventing three hundred words of explanation, and still she wasn't satisfied. I turned the question back on her to give myself time to think.

"Come, come, Brother Leon—do no hypotheses suggest themselves to you? What are your thoughts?"

Brother Leon would have scratched her beard quizzically at this point, had she been a real monk. Instead she gave me what I felt to be a less-than-convinced look and said:

"I think it would all become a lot clearer if we had Chief Galahad to lead us."

CHAPTER THIRTY-FIVE

In which the secrets of the laboratory are revealed.

Once again I found myself starting a new chapter in a mood of hurt resentment. I admit I was stung by Agent Dyson's thoughtless words, but I was disappointed too. I had intended her to break the mould—to be neither the helpless female, nor the equally-clichéd gutsy, fearless heroine, but instead to be something more nuanced, something less gender-specific. Yet she was showing all the lamentable traits of a stock female character—constantly deferring to a stereotypical alpha male of higher rank in her professional milieu. Was it any wonder I didn't have female protagonists in my books when that's the way they behave? Next time I'm on a chat show with Germaine Greer remind me to dumbfound her with a devastating critique of Agent Dyson's behaviour, rather than sitting there being made to look an idiot like I usually do.

However, in the interests of keeping the story fast-paced and free of tedious introspection, I shelved my hurt feelings and did my best to instil into Agent Dyson some of the nobility of spirit that had become the cornerstone of my literary endeavours.

"Well, Chief Galahad isn't here, so ner ner nee ner ner."

I don't know—there's just no helping some people.

I looked absently at the geological wonders of the grotto, waiting for the next thing to come into my head. When it did, I was aggrieved to find it was a question from Agent Dyson making a mountain out of a tiny slip in my description of the cave painting.

"Did you say those square things in the picture were plastic pouches for drugs? Since when did the indigenous peoples of America have plastic pouches?"

Whether it was the product of over-zealous training in the FBI, or some innate character flaw, her mania for pedantry was driving me nuts. I was beginning to wish I'd left her pounding monks' smalls in the laundry. As it was, I'd now have to flipping well think of some kind of plot twist to explain the anachronistic pouches. Let me see...

"Congratulations—I was wondering how long it would take you to spot the obvious clue. Lend me you glass again, would you?"

I took Agent Dyson's powerful magnifying glass, hitched-up the skirts of my habit, and bent to inspect the painting minutely.

"Hmmmmm...just as I expected. Every reference to the production of drugs has been overpainted upon the original mural. The colour tones are an authentic match, but to the trained eye the brushwork is entirely different. Here." I handed the glass to Agent Dyson. "Observe the technique that has been used to suggest the transparency of the plastic—the staccato-like attack of the brush, creating an entirely distinctive melange of pointilistic and impasto treatments."

"What could that mean?"

How was I to know? I'd only just invented it. I resorted to monkish obfuscation. "The Lord will reveal the truth when he sees fit. Let us return to COMOEADIA," I added, symbolically holding out the possibility that the book might get funnier.

We indulged in the cliché of retracing our steps until we found ourselves once more in the octagonal chamber through which we had entered the nexus. Around us were seven archways.

"Which shall we take?" asked Agent Dyson, true to character.

"We shall apply our powers of deductive reasoning to determine our next plot twist," I replied. By 'our' powers I meant mainly mine, of course. "Through which of the arches did we arrive in COMOEDIA?"

It was a rhetorical question, designed to prod Agent Dyson into some thinking of her own.

"MAINE."

"Does that suggest anything to you?"

"Perhaps the names of the states indicate the direction the passages take? So Maine would be north east, Texas south, and so on."

Hmmmmm. I was impressed for once. I hadn't thought of that.

"Perhaps. However, the theory suffers from at least two difficulties. One is that the number of states is too great. From any point on the world's surface there are always several US states lying in the same direction. The other is less abstract—in INVESTIGATIO the arch labelled MISSOVRI was directly opposite that labelled VTAH, even though both the named states lie in the same direction from Clarkesville. For your theory to be true, one of the two passageways would have to double back and run parallel to the other, which seems hardly likely.

"A more promising theory is that the names of the states correspond in some way to the names of the locations that may be reached via the passages. Take MAINE again—we arrived at that arch from the morgue, which suggests that the first letters of the two names are linked. That being so, LOVISIANA should lead to the laboratory. Let us test the hypothesis."

We entered the arch so named, and followed the dank twisting passage for some hundreds of yards before it rose steeply to meet a short flight of well-worn stone steps, at the top of which the outline of a trapdoor could clearly be seen. Agent Dyson mounted the stairs noiselessly, like a mountain goat wearing sandals with ultra-soft soles. From her capacious robes she extracted an FBI-issue spying device, consisting of a bundle of optical fibres that could be used to see through small apertures, a gizmo I had cleverly invented as I typed the sentence. She inserted it between the leaves of the trap-door to inspect the area above them. All must have been clear, because she returned the device to its designated pocket, lifted a flap of the trap-door, and beckoned me to follow her past it.

As I entered the laboratory, I remembered examining its interior through a huge keyhole when standing in the snow with Como. Who would have thought, all those chapters ago, that I would now be rising through the trapdoor in the company of a beautiful FBI agent? And even if someone did, I bet they never imagined that the beautiful FBI agent would be stupidly besotted with Como and oblivious to my less conspicuous charms. Such is the sad unpredictability of the style of spontaneous literary creation which I have made it my unbending rule to adopt.

Abandoning my embittered ruminations, I re-assumed the character of the world-renowned scientist and went quickly from bench to bench to assess the nature of the work undertaken in the laboratory. I videoed everything of note with my iPad, so there would be an irrefutable trail of evidence should any legal proceedings arise from our investigations—an unlikely outcome, I admit, given that my books usually end with all the baddies dying in some freak event that miraculously saves me and Como from certain death.

"Note, Agent Dyson, the contents of these test tubes. Unless I am mistaken, they are the parts of a rose that are responsible for creating its scent."

I removed the bung from one of the tubes and used tweezers to extract a small quantity of the contents, which I fixed with a neutral ether base and smeared on a glass slide. With deft flicks of my fingers, I activated the scanning electron microscope, slid in the slide, and adjusted the mirror at the bottom to reflect maximum light through the sample. Putting my experienced eyes to the cups, I twisted the focussing rings to create a faultlessly sharp image.

"Here."

I invited Agent Dyson to look for herself. As she bent to the powerful magnifying instrument, I addressed my comments to her right shoulder. I'd show her that Como wasn't the only person writing impressive articles in specialist journals.

"The long-chain carbon molecules from those rose samples are unlike any other aromatic compounds known to science. You may have read my summary of the field, in last month's International Journal of Olfactory Neuroscience, in which case you will know that all plant-based aromas share a common molecular backbone which facilitates the transmission of bicodal suppressants at neural boundaries within the left occipital cruvex. In this case, you will see that the third carbon ring from the left has a covalent bonding with a free radical ester induced. What does that suggest?"

"Why..." Agent Dyson raised her queenly head from the microscope, her face conveying the astonishment she felt at my masterful revelations "...that's highly suggestive of the limbic reward mechanisms in many recreational drugs!"

"Exactly. Imagine a rose whose intoxicating scent could generate an addictive sensation of well-being. Consider the fortunes to be made from such an innovation."

CHAPTER THIRTY-SIX

In which the duo are discovered.

At last we were getting somewhere. At last the rambling rose plot was starting to bloom. I punched the air to betoken my pleasure at reaching a major crux, accidentally knocking over a stack of wire baskets that had been on the bench beside me. We knelt to collect the contents I had spilled on the laboratory floor—rectangles of clear plastic, just like those Como had found in the safe at the bothy.

"I wonder why they'd have so many screen protectors?"

"Screen protectors?"

I stared at Agent Dyson, then at the pieces of plastic in my hands. Screen protectors? So that's what they were— screen protectors for smartphones. My mind started to race. Well, actually, it was probably more of a crawl. Why indeed? I flexed one of the pieces of plastic, then held it up to the light. Nothing. Then I had an idea.

"Pass me that scalpel."

I cut a corner from the screen protector and started to mount it on a slide. If there was anything to be seen, the tunnelling electron microscope would reveal it. Or did I say it was a tunnelling neutrino microscope? I was too excited to check. I could scarcely believe that in just a few moments the microscope would reveal some decisive fact, perhaps the final clue that would allow me to clear-up the mystery of the abbey well before the cameras arrived for the celebrity opening night. Having inserted the slide with trembling fingers, I was on the point of activating the microscope's vacuum extraction pump when a hiss from Agent Dyson froze my hand.

"Someone's coming."

I did what I usually do when confronted with the kind of unexpected threat that would startle an ordinary mortal—I flapped my arms in a complete panic, and flip-flopped indecisively about whether to run to my left or to my right. Luckily Agent Dyson had more presence of mind—she grabbed the girdle of my habit and pulled me down to join her behind the raised flap of the trapdoor, putting her finger to her lips to instruct me to be quiet. I got the general idea that she meant us to scarper down the passage behind the back of whoever was about to enter the lab. I readied myself for action and tried to suppress the noisy gulps of my breathing.

We heard footsteps approaching along the passageway. It sounded like two people—double the chance of being seen. I crouched more tightly behind the flap of the trapdoor—a flap which seemed ridiculously inadequate to hide us from view. The footsteps were now coming up the stairs. My heart was thudding. My mouth was suddenly bone dry. Two gowned figures swished past, their knees about a foot from my face. They seemed to be carrying boxes. I felt a sharp nudge at my back—the signal from Agent Dyson to leap up, to whip around the flap, and to vanish soundlessly down the passageway before the newcomers had a chance to see us.

I leapt up. I whipped around the flap. I was a millisecond away from vanishing soundlessly down the passageway before the newcomers had a chance to see us, when the trailing edge of my cloak caught on the corner of the flap and brought it crashing down with a noise like the trump of hell, simultaneously alerting the newcomers to our presence and blocking our escape.

I stared at the monks who had turned to face us—huge brutes with heavy cruel features and fists to match. With unflappable deliberation, they put down the boxes they were carrying and came towards us—tough professional thugs acting as if the surprise appearance of intruders was something they could handle in their sleep. I was beginning to see Agent Dyson's point about Como—there are definitely times when it is comforting to have a gigantic, short-tempered sidekick.

"Get the flap." Agent Dyson sprang between me and the would-be assailants.

I froze.

Agent Dyson vaulted onto one of the benches.

"Get the flap!"

I was too busy checking my contract with Barney on my iPad. It has strict clauses limiting the treatment of violence in my books—something to do with a deal he has to sell them as primers to elementary schools. I was hoping I could rely on them to stop myself from getting mashed to a pulp. Hmmmm... it seemed violence was allowed provided it wasn't graphically depicted. I decided the best course was to close my eyes.

I can't quite remember the exact order of the subsequent events. The sounds I heard included grunts, unbrotherly oaths, the echo of light fast footsteps on a laboratory bench, the smashing of vast amounts of glass, and two sickening crunches of the sort made by a hard object swung fast against a human head. Then there was quiet except for the deep panting of someone recovering from unexpected exertions.

I opened a tentative eye.

Agent Dyson was looking down at two unconscious figures on a floor littered with broken laboratory equipment.

I was all for running away before they woke, but Agent Dyson said they'd be out for at least an hour, and we should check them for clues—which is how we found they were both carrying mobile phones in an abbey that didn't have any phone reception. She put them in her pouch.

"I know these guys," she said. "They're Brothers Tony and Vinnie—they're always hanging round with Brother George."

I wondered whether I needed to remind the readers that Brother George was the grumpy one on the council of elders who had objected to the presence of Como and I in the governance chamber. Or should that be Como and me?

"Let's see what's in these boxes." Agent Dyson's timely interruption put a stop to my dithering.

I gave her a hand to clear a space on the bench, then lifted the boxes—one light, one heavy.

The light one contained tens of those sealable transparent plastic bags, about three inches square, in each of which was what looked like tiny parts of a flower and a strip of paper with a long sequence of characters printed on it. The heavy one was full of smartphones. I had to read that sentence twice to make sure I meant it. Smartphones? Why smartphones?

Evidently Agent Dyson was as confused as I, as she just stared at the jumble of phones. Then she started taking them out and spreading them on the bench. They were a miscellaneous collection, with models of every type from a range of manufacturers. Some looked new; others were scuffed with use. There seemed nothing remarkable about them at all, apart from the remarkable fact that they were together in a box carried by a thuggish monk.

"None of it makes sense," said Agent Dyson.

I supposed she was talking about the contents of the boxes, but now I think about it, she might have meant the whole book.

"Maybe they're stealing phones and reselling them," I ventured.

"But why bring them to the lab? And what's with all the flower samples?"

She was right—none of it made sense.

I remembered I'd been about to examine one of the screen protectors. The electron tunnelling microscope had been knocked over in the scuffle with the baddies. I righted it and switched it on, anxiously inspecting its various knobs and dials to check nothing had been broken. All appeared in order. I could scarcely believe it—once again I might be moments away from solving the mystery of the abbey.

I pressed the switch for the vacuum pump—it ran for a few moments then stopped. A flashing red code appeared on the LED screen of the microscope: AF28.

"What is it?" Brother Leon tuned-in to my hesitant movements.

"I think there's a fault."

We found the instruction booklet in a drawer under the bench and looked-up the code in the trouble-shooting section.

"Vacuum reduction error," read Agent Dyson. *"Check for clogged filter."*

"That old problem," I said. "It's always happening with these models. They use a cyclonic separation technique to filter out impurities in the discharge chamber, and it's useless. The older models with filter bags were much more reliable. I suspect it's all the dust that's been kicked-up in your struggle. I'll fix it."

The air was blue for a few minutes as I cursed the manufacturer of the microscope for their short-sighted cost-cutting measures—measures that had caused an entirely unnecessary delay to what could be the most decisive plot-twist in the book. Finally I reassembled the cheap plastic parts and reconnected the extraction hose. I could scarcely believe it—once again I might be moments away from solving the mystery of the abbey. With elated fingers, I pressed the switch for the vacuum pump. The machine settled into its warm-up routine with a satisfyingly consistent hum. My eyes followed the needle on the vacuum gauge as it crept toward the green sector. Yes! Seated in front of the vast control panel, I eased up the sliders that governed the modulus of the neutrino generator. The lights in the room dimmed as the microscope drew its transient start-up current. Huge crackling sparks seared the air between the HT electrodes, and static began to raise the coarse fibres of our habits. Any moment now, the secrets of the screen protectors would be...

Ping!

The machine shut down, a new code flashing red on its LED display: DB16.

With a frantic hand, I grasped the instruction manual and tore through its pages with fingers like the talons of a raptor.

"The electron beam collimator has lost its alignment," I read. *"Activate auto-realignment mode."*

"It must have been misaligned when I knocked it over," said Agent Dyson for the benefit of slower readers. "Can you fix it?"

"It is a straightforward procedure, but it requires a special calibration plate to be inserted in the slide holder. It's usually in a plastic wallet that's kept with the manual."

I leafed through the various papers and booklets in the drawer and found the plastic wallet, but from its limp feel I didn't have to open the wallet to know that it was empty.

"By the Eight Evensongs of St Edward!" I thumped the desk to underline my fury at the sloppy laboratory practices that had gone unchecked at the abbey. "The plate is missing from its wallet—we cannot recalibrate the collimator without it."

"But it must be here somewhere. What does it look like?"

"It is a small thin plate of perforated titanium—about the size of a credit card—embossed with the logo of the manufacturer and the serial number of the microscope."

Agent Dyson hunted diligently through the drawers under the bench, but I knew she searched in vain. I knew that even if the card were found, I would end up writing some other outlandish glitch that would prevent me from using the microscope to reveal the secret of the screen protectors. There was a malicious force at work within the laboratory, a force that was insidiously weakening my ability to write fast-paced comedy plot twists. I broke the news to my comrade.

"I believe our hunt here must be suspended for the nonce. There is a supernatural agency at work to defeat our purpose. I propose we try elsewhere."

Agent Dyson knelt before me as a supplicant. "But surely...if we were to find the calibration plate...what else could go wrong?"

I pointed at the huge list of fault-codes in the microscope's manual.

"Take your pick."

Agent Dyson continued to implore me to have one more go at getting the microscope to work, but I was adamant— for the sake of the reader's sanity we had to abandon this ludicrous sequence of false starts.

Having taken a selection of the mobile phones for later analysis, we returned to COMOEDIA, Agent Dyson leading the way in what I thought was something of an annoyed manner. The octagonal chamber confronted us with its cryptically named arches.

"Where next?" said Agent Dyson.

The answer on my lips was *as far away from Clarkesville as I can get—how about Hawaii for instance?* but I could see that it wasn't going to help us finish the book. The idea that next came into my head was that we should explore the herbarium. I looked at the names of the states above the archways for one that began with an H, and wondered if my readers would spot the irony of it being HAWAII.

"This way."

Agent Dyson followed me down a long, curving tunnel, the floor of which bore the unmistakable marks of the passage of innumerable wheelbarrows. Here and there our lamps showed small dark flakes upon the lino. I went to examine one, lifting it on my finger. It was a dried rose petal.

We continued to follow the passage through an area of intense cold, followed by an area of intense heat, then an area full of spiders, before finding our way barred by an ancient door of stout oak planks. I put my shoulder to it in a decidedly manly fashion, then nursed my arm in a decidedly unmanly fashion.

"The door is unyielding. Perhaps there is some secret mechanism to unlock it."

I ran my fingers around the edge of the door, feeling for some cunningly hidden pressure point.

"Try this."

Agent Dyson pointed her oil lamp at a switch on the wall, above which was the legend PRESSARE UT EGRIDIO.

"I wondered how long it would take you to spot that. Well done."

I pressed the switch and eased open the heavy door.

CHAPTER THIRTY-SEVEN

In which there is more to the potting shed than meets the eye.

The first thing that hit me was the smell—a combination of the floral and the chemical, like an oil refinery on Valentine's Day. We had emerged in the northern section of the herbarium, farthest from the main entrance. Through the stained glass panes of the roof, I could make out the looming bulk of the praesidium some distance to the south. To either side of us, row after row of long trestles carried innumerable terracotta pots in which the root-stocks of young roses were nourished by the finest composts. About fifty yards ahead was the seed hall where the abbot and I had found the freakishly disembowelled herbalist.

I decided to address Agent Dyson in the monkish manner, as it's more fun to write.

"Tell me, Brother Leon, what have you learned about the ways of the herbalist?"

She consulted her FBI-issue tablet.

"According to the gossip in the abbey, the herbalist was a man of strict and unvarying routine. Those who have worked in the herbarium report that his working day would start with prayers in the potting shed."

"Let us repair there at once, immediately, and without further delay."

I was mentally brewing some ideas for several paragraphs in which we sought the potting shed among the labyrinthine passageways of the herbarium, but Brother Leona scotched all that by finding it just to the left of the door we'd come through. As befitted the splendours of the abbey, it was a shed of generous proportions, bedecked with humorous horticultural shed signs, such as *Lettuce Pray*, or *Some like The Stone Age, Some Like The Iron Age, I prefer the Cabb Age*, and others too rude to quote. Inside, among the gardening paraphernalia, we found what was clearly the herbalist's seat—a folding chair in tubular aluminium and plastic, to the side of which a small table bore a china mug with the dregs of a white Frappuccino, a single rose in a shapely vase, an ash-tray containing the butts of several joints, and a recently-thumbed copy of *The Awful Truth about the Herbert Quarry Affair*. Having donned some FBI-issue latex gloves which Brother Leon produced from her pouch, we scoured the shed for items of significance. After ten minutes the only clues I had found were those in an abandoned crossword under the herbalist's chair. I scratched a ruminative armpit. At the start of the paragraph, I felt sure the episode in the potting shed would develop into a lengthy digression, but it was running out of steam after barely a dozen lines. Where else might we find a clue?

"There's something odd about this door."

I hurried to where Brother Leon was examining the shed's door. At first glance it seemed just as any other potting shed door—a softwood frame clad with feather-edge boards—but closer inspection revealed that its edges were very finely machined to fit against a rubber seal around the door-frame; over the boards was some impervious transparent film, while the keyhole was covered by an escutcheon with airtight seals.

We re-examined the shed with fresh eyes. Nowhere was there the smallest gap through which air could have entered or left the enclosed space. The gaps between the floorboards were caulked with alpaca wool soaked in goose fat, while the sashes of the window were sealed with a fast-curing silicon bead. The entire shed was hermetically sealed!

I was about to type a hilariously clever pun about Hermeticism, but Brother Leon interrupted my thoughts.

"There's a sophisticated air filtration unit in the top of this tool cupboard."

I inspected her discovery.

"What you call a tool cupboard is in fact a biosecurity cabinet with integral fume hood. The foil hose you see here takes the noxious vapours." I followed the hose with my eye to where it passed through the shed roof. "Clearly the herbalist performed experiments of sorts in this cabinet— experiments generating effluvia too hazardous to breathe within the confines of the shed."

"He couldn't have." Brother Leon shook her head at me.

"Why not?"

"The cabinet doesn't have any doors."

"What?"

I almost dropped my iPad at Brother Leon's startling interjection. She was right—the doors of the biosecurity cabinet had been unscrewed and removed. I knelt and examined the controls of the cabinet, my powerful mind swiftly analysing the implications of Brother Leon's discovery. It could mean only one thing—the entire potting shed was a biosecurity enclosure. Whoever was doing the experimenting was inside the shed with the fumes.

CHAPTER THIRTY-EIGHT

In which Marco recreates the last moments of the herbalist.

I staggered backwards under the impact of my thoughts and flopped in the herbalist's folding chair. What could it possibly mean? How could I have written it? How on earth was I to get the book to 75,000 words before the grand celebrity opening, while astonishing plot twists were springing up faster than I could make sense of them?

I raised a hand to forestall any questions from Brother Leon and performed my hatnu yoga breathing ritual to calm the agitated surface of my mind. There...

At peace, relatively speaking, once more, I proposed to Brother Leon that we should try to recreate the herbalist's final movements.

"So," I said, still seated in the herbalist's chair. "The herbalist enters his beloved herbarium as he has done on countless other mornings. He heads directly to the potting shed, as is his wont. He places his Frappuccino on the table here and..."

"Where does he get the Frappuccino?"

That was a good question.

"Good question, Brother Leon. I have noted it on my iPad to follow-up later if we run short of other leads." Fat chance of that. "Where was I? Yes, he places his Frappuccino on the table to his left. He peruses the morning paper. He..."

"Where does he get the morning paper?"

That was another good question.

"Another good question, Brother Leon. I have noted it on my iPad to follow-up later if we run short of other leads. Where was I? Yes, he peruses the morning paper. He turns to the crossword, and cracks several of its fiendish clues. Then, craving greater intellectual stimulus, he abandons the paper under his seat and gratefully returns to the pages of his favourite book."

I picked up the herbalist's copy of *The Awful Truth about the Herbert Quarry Affair*, the brilliant debut novel that had broken all records and made me a literary megastar. Drawing comfort from its touch, I continued my speculations in a more confident mode.

"Engrossed in his reading, he absently sips his Frappuccino until it is gone. Moved by the book's timeless themes of human drama, he contemplates the beauty of the rose, perhaps mentally composing a rhyme—*the beauty of the rose, the beauty of the prose*. Then, something happens—something out of the ordinary, something that causes him to interrupt his routine, to abandon his beloved book. He stands. Something is afoot in the herbarium."

I stood and walked warily out of the potting shed, my mind inhabiting the persona of the herbalist on that fateful morning. Brother Leon followed me, some instinctive compulsion animating her limbs—the small hairs on her queenly neck rising at the eerie spectacle of my performance.

"He walks between the serried trestles, the trestles upon which he has tended his roses with endless devotion. Something is drawing him to the seed hall. Something he sees, perhaps. Or something he hears. Or maybe something he smells? Upon gaining the seed hall, he reaches the supreme moment of crisis. His mind is unhinged by some miasma of evil, some overarching malignancy. He races here to the centre of the seed hall. He chalks upon its cold stone flags that most cabalistic of signs, the pentagram—the symbol of the five holy sins, of the five seeds of Chronos, the five wounds of Christ, the five joys of Mary, the five fingers of the flirting pharaohs. His mind aflame, he takes his pruning knife, the knife that has caused growth to spurt from the stems of countless roses, and he plunges it into his belly, ripping the flesh of his abdomen in one spasmodic stroke. He staggers and falls. But one final act must he perform. One crucial warning must he give to his brethren at the abbey. As his life oozes away he takes his own slimy entrails in his hands and arranges them to form the word CAVE. Perhaps then, his work done, his hands scarlet with his blood, he lies back and makes his peace with his creator, begging merciful forgiveness for the mortal sin of suicide."

Having acted out the herbalist's movements, I was lying on my back in the pentangle. I looked up at the images painted upon the glass panes of the herbarium roof, imagining how they must have appeared to the dying monk—a smiling Clark Gable, a custom Fender Telecaster in cherry, a teak Chris-Craft speedboat against the Amalfi coast, the face of a Vulgari watch, the first class lounge of JFK airport before its facelift in 1998, CoCo Chanel outside the Ritz, and tens of other incongruous vignettes of celebrity life. I struggled to imagine the herbalist's final thoughts, or the malign influence that had led him to his death.

"What evil agency could have been at work?" I said. "What demonic manifestation could have triggered the herbalist's self-destruction? What absolute eminence of evil? What supreme surge of Satanism? What aprochryphal apparition?"

"And where did he get the chalk for the pentagram?" said Brother Leon.

I sat up and examined my filthy toenails as an aide to thought while I considered Brother Leon's question. It clearly wasn't enough of an aid to thought, as I couldn't decide whether the source of the chalk had the potential to be a pivotal clue or was just an irrelevant detail. What I needed was an entirely unexpected development to cue the start of a new chapter, which is why I looked up from my besoiled feet and saw through the stained glass an indistinct object hovering above the herbarium.

CHAPTER THIRTY-NINE

In which Brothers Marco and Leon discover they are being watched.

It was a small drone, directly above us. I drew Brother Leon's attention to it with a 'psssst' and an upward nod of the head.

"Look up, but don't make it obvious."

Brother Leon looked up.

"Do you see the drone? Someone is interested in our movements. I wonder how long it has been hovering there."

"What makes you say it's watching us? It could be doing something else."

"Such as?

Brother Leon shrugged her lissom shoulders. "Maintenance checks, maybe—looking for cracked panes that need to be repaired."

I raised an eyebrow of the utmost scepticism. "What would you say was the area of the herbarium, Brother Leon?"

Brother Leon re-shrugged her lissom shoulders. "Ten acres, maybe."

"Assuming so, the odds of a maintenance drone being interested in the few square yards of glass directly above us are several thousand to one. And why would it hover there, since there are evidently no damaged panes hereabouts? No, Brother Leon, the contraption's presence is assuredly linked to ours. In any event, we can put the point to the test. Follow me."

I grabbed several seed packets from a nearby rack, and strolled along one of the many winding paths from the seed hall, leaving a trail of seeds so that we might re-trace our steps should we lose track of our position in the labyrinth. Notwithstanding the many twists and turns of our random walk, the drone patiently followed our movements. I crossed my fingers and hoped the readers were following also.

"Our little experiment puts the question beyond doubt, Brother Leon—the drone is definitely tracking us."

"What shall we do?"

"We shall turn the tables, and track it. Let us aim for the main exit, but in a manner that suggests we are examining specific beds here and there upon our route. Come."

I led Brother Leon southwards through the vast greenhouse, stopping now and again to give the impression to our airborne tail that we were inspecting particular crops. I explained my plan to Brother Leon as we walked...

"By engaging the interest of its pilot, we will ensure that the drone follows us for as long as it can. Inevitably, however, the battery powering the device will become exhausted. The pilot will need to bring their baby home for recharging, so we need only to follow it by eye to see where it lands."

"But..."

I held up a hand to shush Brother Leon. I knew what she was going to say, and my natural modesty forbade that she should say it. *But that's incredibly brilliant, how did you think of it so quickly?* Or words to that effect. With another nod I indicated that we should continue our clever charade, and within ten minutes we had reached the main entrance, or, rather, exit, of the herbarium. The drone still hovered overhead.

"Now, Brother Leon, we approach the end game. Let us pretend to be making minute examinations of the fixtures near the exit, all the while keeping the corner of an eye upon the drone. As soon as we see it leave, we will run outside and see where it lands."

"But..."

I held up another forbidding hand. Now was not the time to indulge in fawning compliments. I was just about to tell Brother Leon that while I might be a genius, I was not a conceited one, when the drone crashed through the roof.

CHAPTER FORTY

In which Marco enters the crypt.

But that's what I was going to say," said Brother Leon, as I shook the splinters of stained glass off my habit. "Why would the perp give themselves away to save a drone worth a few hundred dollars? Surely they'd just let it crash when the battery died."

I felt an utter idiot. What I really needed was time to think up a witty rebuff to her tactless assertions. I don't suppose you could put the book down for half an hour? No, I thought not. To hide my embarrassment, I bent to examine the drone.

"No matter, Brother Leon. I had thought of the possibility, naturally, and the perp has played straight into my hands. We will simply dust this object for prints and DNA and whatnot, and..."

I stopped talking, because there was a noise I wasn't sure how to spell, like *whooerftt*, following which flames burst through the sides of the drone. Before I could gather enough of my wits to stop it, the fire burned the plastic shell of the device to a shapeless black blob.

I stared at the blob.

"Hmmmm. Just as I suspected. A self-destruct function. Clearly, Brother Leon, we are dealing with a foe of exceptional cunning. However, they will find they are no match for Marco Ocram. Come."

I strode purposefully from the herbarium, hoping to give Brother Leon the impression that I knew where I was going. We trudged through the snow towards the praesidium, where we were met by the abbot.

"Ah, Brother Marco, Brother Leon. I trust you have spent the afternoon performing the Lord's work. Brother Leon, if you could leave us, I must consult with Brother Marco in private."

Brother Leon bowed and withdrew. The abbot beckoned me to follow him along the corridor.

I found that our destination was to be his quarters, at the door of which he invited me to enter. His was an enormous penthouse cell, with stunning views of Mount Clark. It was decorated and furnished with no regard to cost, and entirely in conflict with at least nine of the ten tenets of feng shui. The abbot led us over a series of ancient oriental rugs to the bar, where he mixed a stiff Manhattan for himself, and a Moscow Mule mocktail for me.

"To the Lord's health."

We raised our glasses to the abbot's holy toast and retired to the lounge, where an array of easels bore a range of paintings, each with a yuletide theme.

"How charming. Are these your work, Your Sublimity?"

"No, no, Brother Marco—they are submissions from the brethren for the annual Christmas card competition. Here you see the shortlisted entries, from which I will choose five to become the subjects of the abbey's Christmas cards. It is a valuable honour to be chosen, as the artist receives ten percent of the profits as a royalty."

I walked from easel to easel, eyeing the pictures. Each seemed the indifferent work of the tiro or the talentless, until I reached one that shone among the mediocrity like an especially bright advent candle. The subject of this glorious artwork was entirely abstract and superficially meaningless—much like a certain author's books—but to the trained eye the artist's technique was instantly recognisable, the staccato-like attack of the brush creating an entirely distinctive melange of pointilistic and impasto treatments.

"I see you are admiring Brother Crispin's work. He has an exceptional talent, has he not?"

"Indeed, Your Magnificence."

So, Brother Crispin was the artist who had modified the cave painting. Hmmmm. I paused, to let the readers absorb the significance of my conclusion, before writing that the abbot invited me to settle upon an antique Chinese sofa in quilted panda-skin.

"Tell me, Brother Marco, what have you learned about the mysterious events at the abbey?"

I decided it wasn't possible to recap all the absurd nonsense from the last forty chapters, so I responded in vague and general terms.

"There is much evil at work, Your Sublimity. The devil himself could not concoct a more sinister brew. Not since the eight aberrations of Antioch has there been such degeneracy."

The abbot's expression suggested he was unimpressed by my reply. I couldn't blame him—I thought it was rubbish myself. I changed the subject, to divert him from his critical thoughts...

"Can I ask, Your Marvelosity, whether the ordinances of the abbey permit the flying of drones?"

"Drones? They are a curse in the wrong hands, Brother Marco. It is for that reason that drones may only be flown with the permission of the abbot."

"And have you given such permission recently?"

"Let me see."

The abbot walked to a bookcase beside his jukebox, and, feeling under one of the shelves for a hidden catch, he activated a mechanism that caused the bookcase to open away from the wall. Behind was a steel door fitted with every conceivable security device. It was at least two minutes before the abbot had completed the various steps to unlock it—tapping a nine digit code onto a pad, swiping a keycard, dialling a combination knob, pressing his finger against a fingerprint reader, having his iris scanned, donning the domed cap of a follicle counter, writing his signature on a digital pad, and, finally, turning a giant key.

When the thick steel door swung back on jewelled hinges, I saw beyond it a capacious strong-room. Judging by its contents, its purpose appeared to be that of preserving the abbot's secrets, rather than his treasures. There were no items of intrinsic monetary value—no jewellery, cash, bonds, property deeds, objet d'art, relics, and so on. Instead there were files, binders, ledgers, scrolls, codices and various envelopes sealed with wax. The abbot took from one of the many shelves within the vault a large, thick book, bound in hand-scalloped wildebeest hide—evidently a log of some sort. He flicked through its vellum pages. I savoured my Moscow Mule. Now we were getting somewhere.

"I have granted a total of four dispensations for the flying of drones," said the abbot.

"Four! Are you certain, Your Astoundingness?" I'd assumed he would have granted only one, and that it would lead me straight to a perp.

"Certainly, Brother Marco. The entries are in my own hand."

"To whom did you grant the dispensations, Your Holiness, and for what purpose?"

"I granted one to the ornithologist to observe the chicks in the nest of a pair of eagles, one to Brother Kaku to monitor the evolution of snowflakes during their descent from the heavens, one to the cellarer for maintaining a watch on the abbey's sheep when they are put out to pasture, and one to Brother George for a research project concerning lichen."

"Lichen?"

"Indeed, Brother Marco. I was surprised myself when the application was submitted for my approval. However, my brethren reminded me that lichen are some of the Lord's most overlooked handiwork. They grow in profusion over all the buildings of the abbey, and upon the trees and rocks of the surrounding woods, and yet how often do we stop to admire their beauty and variety? I have given permission for drones to be used to survey the distribution of the many species of lichen within the abbey and its surrounds."

Hmmm. It seemed like a pretty flimsy cover story to me. One thing was for sure—Brother George had flown the drone that crashed into the herbarium, and if he was looking for lichen on the roof then I'm William Shakespeare.

"And speaking of the Lord's beautiful handiwork," the abbot interrupted my thoughts, "where is your assistant, Sister Coma? I have not seen her all day. I would not wish her to be alone in the abbey, believing herself a neglected member of my flock."

"I suspect she will be at prayer somewhere, Your Imposingness. I will go to find her, and will be sure to let her know that your thoughts remain with her."

The abbot nodded dreamily, which I took as my opportunity to withdraw from his chambers before I had to write any more nonsense about Sister Coma. Speaking of whom, I would have sharp words to say to Como about leaving me to deal with deadly foes in the abbey while he wasted time on trivial administrative duties back at Police HQ. With such thoughts in mind, I strode along what I thought was the corridor to the reception, but found myself descending a flight of worn stone steps which led to a dark area below the abbey church.

The crypt!

That was one of the locations the secret key-card was programmed to access. Somewhere there would be a door protected by a digital lock. I searched about in the gloomy recesses between the giant stone columns that supported the church above. What caught my eye was some new trunking running high along the walls, trunking which appeared to contain unusually thick electric cables—far thicker, indeed, than would be required to supply the modest power needs of the abbey. What could be their purpose?

I traced the trunking for about a hundred feet, to where it met a turn in the wall. There, the cables disappeared through an opening recently cut into the ancient stonework.

I knew what was coming. Huge electric cables leading into a chamber within the crypt could mean only one thing. It was so obvious I didn't even need to type it. However, I knew Como would give me a hard time if I didn't follow proper police procedure and get evidence to back-up my conviction. I followed the wall through which the cables had disappeared. It led me into the darker depths of the crypt. The slap of my sandals on the stone floor echoed among the arches. I rounded another corner, and there was a heavy oak door. A sign carved in gothic script bore the instruction STRICTLY NO ADMITTANCE. Just as I had expected, there was a digital lock affixed to the jamb of the doorway. I rummaged in the folds of my habit for the key-card. I would open the door, take a few quick photographs of what I knew would be inside, then leave. No-one would be alerted, and I could continue my investigations of the unsuspecting perps. I was just about to swipe the key-card, when I heard the rustle of cloth behind me. I turned. In the gloom were two hooded figures. I couldn't make out their features, but their build and bearing told me they were Brothers Tony and Vinnie, the two thugs from the lab.

"I perceive you are lost, Brother Marco."

He was right, on several counts. I typed some mumbo jumbo to give myself time to think.

"Are we not all lost, Brother? Life is an earthly struggle to find the way to heaven."

Neither figure answered, which was fair enough. They stepped towards me, a disturbing degree of menace in their movements. Sensing imminent danger, I did the first stupid thing that came into my head, as usual. I swiped the card through the reader, yanked open the door, and slammed it hard behind me.

CHAPTER FORTY-ONE

In which the secret of the crypt is revealed.

I was in a chamber darker than the main body of the crypt had been, yet pinpointed with hundreds of red, green, and yellow lights, some steady, some blinking. When my eyes adjusted to the deeper gloom, I saw exactly what I had expected when I traced the path of the heavy cables—the chamber was a computer room, filled with row after row of racked servers. The air was heavy with the hum of countless small cooling fans, and the deeper noise of a powerful air-conditioning system. I strode down the walkway between the racks, and dodged around a corner as the space suddenly flooded with light. The two hooded figures had followed me into the chamber, and I was now their Herbert. Sorry, their quarry. Well they weren't going to take me easily. They were up against a foe of exceptional ingenuity, fiendish cunning, and a complete lack of inhibition when it came to inventing absurd plot twists.

Typing with gusto, and blatantly coping what I'd said about the herbarium, I wrote that the server room of the abbey formed a giant labyrinth, so complex that nine hardware engineers died in its construction, having lost their way among the racking and starved to death. Actually, that's nonsense, because they would have died of dehydration first, but can we please not get bogged down in spurious realism. Where was I...

The labyrinth had taken many decades to construct, so that the computers it housed were not of a uniform type—rather, they varied through the complex in accordance with the age of the their immediate surroundings. The most recently constructed parts had highly hyphenated equipment—cutting-edge servers with octo-core processors, over-duplexed bi-nano memory expansion, and gold-plated prongs on their power-connectors. As I walked deeper into the endless maze I encountered increasingly antiquated equipment, including a computer the size of a house with less power than my iPad. I must have been wandering for an hour or more when I turned between the tape cabinets of an ancient IBM and saw an elderly monk attending to some maintenance job. He did not turn from his work, but spoke thus:

"Who is it?"

Not very imaginative, but at least it was to the point, which made a nice change from the rambling nonsense the abbot was always spouting.

"I am Brother Marco of Ocram, a seeker of truth."

The elderly figure turned toward me, a look of astonishment on his grizzled face. There was a look of equal astonishment on my juvenile face as I saw that his eyes were completely frosted over. He was utterly blind.

"Brother Marco of Ocram!" He felt among the folds of his habit. "Here, please."

With a knobbly finger, he indicated a place where I might sign his braille copy of *The Awful Truth about the*

Herbert Quarry Affair. That ceremony completed, he explained who he was, thus saving me the bother...

"I am Brother Steve, the computerist—the only member of the brethren who knows the ways of the labyrinth. It is fortunate indeed that the good Lord guided you to meet me, otherwise you would surely have wandered between the computers until you perished of dehydration. The air in the computer room is very dry—unlike your jokes." He smiled at his little quip.

"Tell me, Brother Steve. You have no sight, so how is it you find your way within the devilish complexity of the maze?"

"Over the years that I have tended the machines my ears have become attuned to the nuanced differences between their sounds. Without wishing to commit the sin of vanity, I pride myself that I can distinguish between the individual computers more clearly than a sighted brother might."

It sounded an unlikely load of tosh to me, but I went along with it, the alternative seeming to be death by desiccation.

"What brings you to the labyrinth, Brother Marco?"

An instinct told me to be honest with the old man—the instinct of an exhausted writer who had lost the will to dissemble.

"There is evil in the abbey, Brother Steve. There have been seven deaths in as many days, none of them the work of the Lord. I am here to divine the hidden springs of malignity that are feeding the evil. I entered the labyrinth, not knowing it to be such, in order to escape pursuers intent on doing me harm."

"Then you are safe for the time, at least. None of the Brethren would risk penetrating the deeper labyrinth. Your pusuers will have abandoned their pursuit."

I might be physically safe, but I was beginning to worry for my mental health, with all this lunacy. I did my best to reassert a semblance of sanity by asking factual questions concerning the labyrinth. We would have a few sentences of padding, grounded in the exacting technical realism that characterised my best work.

"Tell me, Brother Steve, how is the computarium funded? The licence fees for the software on so many thousands of processors must amount to a holy fortune, leaving aside the cost of the electricity."

A faint smile lightened for a moment the dour features of Brother Steve.

"The abbot funds the electricity from his own purse. He carps about the expense endlessly. But we pay no licence fees, Brother Marco."

"None? Surely the abbot does not countenance the use of pirated software in the very heart of such a place of holiness?"

"No, Brother Marco, we are not pirates. All of the software running within the computarium has been written here, at the abbey."

"All of it? But...but..." I considered the huge range of computer processors I had witnessed in just the small part of the labyrinth I had penetrated so far. The sheer variety of operating systems and other utilities required to manage such a vast collection of computers was unimaginable. "But how can you possibly maintain so many programmes?"

"Programmes? You speak of plurality, where here there is only singularity—the unity of the Lord."

"You mean..." I could barely believe what I was about to type.

"There is only one programme."

So much for exacting technical realism. Well, I'd typed it now, so I'd just have to go along with it...

"Only one programme? But...but..." I was lost for words for the second time in only six paragraphs—a record even for me. I considered the technical challenges of writing a single programme for so many incompatible systems. "How is it done?"

"The systems are indeed all different," said Brother Steve, fondly stroking the cabinet of a 1970's Sperry, "but they all deal ultimately with zeros and ones, as different as heaven and hell. It is simply a matter of writing protocol converters, by means of which we compile our high level code into versions suitable for each target environment."

I picked up on a significant word...

"We?"

"You did not imagine, Brother Marco, that the programme could be the work of one person. Ha!" He laughed at the absurdity of the idea. "The programming is a communal activity, carried out by those members of the abbey with an interest in computing—mainly members of the Nerd order. We hold a coding bee every second Tuesday after matins."

I had an exciting thought.

"Tell me, Brother Steve, is the abbot a member of your coding circle?"

Brother Steve grunted. "Indeed not, Brother Marco— the abbot would not know one end of a computer from the other. He is entirely ignorant of matters technical."

So that was a bit of a let-down. I had another exciting thought—tens of chapters ago, I had inexplicably written that the CVs of the other members of the elder council mentioned various esoteric computing qualifications...

"What of the other members of the elder council? Did they participate in your coding bees?"

"Indeed—they are all devout and expert coders, never missing a meeting of our dedicated group."

That was more like it. I probed further.

"And what purpose does the programme serve?"

"Who knows? The programme is too complex for any single mind to understand. Each member of our coding circle is free to inject their own purpose into our communal effort."

I rolled up my sleeves—metaphorically, I mean, as my habit was technically sleeveless. Something as fishy as a million marlins was going on here, and I was just the person to find out what.

"Might I see the programme? You have a print-out, I assume, for back-up purposes."

"Indeed, Brother Marco, but not here; the print-out is kept where all the abbey's most sacred scripts are stored—in the library."

The library! I could have wept with relief. Here we were, fifty three thousand words after the fire alarm has stopped me from going to the library, and now at last the mindless digressions might be over. I would proceed to the library, where surely the answer to the mystery would be found.

"Brother Steve—at the risk of disturbing your work, could I ask you please to guide me to an exit from the labyrinth? Preferably not the one which leads to the crypt, as my pursuers might still be lurking there."

"As you wish it, Brother Marco. There is an exit by the reception area in the praesidium. Follow me."

As Brother Steve led me through turn after turn among the endless paths, I wondered whether I should include some gratuitous descriptions of the labyrinth, typing, perhaps, of the many bundles of cables, neatly tied and labelled, or the huge stacks of floppy disks that appeared here and there, or the marvellous variety of video display units, ranging from green screens with deplorably low refresh-rates to top-of-the-range 'Amoled' touch-screens, or the echo of our footfalls on the hollow floor, underneath which ran countless miles of ducting, or the abbey's unsurpassed collection of 'Dilbert' cartoon strips, which had been pinned to the acoustic screens which sub-divided the area of the computarium. I decided the readers would probably spot that it was just padding, so I left it out.

I thanked Brother Steve as he let me out of the computarium via a secret passage leading to a concealed door behind the leaflet racks in the reception area, where, by some utterly implausible coincidence, Como was kicking the snow off his sandals.

"Como!" I ran over and patted his beefy back. I'd meant to give him a hard time about leaving me to struggle on my own against the forces of evil, but I was too pleased to see him. "How's tricks?"

"Don't ask, Writer. I just got here after a hell of a day catching up on all the work I've been stopped from doing by helping you."

"Helping me? That's rich. I'm helping you, don't forget."

"Your idea of help and my idea of help are two different things, Writer. So what 'helpful' things have you been up to while I've been working my ass off in the office?"

I thought back to everything that had happened since Como told me to leave the key under his mat. It was too much to even try to summarise.

"It's a bit complicated, Como, but I figure I'm close to blowing the lid right off the mystery. I just need to get into the library. You wanna come with me, or hang around waiting for the abbot to come and offer special religious coaching to Sister Coma?"

"That's a harder choice than you think. It might be more fun to slap down the abbot than put up with the sort of nonsense I'd find in the library with you."

"Como! Don't be such a grump. Come on."

I was just heading to the praesidium door when the bell rang for vespas.

CHAPTER FORTY-TWO

In which Marco scoots after a bad gang.

Damn, it's vespas." I cursed in an unmonkly way, inventing the word unmonkly in my frustration. "We'll have to do the library later."

"What's vespas?"

"Do you know aught about monastic life, Como?"

"I know these freakin' shirts itch." Como scratched among the folds of his capacious robe.

"Vespas, Como, is that hour of the monastic day at which the brethren gather to tour the vicinity of the abbey on motor scooters. It is an ancient and venerable tradition, so we will attract suspicion if we do not participate in a devoted manner. Besides, the vesparium is one of the places on the list of digital locks, so we can despatch two avians with one stone by checking Brother Glaxo's key-card while we are there."

"Where? D'you know where the vesparium is?"

It was a good question. I had foolishly left in the potting shed the leaflet containing the map of the abbey. I was about to write that there were maps on illuminated notice boards throughout the complex, one of which was conveniently next to where we stood, when I thought of a simpler solution.

"We shall just follow the other brethren. Come, Como."

Streams of hooded figures were converging on a cinder path that led to the rear of the praesidium. We followed the path down to the valley floor, where a number of tunnels had been bored into the foot of the cliff upon which the praesidium had been built. The tunnels had been put to various purposes associated with the running of the abbey—staff parking, the storage of props for the Christmas pantomime, and so on. One of the tunnels was the destination for the shuffling line of monks. Parked along its right-hand wall was a swarm of the famous Italian scooters, featuring models of every vintage and colour. The air was thick with the fumes from the little machines and with the idling chatter of their engines and of the monks preparing to ride them.

We gathered through careful observation that each machine carried a plaque with the name of the monk to whom it was assigned, so we sauntered along the line until we found ours. Mine was an unremarkable utilitarian model from the 1980s, in ivory with a black leatherette seat. Como's, however, was a *Speziale* from 1963, in candy pink with a faux leopard-skin seat and handlebar grips. We pulled our allotted machines from their stands, primed their carburettors and kicked them to life.

"Let's separate," I shouted at Como, above the noise of the revving engines. "Keep an eye open for anything suspicious."

Como nodded his agreement and swung his leg over his undersized steed, his knees almost touching the handlebars. He wobbled as the motor of his machine struggled against the combined weight of the scooter and its giant rider. I followed his progress until my eye was caught by some disreputable-looking monks still gathered around their machines just outside the mouth of the tunnel. They had a decidedly shifty apperance. Their greasy habits had death's head logos embroidered across the back. Their beards were long. Their hair was in pony tails. They each wore reflecting sunglasses, and thick-soled sandals with chromed steel studs in the straps. Their scooters had been highly modified, with short, upturned exhaust pipes, ape-hanger handlebars, lowered seats, raked forks, cruciform wing-mirrors, and ultra-wide rear tyres, the treads of which were formed in a pattern of interlocking daggers. They had their names painted in red and white gothic letters upon the fairings of the scooters—names such as *Brother Evil*, and *Friar Fright*.

I couldn't say exactly why, but something about them made me suspect they were up to no good. Perhaps they were linked to the organised crime afoot in the abbey.

I sensed that one of the group had noticed my surveillance, as they turned to look in my direction. I bent to my machine and pretended to be tinkering with its crankshaft or whatever, maintaining my observations through a wing mirror. They finished their cigarettes and beer, and after a few minor scuffles they moved off, the low-frequency thud of their poorly-muffled engines booming down the valley. I waited until they were a hundred yards ahead before following.

For the first mile or so they followed the same narrow road as the rest of the monks, but then forked left. The track they had taken wound up into the forest, hugging the precipitous side of the valley. I kept my distance—the stupid joke I made about their dagger tyre treads allowed me to follow their distinctive tracks in the snow with no fear of losing them. The road became ever more dangerous, with blind bends swerving from sheer drops. On the surface of compacted snow, my rear-end was continually threatening to break free, so I took most of the bends with my feet skimming the snow in case I had to stop myself from toppling.

Up and up we went. I found my mind wandering into thoughts of what might happen next. Perhaps I would trace the baddies to a secret tryst with members of a shadowy crime syndicate. Perhaps they would descend the other side of the mountains and hold up a bank. Perhaps I would find them menacing a beautiful woman, and I would arrive like an avenging angel, scattering her assailants with the force of my commanding personality. Perhaps I would lower a hand to help her onto the seat behind me, and whisk her away to a luxurious hotel where her side of the conversation would weave between questions about my writing and praise for my gallantry. Perhaps...

I was still speculating when I rounded a particularly tight bend with my sandaled feet extended, looking a little like Audrey Hepburn on her bike in *Roman Holiday*, to see the be-scootered riders fanned out ahead of me to block my path.

I pulled the brake as hard as I safely could on the icy road, and slid to a wobbly stop at more or less the centre of a semi-circle of Vespas. Out of a path through the trees to my left, four riders broke cover and circled behind me, cutting off my retreat. To my right was the ravine—almost a sheer drop. The central rider ahead of me brought his machine forward and stopped a few paces away, his heavy sandals crushing the snow. I could see tattoos on his knuckles—on the left hand they spelled *HATE*, while on the right hand they spelled *HATE*. Not much comfort there then. The red and white Gothic script on either side of his scooter's fairing announced him as Brother Orville.

Orville—where had I heard that name recently?

Brother Orville threw back his cowl, and suddenly I knew where I'd heard the name. The family resemblance was unmistakeable. It was Orville McGee.

CHAPTER FORTY-THREE

In which Marco prepares for an exit in the manner of a Shakespearian character.

Orville McGee sat back on his Vespa, winding one end of a bicycle chain around a meaty fist.

"I've done a lot of praying, Ocram—a whole lot of praying that some day I'd find you, and get even for what you did to the McGees; but never in all my prayers did I think you'd be crazy enough to lay it on a plate like this."

He was right. On reflection it did seem a bit rash to have followed the rough-looking riders on my own. But in fairness, when I started to write this whole sorry escapade, I didn't know their leader was going to turn out to be a McGee—especially not the one McGee who hated me even more than all the other McGees did.

"What were you gonna do next, Ocram—frame Stella? She said you and Galahad were after Uncle Thaddeus—a poor old guy like that. You're sick, Ocram. The elders are right—you need putting down."

Before I could take-in the significance of his reference to Stella and the elders, Orville kicked his machine forward and drove past me, swiping the bicycle chain at my face. I had to drag my Vespa sideways to escape the lash. Another of the riders kicked forward his machine, chain in hand, and followed his leader, again just missing my face with a vicious swipe. One after another, the riders tormented me this way. Each time I flinched from a whipping, I was dragging the Vespa an inch or two closer to the edge of the icy road. When, at last, there was nowhere to go—I had to stumble off the machine and let it drop over the ravine.

Now the riders parked in an arc around me, each maybe fifteen yards away. Orville dismounted first, then the rest. Slowly they converged on me, each with a swishing chain. I remembered what people always said in such circumstances.

"You won't get away with it."

"Won't we?" Orville's voice was full of irony.

"They'll find the scooter. They'll know it's mine."

"And?"

Good question.

"And..."

They came closer.

"I used to be a boxer, you know."

They came closer.

"They'll see your tracks in the snow. They'll know you were here when it happened."

"We saw you skid off the edge, and we circled back to help."

Orville McGee tried a ranging swipe with his chain. The very tip of it cut my left wrist as I held my hands to my face.

"Ow!" I had a brainwave. At last I thought of a deterrent. "Chief Galahad won't believe you. You'll be interviewed by him."

That did it. They stopped dead, their chains dangling impotently. I wish I could paste in a photo, because I can't find the words to describe the looks on their stupid faces as it dawned on them that they would inevitably find themselves alone in a police interview room with Como. And as everyone knows from reading my books, no-one wants to be alone in a police interview room with Como.

Warily they stepped back from me, slowly and evenly, as if I were some unstable menace they were anxious not to provoke. Then they turned and ran, throwing horrified glances over their shoulders. Some of them slipped as they reached their Vespas, and clawed themselves upright, frantically kicking their machines into life. The quiet mountain air was once again violated by the unnatural buzz and roar of the engines, as the whole cowardly crew went skidding down the track.

Ha! I rubbed my hands with satisfaction as I watched the last of them disappear around the hillside. A little unbelievable, perhaps, but I had written myself out of a tight spot without having to fall back on some utterly ridiculous twist about earthquakes etc. Yes, all in all it wasn't a bad effort, and I could keep the utterly ridiculous twist for when I really needed it. I knocked the gathering snow off the sleeves of my habit, and was just inspecting the cut on my wrist when a noise behind me caused me to spin.

It hadn't been the threat of Como that had caused McGee and his cronies to scarper. Standing a good foot taller than even Como, its massive paws in the air, a giant bear roared at me.

CHAPTER FORTY-FOUR

In which it is down hill all the way.

Had the bear been, say, a hundred yards away, I might have been tempted to tease the reader with a few digressive paragraphs of an ursine nature. I might have written, for example, about bears' behavioural patterns, physical characteristics, diet, breeding cycle, and so on. I might have written about their geographic distribution, beginning with a world-wide viewpoint, then focusing progressively down through North America to the forested uplands around Clarkesville. I might have written about the sociological aspects of bears—their interrelationship with humans in the modern world. Or about the urban mythology of bear attacks and how to survive them. Or I might have written about this bear in particular, speculating, perhaps, on her recent loss of a cub in a confrontation with hunters, her resulting hatred of human kind, her hunger for soft, warm flesh, and so on. But she was about ten yards away, so I didn't have time for any of that nonsense.

The bear reared again, waving her huge front paws to show the long sturdy claws that would soon make mincemeat of me. If she was trying to intimidate me she was wasting her time—I was already as intimidated as it was possible to be. I did the only thing that might give me a slight chance to escape her slobbering jaws. Very slowly I untied the knot of my girdle and slipped out of my habit, shivering with both the cold and naked terror in just my horsehair undershirt. Holding the habit in front of me, my body paler than the snow, I advanced like an anaemic toreador.

"Nice bear. Nice bear."

Uttering unctuous words to sooth the beast, I took another horrified step. I was close enough to smell her scent—like fresh hay in an abattoir. She snarled an enraged snarl, steam puffing from her capacious throat, the throat down which parts of the Ocram limbs and torso might soon be ingested. I took one more step. It was all a question of timing. Now...

As the bear swung a huge paw for me, I threw my habit over her face. I didn't stop to watch her react. I ran. I'd heard the old tales about bears running twice as fast as humans— and that was fit humans, not someone with a middle-ear problem, running over snow in sandals—but what else could I do? I ran down into the trees. Maybe the bear would be slower weaving between obstacles. Twigs of spruce and pine whipped my skin, but I felt nothing. I ran and ran and ran and ran and ran. The ground fell more steeply now, so my running was more a series of a falls separated by straight-legged rebounds. I could no longer stop myself when directly ahead appeared a stream running fast and straight between sheer banks. It was perhaps only six feet across, but it intercepted my path at such an angle that even my most energetic final bound could not carry me across it, and I plunged into the shocking coldness of its rushing waters.

I touched bottom then quickly surfaced. The water was not deep—I could brush the bed with my feet—but its speed was irresistible. I was being whipped down the hillside at perhaps ten miles an hour in a channel that was evidently man made.

The log flume!

I must have hit the old log flume! God bless Nanny McGee! I could have kissed her. I spun in the water and looked back upstream. Thankfully there was no gigantic bear in pursuit, but a sudden blow to the back of my leg reminded me of the new danger I faced as I was washed down the channel with who knew what hazards waiting to hit me under the surface. I turned onto my back, my head upstream, my legs leading the way. If I was going to crash into anything I'd rather do it with my feet than my skull. I was breathing in rapid panicky gulps. My body was reacting to the temperature of the icy waters. I felt curiously detached. The question of what might happen to me in this mad hurtling downhill rush—whether I might be smashed into a tree wedged across the flume, or sucked into some abandoned sluice—seemed abstract and academic. If I died I died. Physical feeling was leaving me. The corporeal Marco Ocram was fading. My eyes registered my passage under the green-black canopy of the trees, a surreal spectacle from my unique vantage point. I was starting to hallucinate. The trees seemed to be waving me on with the frond-like extremities of their snow-laden branches. Hurry, they seemed to say. Eternity awaits. The current had slowed now, the stream broadening. I spun slowly around, my body following some transient eddy, so that now my feet pointed upstream. Above my blue-white toes I could see the line of the plume retreating up and across the hillside.

I couldn't say how long it had been before I realised that I was no longer moving, that the keel of my body had slid softly into the muddy fringes of a small lake. With the last of my strength, I turned onto my belly and squelched out of the water like some albino amphibian. The movement of my limbs helped unthicken my congealing blood. The air was colder than the water had been. I shivered painfully. After crawling a few yards that seemed like a mile, I had generated sufficient blood flow to risk standing, which I did with the help of a birch sapling. On trembling legs I glanced back—almost a thousand words without a joke. I rubbed my arms to restore my spirits, and looked around.

I seemed to be in exactly the sort of run-down timber yard I'd imagined before Como had driven me into Stella McGee's lumber processing plant. This must be the original McGee mill. I suddenly felt very conspicuous. What if there were more McGees about? My horsehair shirt wasn't quite long enough to obscure the shrunken state of my delicate portions, which appeared to be trying to hibernate in the extreme cold. Most of me was covered in oozing slime. I could just imagine the ridicule to which I would be exposed if a party of McGees found me.

Holding the hem of my shirt as low as I could get it, I explored the old mill buildings, hoping to find some old sacking or tarpaulin I could take to make a cloak. I passed what seemed to have been an office of sorts, and then a storage barn, the roof of which had partly collapsed. The next building had a well-rusted pick-up truck sheltering under years of dust. I climbed inside and tried the starter, but it was as lifeless as my... well, let's just say it was lifeless. I was wondering what might be in the other run-down sheds when I became aware of a low background hum I could just make out against the sound of the stream. It sounded like an engine, and seemed to be coming from a hut about a hundred yards away. There were no human footprints in the snow, and no visible lights, so I assumed I had the place to myself. Emboldened by the thought, I kicked my way through the powdery snow towards the hut, the hum swelling as I approached. The hut's only door was padlocked, but I didn't need to get inside to figure out what was what. The signs were unmistakeable. From a vent just below the eaves, condensing water vapour wisped off into the night. There was a heavy smell of diesel. Clearly a generator was running in the hut. Two cables came through the rear of the hut—one thick, one thin—and were clipped up a wooden pole about twenty feet tall, at the top of which a drooping wire carried them across to what appeared to be the rusting tower of an old windmill, now adapted for another purpose. The cables followed the criss-cross members of the tower to its top, where I could see something I recognised at once—the antenna of a mobile phone cell. It was as I was standing there, looking up at the antenna, wondering why anyone would maintain a mobile phone base-station in a shed in the middle of nowhere, that I first heard the approaching vehicle.

CHAPTER FORTY-FIVE

In which Marco has a miraculous escape from the frying pan.

I was going to start the chapter with the words *I froze*, but it seemed such a stupid thing to say standing knee deep in snow wearing nothing but a wet horsehair shirt. Besides, I only froze for a moment, after which I started banging my head against the wall of the shed. Why did I keep writing myself into these embarrassing predicaments? Well, it was too late for second thoughts—or even first ones—I'd just have to make the most of it.

Headlamps were now sweeping jerkily across the farther quarter of the site as the vehicle made its way down the track. Any moment now they'd pick out the shed, and an oddly clad intruder smeared in mud next to it. I moved round to the back of the shed and crouched against it, immediately wishing I hadn't crouched, as my dangling portions made contact with the snow.

The light grew brighter, and the noise louder. I knew then that the vehicle had to be heading for the shed—the only building still in use on the site. My deduction was confirmed when the headlights stopped moving, the sound of the motor faded to an idle, and two doors opened and slammed shut. I heard voices—gruff male voices—cursing the snow. I gathered they were here on some routine visit connected with the maintenance of the generator. With luck they would complete their work and go. I imagined them going to the rear of their vehicle, raising the tailgate, extracting their boxes of tools, then each of them trudging to the shed, tool-box in one hand, a flashlight in the other, its beam yellowing the white purity of the virgin snow.

The virgin snow!

At the very moment I realised they would see my tracks in the snow, they saw my tracks in the snow. Several sounds told me so. One was the dropping of tool-boxes, one was a change in the tone of their voices, from resentful tedium to aggressive alarm, and one was the unmistakable sound of guns being cocked. Before I had a chance to let the next thing come into my head, the light of a powerful torch swept around the back of the shed and straight into my eyes.

"Stand up!"

It was a voice used to issuing orders. I stood—not quite completely up, but bent enough to hold the hem of my horsehair shirt below the tops of my thighs.

"Put your hands up!"

I put one of them up, palm forward in a gesture of harmless pacification. Not a sufficiently clear gesture, as it turned out.

"Both of them, or I'll shoot."

I could have cried. I raised both hands. The hem of my horsehair shirt rose in sympathy, betraying the shrunken shame of my dangling parts—dangling parts still caked with compressed snow.

The flashlight beams dipped from my face to my midriff. I stood there, trying to muster some vestigial trace of dignity, while the air was filled with coarse jests at the expense of my shrivelled anatomy. Thankfully my face was sufficiently daubed with mud, so at least I could suffer in anonymity.

"Hey, Walt," said one of my captors, between the tears of his laughter. "You know the last time I saw something as pathetic as that?"

Walt was too creased with laughter to do more than wave his gun by way of reply.

"Those pictures of that asshole Ocram in Panama! Haw haw haw haw haw haw."

He was referring, of course, to the episode in *The Awful Truth about The Sushing Prize*, when I had been caught by Tom Cruise's minders sitting with my pants down in a ladies toilet disguised as Tom. They dunked me in the lavatory bowl, flushed it on me, and dumped me in the street in front of the waiting paparazzi, who lost no time in snapping close-ups of my privates. The pictures had made front pages world-wide. Barney told me it was good exposure, but it wasn't the type of exposure I relished. However, the memory of the pictures clearly tickled my tormentors.

"Hey—maybe he's Ocram's brother," said one. "Haw haw haw haw haw."

"Yeah—his little brother!" quipped the other. "Haw haw haw haw haw haw haw haw."

This time they laughed so much that Walt lost his footing, fell back against the shed, and accidentally discharged his gun, the report from which brought down an entire roof-full of snow to engulf the pair of them.

I ran.

I ran toward the headlights of their vehicle. It was a four-wheel-drive pick-up with a crew cab. They'd left the engine running. I leapt in, the warmth of the seat feeling like a fire against my frozen externalities. I locked the doors, reversed in a tight semicircle, and tore off down the track. In the mirror, I could see two snow-covered figures receding, their arms waving in gestures of impotent fury. Ha! That would teach them to mess with Marco Ocram. Suckers.

I smacked the rim of the steering wheel to betoken my jubilance. At last this ridiculous digression was over, and I could get back to the main strand of my plot. Having adjusted the nozzles of the air vents to direct a reviving stream of warmth to my middle portions, I was just starting to puzzle over the workings of the sat-nav when something hard and gun-like pressed into the back of my neck.

"Stop right now or I'll blow your freaking brains out."

It was a voice I knew. A voice I'd last heard against the noise of an electric-blue helicopter.

CHAPTER FORTY-SIX

*In which Marco conveniently remembers something he
forgot to mention several chapters ago.*

H*e just writes the first thing that comes into his head*, the
critics scoff, *how easy must that be?*

Easy? Easy? Put yourself in my snow-caked sandals for
a moment, and let me know if it seems *easy*. Indeed, if ever
you find yourself in a bar, perhaps, or a book-club meeting,
and some ignoramus with a Neanderthal brow ventures the
brainless opinion that writing like Marco Ocram is easy,
grab the nitwit by the scruff of the neck and rub his face in
the concluding paragraphs of Chapter Forty Five of *The
Awful Truth about the Name of the Rose*. How many other
authors would have written themselves into my harrowing
experiences in the old mill, and, having done so, allowed
Stella McGee to be sitting with a gun in the back of the
vehicle in which they were just about to make a getaway to
warmth and comfort? I can tell you how many—as many as
you can count on the fingers of one foot. I, however, have
the commitment of the true artist, and will allow no extreme
of personal discomfort to prevent me from writing the next

thing that comes into my head. Thus are brilliant stories born.

Accordingly, I put my hands in the air and let the pick-up coast to a stop in a drift of snow.

"Let's just rest here nice and easy 'til the boys arrive," said Stella McGee, her gun no longer resting against the back of my head.

I rested there nice and easy, savouring the feel of the warm air from the dashboard vents, knowing it might be the last warm air I would feel for a while. Through the mirror I saw the boys coming along the lane. As I had hoped, they walked in the tracks left by the pick-up rather than waste effort pushing through the deep snow either side. What Stella didn't know was that I'd knocked the gears into reverse and was sitting with my foot on the clutch. The boys were about twenty paces away. Fifteen... Ten... Five... Now!

I floored the gas and yanked my foot off the clutch. The pick-up reared like a reversing kangaroo. Stella McGee flopped between the front seats, her gun rattling into the passenger foot-well. I heard and felt the boys meeting the tailgate of the pick-up, but I didn't spare the time to look. Leaving the truck trundling in reverse, I pushed the door wide open and belly-flopped into the snow.

Ooomph!

Winded by the impact, and nurturing a potential crop of chilblains in my private area, I crawled to my knees then hopped into the trees, wondering why I hadn't grabbed Stella's gun. Depending on the state of the boys after their impact with the truck, I might have a few minutes before they started following my trail in the snow, then I'd be the proverbial seated duck—a shivering blue one. Think, Marco, think! As I stumbled randomly through the snow, I clutched the leather pouch on the cord around my neck. The comfort and inspiration I drew from the feel of the special pen was like an injection of some magical elixir.

Immediately, I saw an unnatural outline among the trees. It was... yes... it was a concrete pylon for a ski-lift—the ski-lift Stella McGee had mentioned in our helicopter tour. The engine house must be close by. I traced the line of the overhead wire down the hill. There was a low concrete structure—the building from which the ski-lift was powered and controlled. I leapt toward it through the snow, like a caribou chased by wolves, trying to remember whether Stella McGee really had mentioned the ski-lift on our helicopter tour or whether I'd just imagined it. Okay, maybe she hadn't—but does it matter? I'm freezing to death, so can we please all just pretend she mentioned it. And, now I think about it, can we please pretend she said it was still scrupulously maintained by the Clarkesville County Mountain Rescue Volunteers for the purpose of facilitating the descent of casualties, and she had conveniently described to me the manner of its operation. Good. Now, where were we? Oh, yes...

At a sweeping glance my agile mind took in the features of the winding room. It was just as Stella had described—a single lever controlled the movement of the system, directing an outflow from a fast-flowing stream onto one side or another of a paddle wheel, the chosen side determining the direction in which the chairs of the ski-lift circulated. The complex mechanism was gleaming with recently applied oil and grease. I praised the Clarkesville County Mountain Rescue Volunteers. Such selflessness. Such devotion to ones fellow humans. Such foresight. As soon as I got out of this mess there'd be a big check on the way to their HQ. What might they do with my huge endowment? A new Marco Ocram wing on the winch house, perhaps, providing every conceivable amenity for the ski-lift maintenance crew.

Curtailing my philanthropic speculations, I heaved on the lever. It wouldn't move! It was padlocked just above its pivot. I cursed the busybodies of the Clarkesville County Mountain Rescue Volunteers. What if it had been an emergency? How were casualties to be brought down the mountain with a padlocked lever? Through the trees I saw the glint of torchlight. My head-start had been shorter than I'd hoped. Then I saw it. A yellow and black box at shoulder height on the rear wall of the winch-house, emblazoned with the legend *In Emergency, Break Glass.*

It was an emergency. I broke the glass.

In seconds I'd extracted the key and undone the padlock, hurling it aside. I yanked the lever. A water-worn oak baffle swung round into the channel, diverting a solid spume of water onto the paddles of the wheel. Slowly the machinery responded to the flow. The trusty waterwheel turned a heavy square axle hewed out of a giant log of straight-grained hemlock. The axle drove a crown pinion, cunningly linked to a sequence of synchromesh gears ground to the most exacting tolerances. The gearbox turned a complementary pair of offset lay-shafts to which a helical worm-drive with centrifugal governors was connected by a tight-fitting gudgeon pin stamped in three places to show its rated breaking stress. The worm drive engaged an endless mobial screw which directly drove the main cast-aluminium bull-wheel around which the hawser of the ski-lift was tensioned by a system of weights and pulleys. In moments the ski-lift was up to speed. My heart rejoiced to think I would soon be scooped out of this horror and conveyed back to the abbey.

But wait! What was to stop Stella's thugs from simply switching the flow of the water to the other side of the paddle-wheel to reverse the circulation of the chairs? I could picture them making more of their crude jests as I was carried straight into their arms, so to speak. I ran back to the lever. It was a sturdy pole of Ash held by a bolt in a steel socket. I quickly spun off the scrupulously oiled nut, extracted the bolt, and twisted the pole out of its socket. I would carry the pole with me and see that it was returned to the mountain rescue people along with my check.

Dashing to the platform from which the chairs of the ski-lift could be accessed, I grabbed a hi viz tabard that had been hanging from a nail, knotting it around me like a dayglow diaper. It had the words *DUTY MANAGER'S BRAKE ASSISTANT* printed upon it. Perhaps I would add an extra thousand dollars to the endowment to provide for a new tabard to be procured on an annual basis, with a tasteful embroidered badge bearing the logo of my charitable foundation, possibly with...

Here came the next chair.

I brushed the thick of the snow from its seat and jumped aboard, clutching the Ash pole with one frozen hand and the upright of the chair with the other. Swaying slightly, the chair rose from the platform and was soon up among the treetops, winging me ever farther from McGee territory. Down at the winch-house, the beams of the torches flicked this way and that, sometimes flashing up the hillside towards me, but they were too late. I was safe.

Safe?

With horrified eyes I glanced down at what had now become at least a fifty foot drop below the chair, the chair that the idiots of the Clarkesville County Mountain Rescue Volunteers hadn't seen fit to equip with a harness, or even a restraining bar. My inner lemming was having a field day. If I were just to relax the grip of my hand and slide forward I would plunge to certain death.

I cursed.

I cursed Como for talking me into this stupid story. I scrolled back to the start. There, in black and white, were his very words: *It's just what you said you needed—complete rest.*

I cursed.

I cursed myself for believing him, for listening to Herbert Quarry, for writing the first things that came into my head without a thought for their consequences. Why had I written that this was a simple chair-lift, when with five minutes on Wikipedia I could have cut and paste an entire chapter on the workings of some complex overhead transportation system with luxurious heated gondolas? Why hadn't I even had the brains to write that the cabinet containing the key to the lever had also contained other basic items for use in emergency? A space-foil blanket, perhaps, or glucose pills. Sheepskin slippers. A dressing gown. Thermal mittens. A hot water bottle, with pre-installed water kept permanently hot by a thermostatically controlled probe. A sleeping bag quilted with finest armpit wool from virgin yaks.

My thinking spiralled in on itself with ever more ludicrous fantasies about the contents of the cabinet. I was losing what was left of my mind. I could see hundreds of lights ahead. Had Stella McGee sent an army of thugs ahead to await me? No—it was the abbey! The ground was getting closer. My sandals were starting to skim the snow. Time to bail out.

I flopped out of the chair face forward, hardly able to believe my ordeal was over. Using the Ash pole as a crutch,

I dragged myself to my frozen feet, and hobbled over the cobbled courtyard. Every part of me was rimed. Two figures were coming toward me, one slight, one huge.

"I don't know where you got your fancy shorts, Writer, but they suit you to a tee."

As Como bent forward to pick me up, I looked down at the loincloth I had fashioned out of the tabard. Snow and folds of cloth had obscured most of the letters of *DUTY MANAGER'S BRAKE ASSISTANT*.

Only *DUMBASS* remained.

CHAPTER FORTY-SEVEN

In which some loose ends are tied up.

I was so exhausted from my creative writing about my suffering in the snow, that I forget I was meant to be heading for the library, and I fast-forward to a quiet corner of the refectory, where Como, Brother Leon and I were huddled with our hoods up. We were eating dried bread, and digesting the news that Orville McGee had been taken into town by ambulance, having suffered a freak accident when Como had accidentally picked him up from behind, accidentally carried him to a stairwell, and accidentally thrown him down it. Como's actions had been a little unorthodox, perhaps, but I needed Orville out of the way, and didn't want to waste all our time on a load of boring police procedure about arresting him and whatnot. Instead, I decided to write a few paragraphs of explanatory dialogue to help me make sense of the plot...

"As I see it," I said, "Someone's making drugs and running them out of the abbey via the bothy."

"That doesn't stack-up," said Agent Dyson. "The bothy's too remote, and too isolated. If you want to make money from drugs you need to make them in volume—a much bigger volume than you could shift through occasional trips to the bothy."

"I agree," said Como. "And the wall safe we saw was too small. The bothy doesn't make any sense as a drop for routine shipments. Mind you, nothing else makes sense in this stupid book."

"So why would anyone bother to use the bothy?"

Como and Agent Dyson let my question hang. So much for helping me make sense of the plot—all they had done so far was to point out its contradictions. I tried another tack.

"What about the screen protectors? Where do they fit?"

No answer.

"And how's all this going-on under the nose of the abbot?"

No answer.

"And why's there a mobile phone base station down at the old mill, when the only other place within range is the abbey?"

No answer.

I can't be sure, but I think that asking questions to prompt discussion is known as the Socratic method, after a Greek philosopher. I pity poor old Socrat if he had the success I was having. No wonder he topped himself. Thankfully hemlock wasn't on the menu, or I'd have ordered a double.

"Speaking of mobile phones," said Agent Dyson, "I inspected the ones we took from the lab. None of them has been used recently to make calls, but they've all had a particular app installed in the last two days, and the app doesn't make any sense."

"Let me see."

I powered-up the proffered phone, and Agent Dyson pointed out the app, *RosaHi*. I tapped its icon—a stylised rose flower—to find the app contained only two menu choices. One, labelled *'My account'*, presented the usual tedious processes for setting up a payment card, and so on. The other, cryptically labelled *'Activate'*, seemed only to display a larger version of the rose logo. Agent Dyson had been right, for once—none of it made any sense.

"I think the abbot knows about the drugs," said Como, easily breaking the overcooked-noodle-like abstractions which passed for links in my chain of thought, "but he thinks there's something he doesn't know, and there's something that's stopping him finding out, which is why he's given you free rein to investigate. You dig something up, thinking you're investigating the suspicious deaths, when really you're being his puppet."

I'd never heard such preposterous nonsense. *Moi*, a puppet of the abbot?

"I suppose Como," I said—and if there was a touch of asperity in my tone, who could blame me?—"you'll be formulating some theory about the abbot having learned something in the confessional, and being bound by the sacred chains of confidentiality not to act upon what he has heard, he instead commissions me to report it to him independently."

I waggled my head in disbelief. How could such utter nonsense ever appear in print?

"You got a better theory?" said Como, flogging Socrat's dead horse.

"I've one," said Agent Dyson. "Suppose the abbot knows about the drugs, and he's in on it. But he's only been here two months. Suppose he thinks whoever's behind the drugs thing is holding back on him. Suppose he thinks he's being short changed. Why wouldn't he want someone investigating what's going on and reporting back to him in confidence?"

I put my finger on what was wrong with the Socratic method as a technique for developing a plot. Underlying it was the assumption that thought and logic were the intellectual tools to be taken from the box. What use did I have for them? It was like asking Picasso to paint by numbers. I brushed the breadcrumbs from my lap, wondering if my readers would appreciate the metaphor of sweeping away trivia, or whether I'd have to point it out to them. What I needed now were some bold impressionistic strokes. I raised my head. Across the refectory the abbot was stumbling towards us, his face red from his exertions.

"Brother Marco," he said between his gasps, "thank Heaven I have found you. I have been looking everywhere. You must come quickly. A figure has appeared on the footage from the security cameras."

CHAPTER FORTY-EIGHT

In which patience is not a virtue.

On the wall of the securarium the red second-hand serenely swept the face of the clock, the clock that had recorded two stultifying hours since we had first arrived in response to the abbot's breathless exhortations. A figure had indeed appeared on the footage from the security cameras, but it had appeared at the edge of the field of view. All we could see was that it was a hooded monk. Perhaps at some point the monk would turn to face one of the cameras—we didn't yet know, as we were having to review the tape a few frames at a time, between each glimpse removing the tape, dismantling its case, manually moving it forward, then reassembling its case. It was a torture. If we moved the tape forward too far between viewings, we might miss a momentary glimpse of the monk's features. If we moved it too little, we squandered yet more time with a wasted cycle. To think that there on the tape, possibly within a few inches of the frame we had just viewed, there might appear the face of the hooded figure, unmasking, perhaps, the very person responsible for triggering the hideous death of the herbalist—it was agonising.

Como, Brother Leon and I paced back and forth, punishing our sandals with our impatient tread. The air was thick with tension. At last we found a sequence of frames in which the head of the hooded figure was starting to turn to one of the nearer cameras. For each of us, life had become an unbearable succession of small angular movements—the advance of the second-hand, the twist of a pencil in the spool of the tape, the turns of the screws in the body of the cassette, the soles of our sandals twisting on the worn stone as we paced about the room. Finally we had reached the supreme moment at which the face of the figure was shown full-on upon the screen. We clustered around the monitor, straining to identify the features, but the image was just too vague. All the waiting had been in vain.

Collectively we cursed, smote table tops, punched walls, snapped all visible pencils, tore papers into shreds, dashed our drinking vessels into shards upon the stone floor, squeezed our scalps, kicked waste-baskets, tugged loose the knots of our ties—no, we weren't wearing ties—tugged loose the knots of our girdles, and beseeched the heavens. No clichéd activity betokening extreme disappointment and frustration was left unperformed. Then, at once, a radiant smile chased fury from my face.

"By Jiminy!" I smacked a fist against a palm. "Como, do you remember the Herbert Quarry Affair?"

It was a rhetorical question—of course he did.

"Do you remember at the trial, when Harry Rex Horgan showed the blown-up photographs?"

"By Jiminy yes!" Como smacked a bigger fist into a bigger palm, causing two coconuts to drop on the abbot.

"Quick, quick!" I snapped my fingers for one of the security monks to pass me their copy of *The Awful Truth about the Herbert Quarry Affair*. I flicked through it to find the chapter in which I used my legendary abilities as a hypnotist to regress Como to recall the details of the famous court case, the outcome of which hung upon vague images in a photograph. Herbert's fancy lawyer, Harry Rex Horgan, had commissioned a company to use a special technique to enlarge the photograph in a way that revealed its hidden details, and the technique was...I scanned the pages for the name of it...

"Chained pixel interpolation!"

The abbot crossed himself. "Good heavens, Brother Marco. What is this sorcery of which you speak?"

"Not sorcery, Your Superlative, but merely the appliance of science to photographic images. I believe we will solve this mystery before evensong. We need merely to apply the technique of chained pixel interpolation to the vague image of the monk, and I am certain that his identity will be revealed. If I may..."

Without awaiting the abbot's permission, I unplugged the screen of the security console, and connected my iPad as a substitute for it. With many years of experience in every aspect of information technology, it was the work of moments for me to bring up the blurred image of the monk's face and save it as an uncompressed bit-file with maximum colour depth and enhanced rendering meta-properties. All we needed now was a chained pixel interpolation app.

"Who knows the wifi code for the abbey?" I asked no-one in particular.

Nobody knew.

"I recall, Brother Marco, that the code is printed on the rear of the menus in the refectory."

Making no concessions to the abbot's superiority and dignity, I smote the desk with my fist.

"What are you waiting for? GET THAT CODE!"

We paced around the room until the breathless abbot returned with a copy of the menu. I entered the wifi code—666—and signed-in to my app-store account. It took four minutes. I checked the speed of the Internet connection—it was as fast as a dead snail in tight shoes. Another four minutes took us to the page showing the chained-pixel-interpolation apps. I picked the smallest one—thirty eight megabytes—and clicked to download it.

Time after time we stared at the clock. Time after time we paced about the room. Time after time we muttered exhortations to the gods of the Internet to speed the glacial flow of bits down the line. At last the download finished. My fingers atremble with excitement, I clicked the options to make the app perform its magick on the blurred image from the security camera. I could scarcely believe that we were now perhaps just seconds away from a momentous revelation—one that would reveal a pivotal clue about the death of the herbalist, a clue so decisive that the entire case could be sewn up before the celebrity opening.

The app having completed its task, the egg-timer on the screen of my iPad stopped spinning. Appropriately too, for indeed time seemed to stand still for us as we stared at the screen. Where there had been a vague blurred impression there was now a crystal clear rendition of the face of the hooded figure who had entered the herbarium shortly before the death of the herbalist. It was the face of...

...the herbalist.

CHAPTER FORTY-NINE

In which Como assembles his team to little effect.

Having repeated all the pencil-snapping and girdle-loosening to betoken our extreme frustration and disappointment at the inevitable anti-climax, we repaired to the refectory, where we decided to start a new chapter with a vote about next steps. It was a split vote, as it happened. Como voted to drag the elders down to police HQ and give them the third degree. Leona Dyson voted to flood the abbey with FBI agents. I voted to spend a week in the isolation tank in the abbey's spa complex.

I raised a hand to quell the fractious argument that broke out following the inconclusive poll. I announced to my characters that the time had come for that clichéd event I had been hoping to avoid, even though experience told me it would have to come sooner or later. Without further debate, therefore, we piled into my black Range Rover with tinted windows, drove directly to police HQ, ordered more pizzas and coffee than we could possibly consume, and plonked ourselves in Como's big conference room for a case conference.

Yes, yes, I know. It's dreadfully tedious. You expected better of me. If you wanted to read a boring police procedural, there are plenty of other writers who make a better job of it than I. Honestly, I did my best to avoid it. I'll try to make it as short as I can...

The conference room was crowded. Every member of Como's crack team had been allocated crucial investigative tasks I'd been too busy to write about earlier. Now was the time to reveal a series of new insights that would allow me to make sense of my hopelessly tangled plot. Como brought the meeting to order, and turned to a fresh sheet on his writing pad, ready to record the information his team was about to impart.

"Okay, what have we got? Let's go round the table. Kojak?"

Removing his lollipop, Kojak consulted his notebook. "We tracked the numbers on the phones taken from Donny and Jeb at the bothy. Mostly they're calls to unregistered mobiles, but there are several to the switchboard at Stella McGee's lumber yard. The Walther KKK's untraceable—its serial number's been filed off."

"Good work, Kojak. What about you, Ness?"

"Nothing yet, Chief."

"Columbo?"

"Nothing here either, Chief."

"Hutch?"

"Nothing yet, Chief."

"Cagney?"

"Nothing yet, Chief."

Como rolled his eyes. "Crockett—you got anything about Falconi yet?"

"Nothing yet, Chief."

"Drebin?"

"Nothing yet, Chief."

"Garibaldi?"

"Nothing yet, Chief."

"Lacey?"

"Nothing yet, Chief."

"McClane, what about you?"

"Nothing yet, Chief."

"Wallander?"

"Nothing yet, Chief."

Como threw his pad down in disgust at the lack of progress. "Jesus H Christ."

"Nothing yet, Chief."

Having completed the turn around the table, Como looked across at me with a less than affectionate expression. "Ok, you wasters, get out of here. I don't want to see any of you back in HQ until you've got something useful to report."

The abashed team shuffled out, while Como scratched his head with both hands.

"What now, Writer?"

It was a good question. I'd counted on his team throwing up some answers, but I hadn't managed to think of any for them to throw up. Typical. If you need something done, you have to do it yourself.

"What now, Como, is that we go back to doing this the hard way. Throw me those pens."

Como threw me the special pens that could be used to draw on the big glass screen that formed one side of the conference room.

"And throw me those photos too."

Como threw me my copy of the stack of photos that had been distributed to each of the conference participants. I shuffled through them until I found the one I wanted, and stuck it on the wall.

"This is Brother Wayne, the young novice found dead at the foot of the praesidium. What do we know about him?"

Three hours later, all of the photos were on the wall, and I'd drawn arrows between them to denote their logical linkages. Who said a second marriage was the triumph of hope over experience? They could have been talking about my case conferences with Como. Usually Como leads them, and they never throw up any new insights. So I thought that for a change I'd have a go at leading this one, but it didn't throw up any new insights either. We just ended up with the usual tangle of arrows that seemed to connect everything to everything else, increasing the sense of utter confusion we were feeling when confronted with a summary of all the nonsense of the last forty-odd chapters. I looked at my watch. It was late. With the big celebrity opening just a day away, I didn't see how I was going to wrap up the case beforehand. However, there was one last hope...

"Let's sleep on it," I said.

To judge by Como's lack of response, he already was.

CHAPTER FIFTY

In which Marco announces a theory to his stalwart comrades.

We were approaching the grand opening. The sky above the abbey was dark with helicopters, as the world's top celebrities flew in for the big event. No press were allowed inside the abbey, so across the valley the news-hungry media had installed cameras equipped with the most powerful telephoto lenses, all currently focussed upon the red carpet from the abbey's helipad. Junior monks with brooms were engaged in a constant battle with the increasingly heavy snow, snow that was settling on the carpet as fast as it could be swept away. I took in all this with a glance through the unglazed window of my cell, as I brushed my teeth, nudged my afro into shape, and completed the other personal tasks of the impeccably groomed monk with important business afoot.

The important business in my case was, of course, the grand denouement. In the next twenty four hours the case would be solved, the villains arrested, and I would become free once more to experience the overdue period of complete rest that the doctor had ordered on Page One.

There. I settled my girdle at a raffish angle, and was ready to face the world. I checked the time. Exactly three minutes before my scheduled meeting with Como and Brother Leon. I shouldered my satchel and headed for the refectory.

My comrades were hunched over a corner table, picking at their breakfast in a desultory manner. Was it nerves? Excitement? The thrill of appearing in the closing chapters of what was sure to be a new mega-seller? I slid onto the bench next to Como's huge bulk.

"Well, mon braves, are we all geed-up and ready to kick ass?"

Como pulled off a piece of his dried bread, and flicked it through a nearby window.

"What makes you think we're gonna be kicking any asses, Writer? The only ass damage we're likely to see is from sitting on these stupid benches day after day and getting nowhere."

"Now, now, Como; do not let your natural sunny disposition be o'ershadowed by circumstance," I said, leaving out the v in an attempt to sound poetic. "I told you we should sleep on it, and, having followed that advice, I have a theory."

"A theory, huh? You want us to get all excited because you have one of your theories?"

"Not any old theory, Como, but a real humdinger of a theory." And it was too. I had thought of it in the night when I'd got up to have a pee, and I was so excited by it I had hardly slept since. "Listen to this."

We hunched over the table for added secrecy while I explained my theory, following which I sat back and waited for the applause.

"Crypto narcotics, delivered in roses and activated by smart-phones?" said Agent Dyson, with a touch more cynicism than I had hoped for.

"Absolutely. It fits all the facts. Why else would you have a computer-room in the crypt, a facility to create new rose-scent molecules in the lab, a hermetically-sealed test facility in the potting shed, and boxes full of mobile phones all with an app that does nothing but offer an 'activate' option?"

Como put a finger to his temple to suggest I had at least one screw loose, and possibly more. I ignored his offensive gesture.

"Just imagine it. New varieties of genetically engineered roses, superficially indistinguishable from any ordinary rose. Their scent molecules have been designed to be manipulated by tiny changes in the electric field around a smart-phone screen—changes generated by the special app. The pathetic drug-addict buys a bunch of these evil roses, carrying them home as if an innocent gift for a loved one. Once inside, she plucks off one of the dainty heads, crushes it against the screen of her phone, clicks the activate button, and the special app does the rest. Thirty seconds later she's sniffing the screen to get the latest addictive high. Imagine the money that could be made by whoever owned that trade."

"Writer, if that's your best theory, then I vote that we all go and spend a week in that isolation tank."

"Chief Galahad's right," said Agent Dyson, in what amounted to a total revolt by my characters. "The theory's way too speculative."

"If speculative means completely freakin' nuts, then I agree," said Como. "Even if the theory wasn't total crap, which it is, it still doesn't explain any of the murders."

That was true. I picked in a desultory way at some of Como's breakfast. The theory had seemed brilliant when I thought of it last night, but now it was typed in black and white it wasn't quite as convincing as I'd hoped. Still, there was one way to check it out.

"What we need to do is get into the library. Brother Steve said there's a print of the computer program there, so we just need to examine it to see what it does."

Como looked at his watch. "Okay, we'll give it a go. It'll keep me out of the abbot's way, at least."

We rose from the crude trestle table, and made our way to the library.

CHAPTER FIFTY-ONE

In which there is a catalogue of digressions.

Stay here and keep an eye on the indicator of the elevator. If it looks like anyone else is heading up, come and find us."

We were on the third floor of the praesidium, at the entrance to the abbey's famous library, at either side of which stood a magnificent lion moulded in the finest expanded polystyrene, one named Impatience, the other Apathy. Having given Brother Leon her instructions, Como and I pushed through the turnstiles into the library's stunning beaux arts reception area, beyond which an enormous pair of doors in mahogany-effect Formica led into the collection chamber. The library was famed throughout Christendom for the number and rarity of the documents it contained—documents which, if stacked one upon the next, would reach to the furthest star in the heavens. Where in this vast store might we find the computer print-out?

"Our first task, Como, is to find the catalogue, otherwise we might spend an eternity searching at random among the shelves, and that always makes me want to go to the toilet."

"What about over there?"

Como pointed at the librarian's desk, upon which sat a huge book, evidently a log of some sort. I hastened to it.

"No, Como. I am afraid this is the journal in which the librarian records which books have been viewed by which of the brethren."

It was a disappointment, but it did give me a good idea for a plot twist. I leafed through its pages to the most recent records. A surge of excitement surged through me as I saw among the myriad mentions of *The Bible* and *The Awful Truth about the Herbert Quarry Affair*, seven immensely suggestive entries.

"Como, Quick! Look here."

It took Como's powerful police intelligence only milliseconds to clock the significance of what I had seen. Each of the brothers who had died in the last week had done so within 24 hours of viewing the same book!

CHAPTER FIFTY-TWO

In which Marco gets with the programme.

I started a new chapter to underline the significance of our find and to give myself time to think what to write next. Not enough time, as it happened, because I'd no idea. I fell back on my standard practice under such circumstances and typed the next thing that came into my head. Where it came from I cannot say (or not without admitting to plagiarism).

"I know, Como—what about this for a theory? Perhaps the book has pages soaked in a highly persistent and effective poison, so that those who touch its pages die within the day."

"Yeah, good one, Writer. Better than the usual crap you write. But aren't you forgetting something?"

"What?"

"None of the dead monks was poisoned. One was pushed out of a window, one disembowelled himself, one was stabbed in the back by a forklift, one died of a natural causes, and you never got round to typing how the aycharchivist was killed."

Hmmm. It was a good point. However, this was no time for pedantry. My writer's instinct—aided by the word-counter at the bottom left of the screen—told me we were finally reaching the denouement. In just a few paragraphs, perhaps, we might find some devastating clue, yet here was Como picking holes in things. Typical. Is it any wonder the police take ages to solve crimes?

"Never mind that now," I told Como. "Let us seek the truth within the library. Let us find the catalogue and look up the book in question."

Cunningly I avoided mentioning the name of the book, a move that would heighten the sense of anticipation in the minds of my readers, while giving me more time to decide what to call it.

We searched high and low around the desk of the librarian for the catalogue, keeping an entirely open mind about whether it would be a single huge book, a collection of books—huge or otherwise—a series of drawers labelled with ranges of letters in alphabetical order, such as 'A – D', 'D – F', and so on, or a computerised catalogue of some sort. Even so, we found nothing. Then I spotted a long trestle table against the northern wall of the reception area, upon which were arrayed at least a dozen microfiche readers.

For the benefit of the younger members of my audience, perhaps I should explain what a microfiche is. After all, I wouldn't want anyone to be prevented from following the crystal clear plot by my clumsy use of antiquated terminology...

In the days before it was possible to store vast amounts of information on a phone, one problem with recording information was the space it took on paper. The librarians of the medieval period overcame this difficulty through the invention of the microfiche, a rectangular card of clear plastic—about the size of a screen saver for a smart-phone—upon which they would write information in an incredibly tiny hand, using quills made from humming-bird feathers sharpened to an unimaginably fine point. The microscopic writing could be discerned only by placing the microfiche in a special magnifying device—the microfiche reader.

"Aha!"

The sentiment burst from my lips as I found an old shoe-box in a side drawer of the librarian's desk, in which a few thousand microfiches were separated by card tabs lettered from A to Z. I carried the box to the nearest microfiche reader, and inserted the first of the cards from the S section. I bent to adjust the eyepieces of the reader, and my heart fell as I scanned the weird symbols they revealed upon the microfiche.

"It's no good, Como. The catalogue entries are written upon the microfiches in some obscure code."

I sat back on the bench, mentally defeated by my discovery.

"Let me see," said Como.

I shuffled along the bench to let him sit beside me. While he wasted his time examining the microfiche, I wondered about the strange symbols inscribed upon it. Might they be some cabalistic ritual language? Or could they be a secret of the abbey, handed down from one librarian to the next? Or perhaps they were...

"Obscure code, huh?" Como interrupted my thoughts. "You had the slide in back to front. Here."

He slid aside on the bench to let me take his place. I bent once more to the microfiche reader. I could now make out the list of book titles written upon it in alphabetical order. None of them was the book I sought. By means of a calculation too implausible to describe, I figured that I needed to skip forward another three microfiches. I selected the appropriate piece of plastic, slotted it in the reader the right way up, and scanned its contents.

There was the book, and the details of its location.

"We need to find shelf 196d," I told Como.

Arising from the bench, we ran across the reception area and pushed open the doors to the reading chamber, the huge room that housed the library's main collection. It was arranged like a giant feather, with a long central corridor, off either side of which, like vanes, were angled innumerable passages, lined with Ikea's finest shelving units, each loaded to within an ounce of its safe working load with its burden of books.

We walked down the central corridor until we found the number 196 stencilled upon the upright of one of the bookcases. The shelves were labelled from A to J.

"Shelf D will be the fourth one down. We'll have to find a ladder."

We scouted in the neighbouring passageways.

"The ladder could be anywhere," said Como. "I got a better idea."

Como explained his better idea, which I reluctantly agreed to put into practice. Unstrapping my sandals to obtain a better grip, I climbed onto a table, and thence onto his lowered shoulders, and he hoisted me upright, where I tottered fearfully.

"Don't forget my middle ear problem."

"I won't let you drop." Como fastened his huge hands around the tops of my shins. "Just keep your knees locked."

Shelf D was about fifty yards long. Como started walking along it, I standing unsteadily upon his shoulders.

"Not so fast, Como. Some of these titles are hard to read. Just a mo."

Como stopped. I picked out one of the books.

"You found it?"

"No, but I spotted a baking book my Bronx mom might like."

"For fuck's sake, Writer, can't you concentrate for a minute?"

"Sorry, Como." I put the baking book back. "Keep going."

We continued along the shelf, my head canted painfully as I read the titles on the spines of the numberless books. There seemed to be no order to the sequence in which the books were stored. I had to check every one we passed, including, for example, a 13th century treatise on aeromancy, a passable facsimile of the *Book of Kells*, a maintenance manual for a 1957 Chevy pick-up, the original manuscript of *Hamlet*, signed by Frances Bacon, a book-club edition of *The Three Musketeers*, a 1966 Monkees annual, a practical guide to picture framing, volume seven of *Trump's Guide to Diplomacy*, and so on. It was almost fifteen minutes before I found what we were after, wedged between Pascal's *Pensees* and a book of practical soldering advice entitled *Red Hot Tips*.

"Got it! Get me down."

Como carried me over to the table, and stooped so I could step off his shoulders. I jumped unsteadily onto the floor, and showed him the cover of the book. *Scents and Insensibility*, by Professor Hardiman.

"You better watch what you touch, Writer, with that poison page theory of yours."

"Good point, Como. I don't suppose you've any of those police evidence gloves?"

"In this?" Como lifted the skirts of his habit.

"Never mind. I'm sure there's no poison," I said, hoping I wouldn't accidentally change my mind and find I'd given myself a fatal dose. "Let's take a look."

We sat aside each other on the bench and leafed through the book. It was a slim monograph on the similarities and differences between the physiology of the human sense of smell and the mechanisms of intoxication and addiction associated with narcotics. Several passages within it were heavily underscored in red pencil. I read them word for word, whispering to myself.

"Looks like your narcotic rose theory is just as dumb as your poison page theory."

Como was right. Professor Hardiman's work made it clear that the molecules that caused us to smell perfumes were as different as could be from those that caused mental highs. There was no way narcotics could be engineered from the scents of roses, even with the sort of equipment I'd seen in the lab with Brother Leon. Speaking of whom...

"Let's tell Agent Dyson what we've found."

I walked back to the elevator with Como, thinking obsessively about the significance of our find, so obsessively that I made a glaring continuity error by forgetting that I'd left my sandals behind.

"What can it mean?" asked Agent Dyson after we'd explained our discovery.

The obvious answer was that we were in a book written by a complete idiot. However, I didn't want to demoralise my characters, so I thought of something superficially plausible...

"It means that five people have died because they learnt something, from the book, that was a threat to one or more other members of this establishment. Who and why we will shortly discover."

"How's that then?" said Como. "Seems to me you've been here a week and this case gets weirder by the day. At this rate you ain't gonna wrap it up in under a year."

"Cynicism doesn't become you, Como. Trust me. What did we originally come to the library for?"

"You expect me to remember that, after all the craziness we've just been through?"

"The computer program," said Brother Leon.

I nodded appreciatively. At least one of my characters wasn't being a complete asshole.

"Exactly. Let us find the computer program and assess its contents. Come."

Forgetting this time to leave Brother Leon guarding the elevator, we went into the library and repeated all the nonsense we got up to last time. To spare all our sanities, I won't re-write the sequence *in toto*. We found the location of the computer program, after some initial confusion about whether it would be catalogued under C or P, and this time I suggested that Agent Dyson climb upon Como's shoulders, reminding my comrades of my middle ear problem.

The program proved to be a thick sheaf of continuous paper, closely printed in classic computer characters, with enchanting monastic illuminations at the head of each page. I assessed it with an expert eye.

"There are thousands of lines of computer code. This will take some hours to read. Ooops. Pardon me." Through a loud gurgling noise, my digestive system reminded us all of its presence. "I think I need something to eat. I'm starting to get the wobbles. Let's go to my cell. We can grab some food on the way."

My suggestion meeting with the unanimous approval of all present, we took the elevator to the ground floor, bought coffees and various sugar-filled snacks from the vending machine outside the refectory, and headed for the dormitory block where my Spartan cell awaited.

"Wow!"

My exclamation was prompted by the sight that greeted us as we reached the exit of the praesidium. While we had been in the library, a snowstorm of unprecedented heaviness and ferocity had swept up the valley. Already there were at least three feet of fresh snow, and nothing could be seen in the swirling whiteness beyond a few tens of yards.

"Good job all those celebs arrived early," said Como, "or there'd be no one at the big gala dinner."

We waded through deep drifts to the dorm, where we shook the snow from our habits, and kicked it from our sandals, my sandals being miraculously back on my feet, even though I'd forgotten to write about putting them back on in the library. The corridors in the dormitory block were full of jostling people, the retinues of the recently arrived celebrities—stylists, dieticians, councillors, personal trainers, investment advisors, feng shui consultants, manicurists, pedicurists, publicists, ghost-writers, agents, karma gurus, lawyers...

Agents!

What about Barney? Would he be here? Was it likely he'd leave New York to come to dumpy old Clarkesville? On the other hand, with so many of his celebrity clients coming to the grand gala dinner, surely he would want to be here to schmooze them and frighten away his rivals?

I was still dithering about whether to include Barney in the scene, when he took the decision out of my hands, with a slap to the middle of my back.

"Markeeeey! How's it going? I thought I recognised my best boy under that hood."

I told him how it was going.

"That's my boy. And how's the big guy?" Barney offered his hand to Como. "You in good shape, Chief?"

Como told Barney he was in good shape.

"That's my boy. We need you on top form. Can't have a Galahad adventure without Galahad being on top form."

"Too right," said Como, with a thumbs up. "But you'd better tell the Writer there so he doesn't forget it."

"Forget it? Forget it? He won't forget it. Markey baby knows you're the star, doncha Markey?"

I thought I'd better interrupt all this bigging-up before it went to Como's head.

"Como's here in disguise, Barney. No-one's meant to know he's the real Como, otherwise we might tip-off the crooks."

Barney tapped the side of his nose. "I getcha. No-one will hear he's Como Galahad from me." Which was ironic, since he'd already shouted it to half the people in the building. "You guys come along to my suite, and we can talk in private."

"I didn't know they had suites in the dormitory block," I said.

"Are you kidding? I'm not staying in the dormitory block. That's for idiots. We're in the celebrity wing. Come on."

We followed Barney down a corridor or two, and through the security doors to the celebrity wing, where all was subdued lighting, tasteful objets d'art and calf-deep carpeting. En route, I introduced Barney to Agent Dyson.

"Charmed," said Barney.

Barney's suite was almost as extravagant as the abbot's quarters, albeit more tastefully decorated. He shooed out his underlings, and we sat around a low glass table near a roaring log-effect electric fire.

"So, Markey babes, how's the book coming along? You get everything nicely teed-up for a big show-down at the gala dinner?"

I wasn't sure what to say. I didn't have the heart to tell him he'd annoyed me so much that I was hell-bent on solving the case before the big opening. I decided to be evasive by telling the truth for a change.

"I'm not sure, Barney. It all depends on this." I patted the thick wad of computer paper I'd been carrying under my arm. "It's a computer program I need to analyse."

"Well what are you waiting for? Analyse away, kiddo. I'll keep Agent Dyson and the Chief entertained."

Barney led Leona and Como to his lavishly stocked minibar. I rubbed my exhausted temples, then started to fan through the computer print-out, making notes here and there of its salient points. It was demanding work, calling for every ounce of concentration to decipher the meaning of the complicated coding. Just to give you a taste, here's a sample of what I was having to deal with...

```
IF, THEN, ELSE
GOTO LINE 13
RUN ALGORITHM C
FLUSH BUFFER
SET ARRAY VALUES DOUBLE BINARY
HELLO WORLD
HEXIDECIMAL = TRUE
REWIND ALL TAPES
DISPLAY TEXT = "Are you sure?"
FOR J = 1 TO 517
PI = 3.142
```

```
SUNARRAY (J) = prIMeFACTOR
NEXT K
GOSUB 2000
OBJECT CLASS = DEF(PI**2);CHECKSUM
ON ERROR SET FLAG 'NOPRIME'
DECL STACK FIFO
CONTROL ALT DELETE
```

And that was one of the clearer parts. My task was compounded by the continual distracting chatter from the minibar. There, under Barney's prompting, Como was regaling an overly-impressed Agent Dyson with exaggerated claims about the part he had played in helping me discover the awful truth about various sensational criminal cases. The way he and Barney were going on, you'd think Como was the hero, while I just wrote stuff down. The last straw was when Como dropped his habit to his waist to allow Agent Dyson to see—and feel—the two bullet-holes he'd got when he dived between me and a gunman to save my life in *The Awful Truth about The Sushing Prize*. And, of course, Agent Dyson was just lapping it up. Huh!

Through gritted teeth I continued my analysis of the program, cursing the sloppy practices of its authors, who had included no explanatory comments, and who indulged in what we programming gurus call 'spaghetti coding', which results in no clear logic for the reader to follow. Yes, yes, I know—point taken.

Eventually, however, the puzzle of the program was resolved by my penetrative intellectual powers. I now knew why the members of the elder council had been devoting their time to the coding bees. I refolded the fanned-out computer paper, and retracted the tip of my propelling pencil. The gesture was not lost on my companions.

"You done there, Markey?"

I rose majestically from the settee, and adjusted the girdle of my habit.

"Como, Agent Dyson—if you are not too busy, perhaps you could spare the time to accompany me to see the abbot. Excuse us, Barney, but there's something I need to do."

"Well don't take too long about it, Markey boy—you've a big ending to write, remember?"

CHAPTER FIFTY-THREE

In which there are revelations.

*P*ax in nobis, jam profundis."

We were in the governance chamber. Como, Brother Leon and I were seated at one side of its ornate conference table, while Brothers Crispin, Alfonse and George—having repeated the ritual chant of the abbot—glowered at us from the other. At the head of the table, in his special executive chair, the abbot initialled a scroll to record the start of an emergency meeting of the elder council—a meeting he had convoked at my request in a chapter I had been too tired to write. Besides, I didn't think you could be bothered reading a load of padding about the walk to the abbot's suite, and the scene in which I made up a story to mislead him into holding the meeting. Speaking of which...

"Fellow elders," said the abbot. "I thank you for your forbearance in joining this meeting at short notice. Brother Marco tells me he has news of such import that it must be heard at once so we may decide how to act upon it before the gala dinner. Brother Marco..."

He gestured to indicate that I had the floor. Standing, I cleared my throat with an ahem of immense gravitas.

"Your Sublimity. Fellow Brethren. I have a story to relate—a story that sadly does not end with its characters living happily ever after."

The elders shifted uneasily in their seats. I crossed my fingers and hoped the readers weren't shifting uneasily in their seats too.

"The story begins with a tragic event—the unexpected death of the last head of the abbey, Abbot Croesus. The old abbot had been as generous and as credulous as he had been rich. He had willingly indulged the whims of his brethren on the elder council, investing millions of his own money to convert the crypt into a leading-edge computing centre. He had not queried the need for the huge expenditure. His sole pleasure was the contemplation of the Lord's word.

"Upon the tragic passing of Abbot Croesus, the elder council faced a crisis—how were they to find a new abbot who would be as free-spending as their deceased benefactor had been? How could they find a sucker to continue to bankroll their expensive computing hobby?

"I imagine it was in this very chamber that the problem was discussed, and a solution finally ironed out, with you, Brother George, in the chair as acting abbot, and you, Brothers Crispin and Alfonse, his willing conspirators."

The glowers across the table had deepened as I was speaking. Brother George pushed back his chair and stood, shaking with rage.

"Are we to sit and be ridiculed by this...this idiot and his preposterous nonsense?"

Preposterous nonsense was a bit harsh, but I suppose he had a point. The abbot, however, was hungry for the revelations I had led him to expect, and barked at Brother George to be seated. I took that as my cue to continue.

"It was decided that a cover story should be invented, one which—to the right investor—would justify the continued expenditure on the datacentre. The story that was devised was supremely cunning—bizarre, but plausible enough to the right audience, and attractive too. It would be put about that Brothers George, Crispin and Alfonse were on the edge of a breakthrough that would send shockwaves through the world of illegal narcotics. Rumours would be started of a new way to deliver fixes to addicts. Scent from genetically engineered roses, smeared on the touch-screens of smartphones, electronically activated by an app with built-in cryptographics. The special roses—indistinguishable from any others—would sell at normal prices through florists and supermarkets. The haul would come from the app, which, for a fee, would manipulate the electric field on a smart-phone's screen to alter the scent molecules in the roses to turn them into powerful synthetic highs. The app would handle the payments and give a direct channel to the consumer, cutting out all the expensive middlemen. If it worked, it would be a gold-mine."

Respect was beginning to mix with anger on the faces of the elders across the table, as they acknowledged the supreme investigative reasoning that had led me to penetrate the secret of their dastardly conspiracy. The abbot's gaze darted from one side of the table to the other, as if he were uncertain which presented the greater immediate threat. I continued my explosive exposé.

"But what sort of person would buy the cooked-up story about crypto-narcotics? Someone rich. Someone with the right connections. Someone attracted by the lure of dirty money. And most importantly, someone who didn't understand the digital world but would be too proud to admit it."

I turned to face the abbot.

"And that's when the news broke that a certain individual was about to retire from heading one of the biggest Mafia gangs. A rich individual. An individual with the right mob connections. An individual with a solid track record of handling dirty money."

"Hey!" Como shot up to get between me and the gun that had appeared in the abbot's hand.

"Don't move any of those pretty little muscles of yours," said the abbot. By 'yours' he meant Sister Coma's pretty little muscles, which I though a bit odd, Como's muscles being neither pretty nor little. However, beauty was clearly in the abbot's beholding eye. "I'm not about to shoot anyone, just yet. Finish your story, Ocram."

I waved to Como to suggest he retake his seat, the seat creaking its objections as it retook his huge weight. Remaining upon my exhausted feet, I continued to invent the big reveal...

"Earlier this year, a deal is done between the members of the elder council and their new benefactor—the ex Mafia boss who now finds religion and moves to Clarkesville to be the next abbot. Once again the money starts to flow. The abbot signs check after check for the datacentre, and for countless other expenses seemingly associated with the crypto-narcotics scheme he's agreed to bankroll. Everything seems tickety boo for the scammers, who think they can string along the abbot for as long as they need. But then one of those flukes happens, one of those million-to-one chances that change everything."

All eyes were on me now—those of Crispin, George and Alfonse full of wary resentment, the abbot's alarmed,

Brother Leon's wide with amazement, and Como's on the verge of rolling with accustomed disbelief.

"A young novice, Brother Wayne, is desperate to earn a place as an illuminator. With the Noel exhibition just weeks away, he visits the library, seeking to increase his understanding of the illuminator's art. He peruses the catalogue, and goes in search of *Red Hot Tips*, a book on advanced soldering techniques. As he pulls the book from the tightly packed shelf, out comes the one alongside it— *Scents and Insensibility,* with a lovely picture of roses on its cover. Brother Wayne innocently borrows the extra book, thinking it might interest his friend the herbalist. And interest it does.

"The herbalist has heard the refectory gossip. He knows that the elders have hooked the abbot with their plans for narcotic roses, and now he reads a book that seems to show the plans to be totally bogus. He visits his friend the aycharchivist, and takes a peek at certain CVs—CVs that prove none of the elder council has the specialist qualifications to mastermind the production of synthetic drugs. He shares his suspicions with Brother Glaxo—an expert chemist—who confirms that rose scents can't be manipulated to create synthetic highs, and certainly not by the feeble electric field generated by a touch-screen of a smart-phone.

"Now he's sure the elders are scamming the new abbot. He decides to cut a little action of his own. He goes to the elders and lets them know what he knows. He promises to keep quiet if certain conditions are met—if some of the abbot's money is diverted into modernising the herbarium. But the herbalist can't be trusted. Everyone knows he smokes dope in his potting shed, and when he's high he gets loose lipped. So the herbalist has to die, and so does young

Brother Wayne, and so does the aycharchivist, and so does Brother Glaxo.

"Meanwhile," I turned to the abbot, his face incandescent with rage, "you're getting worried. The story you've been spun about the narcotics scheme seemed so promising when you first moved to the abbey. The brothers had shown you the cave painting, a painting that seemed to prove a long-buried secret about a narcotic rose. They'd explained how the datacentre was needed to generate cryptographic keys to keep the app secure. But you're not so sure any more. The money you're pumping into the operation isn't bearing fruit. You're getting fobbed off by progress reports that always describe breakthroughs tomorrow, never concrete results today. But you don't know enough science or computing to see through the smokescreen of fancy jargon from your friends here.

"So it must have seemed like your fairy godmother was hard at work when I turned-up looking for a rest cure. Suddenly you have one of the world's foremost scientists, IT gurus and criminal investigators on your side." I gave Como a pre-emptive nudge to stifle any guffaws. "Without telling me any of your suspicions, you enlist my help to investigate the evil afoot in the abbey, hoping I'll validate or dispel your suspicions.

"So I get to work, with you at my shoulder. While we're investigating the death of the herbalist, Felonius pulls the tape from the CCTV at the herbarium. He doesn't need to play the tape; he doesn't need to know whether it holds incriminating evidence; he just needs to bluff and pretend it does. He approaches one of the elders, and tells them he has something that ties them to the murder. So Felonius has to be stopped. Now five people have died to prevent the abbot from learning that the scheme he's funding is just a scam—that his money's paying for something else entirely."

I turned to the three elders.

"Do you want to tell him what his dollars were funding, or shall I?"

Defiant silence was their answer. I continued.

"The big IT operation the new abbot had been hoodwinked into bankrolling wasn't to create security codes for the app, it was mining for a new type of crypto-currency. The Bytecoin. Eight times more valuable than a Bitcoin, and eight times harder to create. That's what you were paying through the nose for, and these jokers planned to bleed you dry."

"Crap." It was Brother George who uttered the profane verdict on my explanation. He turned to the abbot. "Are you going to sit there and believe all this made-up garbage? It's just a fantasy. Idle speculation. There's not a shred of proof."

"On the contrary…" I went on to explain what I'd seen in the print-out of the computer programme, the matching brush-marks on the cave-painting and on Brother Crispin's Christmas card, the apps on the mobile phones we'd taken from the lab, the entries in the librarian's log, the scrolls on the floor of the aycharium, and the damning testimony in Brother Felonius' notebook.

"And," I said, staring at Brother Alfonse, "we've found DNA on the bodies of four of the victims that is an exact match for yours." I'd just made that up, but he wasn't to know.

Alfonse kicked back his chair, jerking upright, rage and fear on his face. "Bullshit. You can't pin me for that. I never killed them."

"But I've got the evidence that said you did, Alfonse. So it doesn't really matter—you're going to fry in the chair anyway, whether you really killed them or whether your two buddies here planted the DNA to make it look like you did."

Brother Alfonse screamed a number of unholy expletives far too rude to print. "It was Crispin and George! George tipped Wayne out of the window. Crispin killed..."

"Shut the fuck up!" Brother George underlined his words with a huge slap upon Brother Alfonse's face.

"Okay, I've heard enough," said the abbot, banging the butt of his gun like a gavel to restore order. "I ought to thank you, Ocram, but I'm not in the mood. I've got some scores to settle, the Mafia way, so let's all go outside where we can..."

Before I could decide what we would be able to do when we went outside, Brother Crispin plunged a knife into the abbot's chest.

CHAPTER FIFTY-FOUR

In which Como turns the tables.

Como and Brother Leon ran toward the stricken abbot. Brother Leon followed the routine drummed-in by her FBI training—assessing the state of the victim and the chances of saving his life. Como followed quite different instincts— he lunged for the pistol the abbot had dropped, sliding, with his arm outstretched, on the highly polished linoleum of the ancient governance chamber. Even as Como's fingers grasped for its butt, Brother Crispin savagely kicked at the gun, spinning it away toward his cronies. Como shifted his aim to grab Brother Crispin's ankle, his huge fingers entirely cicling the joint. He wrenched Crispin down, and drew back a mighty fist, ready to smite his cowardly foe...

Conk!

I winced as Brother George smacked the back of Como's head with the gun. Not as much as Como winced as he sat dazed on the floor and felt for his new wound with tentative fingers. Brother Leon, dismissing the abbot as a lost cause, knelt at Como's side and checked the damage.

"Okay. Both of you stand up," said Brother George, clumsily adding the word 'up' where a more stylish speaker would simply have said 'stand.' Como allowed Brother Leon to help him to his feet, as if he were too dazed to rise unaided. A little attention-seeking if you ask me. "Now sit next to your friend." George pointed at me with his gun, reminding them which friend he meant.

Como slowly sat in the chair next to mine, still feigning unsteadiness, the malingerer. Brother Leon took the other seat.

"Very clever, Ocram. You got the story close enough to being right. But you made one big mistake."

I was shocked by his words. Only one?

"What mistake was that?"

"You should have brought reinforcements. Ha ha ha ha ha."

His cronies shared his callous laughter. I asked the question that's always asked when the baddie gets the upper-hand towards the end of a book.

"What are you going to do now?"

"Isn't it obvious? You and your two acolytes know most of the truth. So I'm going to have to kill all three of you."

I felt Como tense next to me.

"Most of the truth?" I said. "If you're going to kill us why don't you tell us all of it? Why don't you put us out of one misery before you put us out of another?"

Which struck me as clever wording from a writer faced with the prospect of imminent death.

"What do you want to know?"

"What was going on at the bothy? Why the private cell-phone network? How's Stella McGee involved?"

I tried to remember the other loose plot strands I needed to tie off, but I was too panicky.

"The one thing you got absolutely right, Ocram, was when you said the cover story was cunning and attractive. So why would a clever conman waste a story like that? You think the abbot was our only patsy? We were selling it to plenty of other fools. The bothy was a drop for samples of synthetic highs we were teasing the other investors with. We told those idiots the chemicals were derived from roses, and they believed us, just like that idiot did." He nodded at the body of the abbot. "Ha! Running the samples out through the bothy made it look like we were trying to keep everything top secret. And none of those dumbasses guessed what we were giving them was re-packaged shit that any scumbag in Clarkesville can get for five dollars. Stella was handling the logistics. It was her idea to have the private phone network— a good way to keep in touch without leaving a trail the cops can follow through the telcos. We just brought the network up now and again when we needed it. That clear it all up for you?"

It seemed plausible to me, who knew nothing about mobile phone networks, drugs, or any of the other technicalities underpinning the plot. I was wondering what the readers would make of it, when Brother George raised his gun.

"Wait! Don't shoot. It's...it's madness. You won't get away with it."

"Wrong again, Ocram. It's easy enough. I shoot the three of you from here. I put this gun in the abbot's hand and fire another couple of shots so he gets some powder on him. I tell the cops the abbot shot you when you revealed his identity, and Brother Crispin here kills the abbot in self-defence before he turns the gun on us."

"But...but... the bullet hole angles will be wrong. The police will know."

"You're sitting on swivel chairs, Ocram. What could be easier than spinning you round? Now no more stupid buts."

Brother George's evil forefinger was tightening on the trigger when Como exploded out of his chair, his hands under the heavy table top, tipping it upright like a huge shield, and charging it forward like the blade of an enraged bulldozer. I heard an incredibly loud shot before Como crashed the upturned table against the stone wall of the governance chamber, pinning Brother George and his cronies behind it.

"You guys ok?"

Como fired the question over his shoulder as he kept the table pressed against the wall. I was too shocked to speak, but Agent Dyson said we were good. Como indicated that we should replace him as the source of the pressure pinning the perps against the wall, following which he looked warily around the edge of the table top. I closed my eyes, expecting another shot, but all I heard was Como saying:

"Okay. Ease off."

We took our shoulders away from the table, and Como pulled it back from the wall with one hand, while holding Brother George's gun in the other. It took us a moment to make sense of the tangle of limbs and habits on the floor against the wall. Brother Crispin was dead, accidentally shot by Brother George. Brother George was dead, his skull accidentally crushed between the wall and the table by Como. Brother Alfonse was alive, but stunned and disoriented. I was feeling pretty stunned and disoriented myself. Just seconds ago I thought I was a certain goner. If it hadn't been for Como's quick thinking and bravery I'd be on the floor oozing blood like Brother Crispin. I gave credit where it was due.

"Como, you saved my life."

"Our lives," corrected Agent Dyson, staring doe eyed at Como. She ran to him, and pressed her face against his massive chest. Typical.

"Yes, well, there's no time for that nonsense. What are we going to do with him?"

By 'him' I meant Brother Alfonse, of course.

Como hauled him up by the scruff of his habit and held him against the wall with one hand, slapping his face with the other to speed his return to full consciousness. They were rather heavy slaps, I thought, hardly in the Florence Nightingale tradition of considerate nursing, but definitely true to the Como Galahad tradition of forceful policing.

"We'll lock him in one of the cells, until we can get some police up here."

I looked at the impenetrable curtain of snow beyond the panoramic bay window of the governance chamber. It might be days before the narrow track up the valley could be cleared, days before official support could arrive. But what did it matter? Utter relief suffused my being. I had solved the case. My iPad said I had typed 74,973 words—almost bang-on my 75K target. I was a Writer fully at peace with himself. Now I could relax. Now I could join my fellow celebrities at the gala dinner of the grand opening.

CHAPTER FIFTY-FIVE

In which Marco's restful evening becomes stressful.

Bottoms up."

We raised our glasses to celebrate the solving of the case, the toast reminding me of the freak accident that had caused Como's backside to be revealed to the late abbot. Around us in the ceremonium thronged the many A-list celebrities here for the grand opening. All had been welcomed, brother and sister alike. The hosteler—who had been promoted to Acting Abbot—had had the good sense to defuse the planned protest by immediately declaring the abbey an equal-rights religious establishment, open to all regardless of their gender or sexual orientation. As a result, a triumphant party atmosphere prevailed, in which the visitors paraded in their finery. Never had the ceremonium been graced by such a dazzling collection of designer habits.

I drained my glass of fizz.

"Well, Como, it all turned out right in the end."

"No thanks to you, Writer. You could have got us killed."

"I admit that it was touch and go, Como, but I never doubted that your strength and courage would protect us." I checked my bespoke Rolex—the one with my Bronx mom picked out in jewels on its face. "Brother Leon is a little late. I assume he's making himself beautiful for you. Or herself, rather."

"For me?"

"Surely you've noticed that the impressionable young thing has been captivated by your manly charms."

"The only thing I've been noticing lately, Writer, is how much trouble you've been causing. Anyway, she said she'd call in to check Brother Alfonse. She doesn't want him hanging himself in his cell."

I raised an eyebrow.

"And you didn't think to help? He's a dangerous felon."

"Don't be sexist, Writer—she can look after herself."

"True." I remembered the trouncing she'd given the two thugs in the laboratory. "Anyway, let's get topped up. I plan to drink myself stupid tonight."

"Won't take much drinking."

As we looked for the nearest waiting-brother with a tray of drinks, the hosteler came rushing toward us. I bowed.

"Congratulations on your elevation, Your Acting Sublimity."

"Thank you, Brother Marco," said the flustered official. "I wonder if I could ask for your support in a delicate matter."

"Of course, of course. What is the difficulty?"

"You might know that the dinner was meant to be followed by a concert which certain of our celebrity guests had kindly agreed to perform."

"Indeed. We have been looking forward to it, haven't we, Brother Como?"

"What? Yeah, sure," said Como.

"The fact is," said the acting abbot, "that I believe some spat has broken out between the musicians as to who should perform the first instrumental solo in the opening number. They have fallen out, and are making excuses not to play. Brother Elton is refusing to play because a sequin is missing from his piano. Brother Ringo is refusing to play because we don't have his favourite tea. Brother Slash is refusing to play because he says he's left his plectrum at his friend's house. And Sister Madonna is refusing to sing unaccompanied. I was hoping, Brother Marco, you might use your influence to persuade them to act for the benefit of our other guests."

So much for my relaxing evening.

"Very well. Where shall I find them?"

"In their dressing rooms to the rear of the stage."

"Brother Como, excuse me for a few minutes. I will be back as quickly as I can. If Brother Leon turns up, explain that I have been called away on important duties for the Acting Abbot."

I raised my cowl, and threaded through the boisterous revellers, wondering whether I should draw the reader's attention to the clever echo of the scene in which I had first met Como in Kelly's bar and diner. I decided not to bother. En route to the stage, I glugged four or five glasses of fizz I swiped from passing waiters. If I was going to have to put up with that bunch of whining prima donnas, I'd need something to help me keep my diplomatic composure.

I pushed between the curtains at the side of the stage and into the darkened corridor beyond. Through the lancet windows the abbey grounds were a spotless blanket of white under the moonlight. Well, not quite spotless. Just entering my field of view, Brother Leon was wading through the waist deep snow. Just behind her was Brother Alfonse, prodding her forward with a gun.

CHAPTER FIFTY-SIX

In which a hundred cameras capture the action.

Bang.

The report of the gunshot shattered the party mood in the ceremonium. The egotistical chatter of the celebrities was replaced in an instant by screams and shouts of alarm. Above the clamour a strident voice called from outside.

"Ocram! Ocram!"

There was a second echoing crack as Brother Alfonse fired into the air to advertise his presence. I saw him press the gun to Brother Leon's head.

"Ocram. I know you're up there. Come down *now*, or she gits it."

Screams of terror greeted this startling pronouncement. I almost screamed myself as I thought how my lovely medieval murder mystery seemed to be morphing out of control into *Gunfight at the OK Corral*. What was I doing, typing this nonsense? Think, Marco, think.

The celebrities rushed as one to the terrace to behold the drama, then rushed as one back indoors to avoid potshots from Brother Alfonse. I pushed through the screaming crowd, slapping faces to suppress the hysteria. I found Como looking over the parapet, his police chief mind absorbing all aspects of the rapidly unfolding scenario. I leant next to him, my writer's mind trying to absorb any aspects of the rapidly unfolding scenario.

"You've gone and done it this time, Writer. You've written us up here with no means of self-defence, no means of escape, no means of bringing in support, and a hundred celebrities screaming in our ears and stopping us thinking straight."

I didn't think I would have been thinking straight even without the hundred screaming celebrities, but I knew what he meant. It was time for leadership. I looked for a gavel to bang, or a buzzer to buzz, or a klaxon to klax, or some other means of gaining the attention of the headless A-listers. Finding no simpler option, I climbed onto the stage, turned the knob of the PA system to eleven, and played a thunderous chord on Brother Slash's electric guitar. My voice boomed through the ceremonium as I spoke into the microphone.

"Brothers and Sisters, listen to me. You are perfectly safe. There is only one way into the ceremonium, and its doors are of the stoutest oak. The evil maniac below is acting alone. He intends you no harm—I am his target. The monk you see by the parapet—yes, the huge one in the dodgy habit. He is not my secretary." I made a sign to Como to throw back his cowl. "He is Police Chief Como Galahad, the bravest and most resourceful law enforcer in the entire genre of crime fiction."

A cheer ran through the crowd. The male celebrities ran to slap Como on the back and shake his hand, while the female celebrities ran to do some other hilarious thing that

I'm too pre-occupied to dream-up, so you'll have to imagine it for yourself.

"Chief Galahad and I have a cast-iron plan to apprehend the perp and to save his hostage. I would ask you please to stay in the ceremonium, to remain calm, and to record the events on your phones, so we will have a solid trail of evidence in the event of any subsequent criminal proceedings."

Given something practical to do, especially something that involved cameras, the celebrities calmed down. They attended to their appearance, and consulted each other about how best to position themselves for the videos being taken. Jumping from the stage, I found myself accosted by the ornithologist.

"Brother Marco, I have my drone with me." He showed me a device he had extracted from his habit—presumably the remote control. "Should I launch the craft to take surveillance footage?"

I considered the pros and cons of his unexpected suggestion.

"Best not, Brother Audubon. The device might arouse suspicion in the mind of Brother Alfonse. I suggest instead you follow the action with the superb binoculars I note you are carrying around your neck."

I patted his shoulder to bolster his morale, and pressed on. Barney appeared from nowhere, and kissed me on each cheek.

"You did it, Markey, you did it. This is gonna be huuuuuuuuge. Just wait till this hits the net. Every producer in Hollywood's gonna be..."

I shushed Barney, and told him to make sure the celebrities got some shots of the action, and not just themselves. There would be time to talk about the reactions of every producer in Hollywood if and when I survived this mess. Speaking of which...

I tacked through the surging crowd to join Como.

"Okay, Writer. What's this cast-iron plan of ours?"

"I don't know."

I'd have to figure it out on the way down.

CHAPTER FIFTY-SEVEN

In which the boys perform the Ocram rope trick.

Okay, Alfonse. We'll do the swap. But we need to do it how I say. Go fifty paces to your right."

Como and I were either side of the main entrance to the praesidium, sheltering behind its thick concrete jambs. I risked a quick look outside. Alfonse was prodding Leona Dyson to wade through the snow ahead of him, in accordance with my shouted instruction. I waited until Alfonse's gun was well out of range before I shouted again.

"Okay. That'll do."

More quietly, I said to Como, "I hope those muscles of yours are up to it."

I put a hand on his beefy arm, then walked out into the waist-deep snow.

The moonlit scene will stay in my mind forever. I regarded it with avid eyes, hungry to absorb every detail of what might be the last seconds of my life. To one side was the looming majesty of Mount Clark, its steep faces featureless under their new burden of snow. To the other was the valley along which I had approached the abbey in what seemed like another lifetime. The snowfall had dampened all ambient sound. All I could hear were my laboured breathing and the regular crunches as I struggled to push my frightened limbs through the heavy mass of white that was now reaching almost to my chest.

Here was far enough. I stopped.

We formed a deadly triangle, one side much longer than the others. At one corner was Como and the safety of the praesidium. At the second was Brother Alfonse—his gun to Dyson's side. At the third, farthest from safety, was me. It would seem a foolproof means of exchange to Brother Alfonse—he could release Agent Dyson to run to Como, while I would be too hampered by the heavy snow to escape him.

"Let her go, Alfonse."

Brother Alfonse pushed Leona away—she floundered toward Como, her glamorous evening habit dishevelled and heavy with snow. Alfonse gave her one last look then struggled towards me, his gun arm held high to stay clear of his bow wave of snow. I stood, a tethered goat, drawing him away from Como and Leona. Any moment, he would be in range for an easy shot. He lowered his gun to point at me.

"Bye bye, Ocram."

Now!

As a feint, I dived into the snow to my right, away from Brother Alfonse. Almost immediately there was a savage bite around my waist, and I slid back to my left. A hundred yards away, Como's arms were pumping like fury, his breath in savage gasps, as he hauled on the rope he had tied around my body, the rope that had slid through the snow behind me on my walk to death, the rope that was now jerking me back to safety.

I was blind. The skirts of my habit trailed over my head as I was dragged over the compacted snow I had trodden from the praesidium. In my deep snowy groove, I was safely hidden from Brother Alfonse, who must now be wading through the drifts to where he had seen me take my dive.

"Quick, he'll be on to us." The words flew from Como as he pulled me to my feet at the praesidium entrance. The knot around my waist was too tight to undo, so we gathered the rope in coils in our hands. I looked back. Alfonse had seen my miraculous reappearance, and was already pushing toward us, rage and effort distorting his face.

"Get in."

Como bundled me into the elevator. Leona Dyson had been holding the doors—she pressed the button for the third floor. I looked at my dim reflection on the control panel as we moved upward. I looked like death. I felt like it too.

After an age, the doors opened.

"Get up the stairs."

The elevator went as far as the library. We had to take the winding stone staircase to the ceremonium on the top storey. In front of a hundred startled faces, Como pushed me inside and slammed the heavy oak doors behind us.

I was bent double, supporting my body with my hands on my knees. I looked up. Around me was a semicircle of shocked celebrities, their phones in hands that tremored with fear and excitement. The hospitaler rushed me a glass of the abbey's famous brandy. I gratefully gulped the fiery liquid, wiping my lips with the wet scabrous sleeve of my tattered habit. I was freed from the rope. With Como's help, I limped to the stage, cheers swelling as the crowd parted to let us through. I sat on the edge of the platform, sucking up the dregs of my will to live, while celebrity after celebrity came to pat my back and take a selfie. After acknowledging their compliments, I got Como to carry me up the steps, and once more took my place at the microphone.

"Brothers and Sisters, thank you, thank you, thank you very much," I waved down their applause. "There may be a gunman outside, but for the next few hours we are perfectly safe in the ceremonium. So let the gala dinner continue!"

Further cheers accompanied my departure from the stage, and every phone was pointed my way as I shook Como's giant hand and was then engulfed by his bear-hug. I kissed Leona Dyson, and the three of us walked out to the terrace.

"How did he get you?" I asked Leona, meaning Brother Alfonse, of course.

"The gun was hidden in the cell. I looked in and saw him lying on the floor. I thought he'd poisoned himself. It's the oldest trick in the book. I can't believe I fell for it."

I wasn't sure which book she was talking about—not this one, obviously, because it had plenty of tricks older than that.

"Where do you think his is?"

"Who cares?" said Como. "He won't get far in the snow. We'll pick him up as soon as reinforcements arrive."

"In the meantime, he can't do us any harm in here," I said, "so let's just enjoy the dinner."

That's when I first smelled burning.

Chapter Fifty-Eight

In which Marco overcooks the plot.

Someone's overdoing the steaks," I quipped. "D'you know, Como, that's what I really fancy just now. A big steak. Have you looked at the menu?"

"I ain't, but after that performance, they should cook us whatever damn thing we like."

"Hear hear."

As if he had read our thoughts, the hosteler banged the gong for dinner. We joined the line of celebs crowding to consult the seating plan before moving to their allotted places on the communal benches.

Leona sniffed, her dainty nostrils widening. "That doesn't smell like food burning."

There was a growing acrid taste to the air. Wisps of smoke were blowing from the terrace. Hardly able to believe what I was typing, I raced to the parapet and looked down. Red, yellow, and orange flames were flicking out from the windows of the library below, their tips tinged with the black roots of the billows of smoke that had started to surround us.

"It's a fire! In the library! Como, try the door!"

Como shot free the bolts locking the heavy doors to the ceremonium and pulled open one leaf. A thick, hot, choking cloud burst into the room. Como threw his cowl over his face and disappeared into the cloud, heading down the winding stairway, only to appear moments later to slam the door behind him.

"No good." He shook his head, his huge chest racked with coughs. "Staircase is full of flame."

"But it's the only way out!"

The only way out. The implications of my words slowly sank in as new screams broke out among the celebrity guests. Evil Brother Alfonse had torched the library below us, the library full of tinder-dry combustibles. How long had we got? The floor of the ceremonium was stone, but would it collapse as the fire continued to grow? Would the flames burn through the oak doors, leaving the stairway to act like the chimney of a blast furnace? Would the fumes enetering through the windows poison us? Would the radiant heat ignite the flammable materials in the room?

In the screaming melee, I struggled to make myself heard, but with Como's help I cornered the hosteler and his obedentiaries. I issued a stream of terse orders. All curtains, soft furnishings, and any other flammable items to be cleared from the windows. Soak those tablecloths. Caulk the gap under the doors to keep out the smoke. Celebrities to breathe through wetted napkins. And more of the same.

We did all we could, but the library was an inferno. The heat through the floor was searing, the fumes choking. A sudden change in the wind cleared the worst of the smoke from the terrace. I ran to the parapet. Brother Alfonse was slowly moving through the snow away from the abbey, looking back now and then to savour his handiwork. Where was he headed? Above the cracking roar of the fire, an unmistakeable noise suggested the answer to my question— the growing beat of a helicopter.

I looked around. There! Against the white backdrop of Mount Clark was a flash of electric blue. Stella McGee's new toy had come up the valley and was manoeuvring above the helipad, angling this way and that to fan the snow from the landing circle. Brother Alfonse was struggling through the blizzard of the downdraft, shielding his face with his sleeves.

I was possessed by a cocktail of anger, shame and self-pity. Stupidly I had allowed a minor character to trap me with no means of escape in a raging inferno. Even more stupidly, I'd condemned the world's top celebrities to share my fate. Barney had undersold things for once. This wasn't going to be huuuuuge—it was going to be huuuuuuuuuuuuuuuuuuuuge. The story was going to be worldwide news for weeks, and I was never going to read it. I pictured my Bronx mom surrounded by tabloids and cake, with no Marco to share them.

Murderous resolve rose to the fore in my mind. If we were all going to die, then Brother Alfonse and Stella McGee weren't going to get away with it.

I found the ornithologist, sobbing in a funk by the bar.

"Where's the remote? The remote for the drone. Quick, man."

He fumbled it from a pocket. I tore it off him and tore back to the terrace. The drone was leaning against the parapet in a corner. I swept the glasses from a table, and set the drone in their place. I looked at the control box, with its central screen. How did the damn thing work? It was complicated enough, but nothing for the scientist who had fixed the Large Hadron Collider. In seconds the drone was away, dancing through the winter air, the screen on the remote showing the view from the on-board camera. At the helipad, the passenger door of Stella McGee's machine had just closed behind Brother Alfonse. The rotors were spinning up. Now the helicopter was starting to rise. Which way would they head? Over the Clark pass no doubt. I had to be right. I was only going to get one chance at this. Yes. The helicopter had spun to face north-west, and was rising to follow the steep sides of Mount Clark, exactly where I had targeted the drone. They were too far away for me to see them directly, so I watched the view from the drone's camera. There was the helicopter, crossing in from the east. We were on a collision course, but the collision needed to be exactly right, or the drone would bounce harmlessly off the bigger machine. Almost there...now! I pushed the joystick forward with a merciless thumb to lance the drone into the tail-rotor of the helicopter.

The display screen was instantly blank. I threw the remote aside and looked at the aerial drama in the moonlight. Stella McGee was fighting her controls. The rudderless helicopter was starting to spin in reaction to the torque of its rotor. Faster and faster, its angular momentum built remorselessly, until the wounded machine spun against the cliff and burst into flames. I watched as the mangled debris ploughed down the face of the mountain.

Now I had my own fate to face.

A giant hand settled on my shoulder. I turned. Como stood before me, his face lined with soot and sweat as it had done once before in another book.

"Looks like this is it, Writer. You done your best, but..."

He didn't need to finish his sentence. I looked into his eyes, and for a moment we were bonded as one—Writer and character, nevermore to star in the spectacular adventures my readers had come to love. I imagined the sadness of the countless readers around the world. Surely it couldn't end like this? Surely there was some way in which I could bring us through this hell, so my millions of readers could enjoy yet another book...

I felt it as a tremble before I heard it. The building shook. I thought it was the fire. I thought the floor was going to collapse, that we would be engulfed in flame and falling masonry. But the noise became a roar, and a sudden wind blew the ceremonium utterly clear of smoke, almost knocking me from my feet. In awe we looked out across the parapet. It seemed the entire side of Mount Clark was on the move, sliding toward us in a solid sheer mass. But then the gigantic cliff of ice collapsed in a boiling sea of white. A mountain's worth of snow was piling down the funnel of the pass, a tidal wave of white powder, sixty feet high. I looked in disbelief as the wave thundered towards us, snapping trees like matchsticks. Obliterating the lesser buildings of the abbey, the wave slammed into the sturdy mass of the praesidium, rushing round it and piling up so that even on the top-most storey we were swamped. My last memory was of Como, shielding my head with his arm, as the river of snow overwhelmed us.

EPILOGUE

Six months later.

It's the latest attraction."

Como poked a finger under his sun-visor to direct my attention to the long line of tourists waiting in the kindly May sunshine to enter Nanny McGee's old mill, which we were passing en route to the abbey.

"Is it true they turned the log flume into a ride?"

"Sure is, Writer. Every time some sucker comes down that thing in a plastic log the McGee's get another twenty bucks. They've a lot to thank you for."

I thought about my ride in Stella McGee's helicopter, the helicopter that had started the avalanche.

"Pity Stella never got to see it. You know, Como, I don't think she ever meant to kill me."

"Shame she never shared that idea with Alfonse."

We left the N66 and took the turn onto the narrow lane that wound up the valley. A lot had happened since I last travelled this road. When news broke of the spectacular events at the abbey, it had gone mega-viral, magnified a hundredfold by the public's interest in the celebrity

341

participants. Producers had been gagging for the film rights, so Barney cleaned-up. The book was rushed into print and hit the top spots world-wide, breaking the records I'd set with *The Awful Truth about the Herbert Quarry Affair* and *The Awful Truth about The Sushing Prize*. There were the inevitable arguments, thrashed out on social media, about what had really happened; and countless conspiracy theories explaining the various loose ends in the plot. The most fanciful concerned the identity of the mole at police HQ—there was no end to the finger-pointing, until Como published a picture of the culprit, a real mole.

"Hard to believe there could be an avalanche," I said, as I eyed the early summer greenery.

Como grunted. "Nothing's easy to believe in your books. That avalanche was spooky alright, putting out the fire but not killing anyone above it."

It was true, the avalanche had been suspiciously convenient.

"But the ends justify the means, Como. Let's not forget that. It's like when you break all the rules to beat confessions out of perps."

"When do I ever do that?"

I ignored Como's protestation. "If I hadn't written the avalanche, we'd both be dead. And all the A-listers. And Agent Dyson. Where's she now—back in the FBI?"

Como looked sideways at me between two tricky bends.

"Didn't you hear?"

"Obviously not. What?"

"She stayed at the abbey. All that shit you wrote fucked with her brains. She decided to be a nun. You'll see her when we get there."

"That'll be nice."

I had my own theory about Agent Dyson. She was probably so awed by the way I was prepared to sacrifice my life to save hers, and by my general heroic demeanour throughout the incredible denouement, that she had concluded she would never meet another man who would live up to the ideal I represented. What else would be left to her, but to join the abbey and remain unwed?

"There it is."

Como interrupted my disgracefully sexist thoughts and pulled up at the top of the rise from which I'd had my first view of the abbey. It was now a major attraction, and the tourist money had been put to good use. A new chain-link fence had replaced the one swept away by the avalanche— its links shimmered in the bright sunlight.

"It looks different. Less menacing, somehow."

"It's amazing what a lick of paint and a rollercoaster can do."

Como ignored the signs to the massive car park, and drove us past the tourist buses and through the abbey gates into the quadrangle where I had diced death with Brother Alfonse. A red carpet had been rolled out, at the end of which the great and the good of the abbey waited to greet us.

We had been invited to the abbey as VIP guests for the annual ceremony at which new varieties of rose were named in honour of those judged most worthy by the herbalist. This year there was only one new rose—a result of the devastation wrought by the avalanche—so its naming would have a special significance.

I stepped out of Como's Range Rover, the day seeming twice as bright beyond its tinted windows. The new abbot offered his hand, which I knelt to kiss.

"Doctor Ocram, we are doubly honoured by the presence of a celebrity author and saviour of our abbey."

I nodded at his words, echoing the second paragraph of the book.

"And welcome to you, Chief Galahad, the man who continues to protect us."

In an extreme breach of monastic protocol, Como shook the proffered hand rather than kiss it, Como having developed an understandable aversion to intimate contact with abbots.

We followed the abbot and his retinue through the grounds of the abbey. All around were signs of reconstruction. The abbey's insurers had almost been bankrupted—not by the physical repair costs, which were high enough, but by the claims of negligence which flooded in from the lawyers of the celebrities, who demanded compensation for the physical and mental trauma to which their clients had been exposed.

As the praesidium was still smothered in conservationists and construction workers, a temporary pavilion had been erected for the ceremony, using only the very finest shuttering-ply and scaffold tubes. We were delayed a few moments while the officials argued about some aspect of the naming ritual, so I stared with interest at the renovations underway at the herbarium.

"Coming along, isn't it?" said a familiar voice behind me.

"Brother Leon!" I gave her a hug.

"It's Sister Leona..." she paused to hug Como too... "now that I'm here officially."

"In which capacity, might I ask?"

"I'm the acting herbalist. They won't elect a permanent holder to the office until a Grand Council meeting in October, but I'm hopeful." She smiled. Her new life suited her—the lines of care and concern had been entirely lifted from her enchanting features.

I was about to ask how the repairs to the herbarium were progressing, but we were ushered into our VIP seats for the naming ceremony. You'll be pleased to hear that I didn't record all the boring details about the preliminaries— the prayers, the chants, the sermons, the ceremonial distribution of forms in which the visitor was asked to rate their visit to the abbey, and so on. I was too preoccupied with my acceptance speech, working through the points I would make about the singular nature of the honour, how the Ocram name would live on for generations in gardens across the world, how the fame of the abbey would spread when *Awful Truth* fans across the world bought the roses bearing my name, and so on. I was just rehearsing the closing remarks, about my Bronx mom being so proud, when the abbot was handed a purple velvet cushion, upon which lay a single rose of unsurpassed beauty and perfection.

Having blessed the lovely bloom, he addressed his audience.

"Today is the first time in the noble history of this establishment that we have had only a single new variety of rose to name at our annual ceremony. This example," he inclined his head toward the pillow, "is the sole survivor of the evil episode through which we so recently passed. Today is also, in my view, the first time that the honour of the name of the rose has been so fittingly bestowed upon a person to whom the abbey owes so much. In accordance with our ancient tradition, the right to choose the name of the rose lay with the acting herbalist alone, but no member of this establishment would have argued against her decision, a decision I now endorse with all the authority vested in me as abbot."

He lifted the rose from its velvet pillow, and I half raised my hand to accept it from him.

"I hereby name this glorious example of the Lord's work, Rosa Como Galahad."

ACKNOWLEDGEMENTS

Aside from Brother Umbert (wherever his soul may lie) who wrote such a beautifully spoofable book, I particularly want to thank...

The authors who kindly took the trouble to read Marco's first book and provide such encouraging blurbs: Alex Austin, S.G. Brown and Minette Walters.

The early adopters (and life members of #ALAS), especially Chris, Jonathan, Noel, and Sarah, who gave us so much fun discussing Marco's weird ways on Twitter.

The fantastic Tiny Fox team for all their help and support.

And Leona, who contributes far more than she knows.

About the Author

Little is known of Marco Ocram's earliest years. He was adopted at age nine, having been found abandoned in a Detroit shopping mall—a note, taped to his anorak, said the boy was threatening the sanity of his parents. Re-abandoned in the same mall a year later, with a similar note from his foster parents, he was homed with his current Bronx mom—a woman with no sanity left to threaten.

Ocram first gained public attention through his bold theories about a new fundamental particle—the Tao Muon—which he popularized in a best-selling book—*The Tao Muon*. He was introduced to the controversial literary theorist, Herbert Quarry, who coached Ocram in a radical new approach to fiction, in which the author must write without thinking—a technique to which Ocram was naturally suited. His crime memoir, *The Awful Truth about the Herbert Quarry Affair*, became the fastest selling book of all time, and made him a household name. It was translated into every known language—and at least three unknown ones—and made into an Oscar-winning film, a Pulitzer-winning play, a Tony-winning musical, and a Golden Joystick-winning computer game.

Ocram excelled at countless sports until a middle-ear problem permanently impaired his balance. He has yet to win a Nobel Prize, but his agent, Barney, has been placing strategic back-handers—announcements from Stockholm are expected imminently (and it might not just be physics and litera-ture). Unmarried, in spite of his Bronx mom's tireless efforts, he still lives near his foster parents in New York.

Be sure to check out his website at www.theawfulauthor.com

ABOUT THE PUBLISHER

Tiny Fox Press LLC
5020 Kingsley Road
North Port, FL 34287

www.tinyfoxpress.com

CPSIA information can be obtained
at www.ICGtesting.com
Printed in the USA
BVHW071246290719
554566BV00003B/197/P

9 781946 501158